PENGUIN BOOKS

TAPESTRY OF THE MIND AND OTHER STORIES

Aneeta Sundararaj trained and practised as a lawyer before deciding to pursue her dream of writing. She has also created and developed a website called 'How to Tell a Great Story'. She aims to make it a resource for storytellers. Her writing has appeared in many magazines, e-zines, and journals. Some of the noteworthy book projects she's worked on include *Knowledge of Life: Tales of an Ayurveda Practitioner in Malaysia, The Banana Leaf Men*, and *Mad Heaven: Biography of Tan Sri Dato' Seri Dr. M. Mahadevan.*

For a while, she contributed feature articles to the lifestyle section of a national newspaper. Many of Aneeta's short stories have been longlisted and shortlisted for and won international literary competitions and awards.

Her most recent and bestselling novel, *The Age of Smiling Secrets* was shortlisted for the Anugerah Buku 2020 organized by the National Library of Malaysia. Incidentally, edited versions of various chapters of this novel have appeared in multiple anthologies, most notably *We Mark Your Memory: Writings from the Descendants of Indenture*, School of Advanced Study, University of London, in partnership with Commonwealth Writers, 2018. Throughout, Aneeta continued to pursue her academic interests and, in 2021, successfully defended a doctoral thesis entitled *Management of Prosperity Among Artistes in Malaysia.*

ADVANCE PRAISE FOR *TAPESTRY OF THE MIND AND OTHER STORIES*

'Aneeta's short stories tell the truth. Through these compositions, the reader gains an insight into the different experiences of social, political, and economic realities of Malaysian life; how they diverge and how they interact—in surprising, amusing, or tragic ways. Furthermore, weaving through these pieces are important threads that, depending on government policy, will strengthen or unravel our nation: among them, mental health, the Federal Constitution and our nation's rich cultural traditions.

Get this book into our schools!'

—Tunku Zain Al-'Abidin
Founding President, Institute for Democracy and Economic Affairs (IDEAS)

'Aneeta Sundararaj's hard-hitting compilation of short stories may be fictional but it is solidly based on real life. Aneeta hits the nail on the head basing her stories on the ambiguous and double standards prevailing within the multi-racial and multi-cultural societies of Malaysia.

Each community, conditioned by the double standards and unreformed practices and beliefs of their communities, is plagued by ambivalent and cruel psychological destiny. Obsessed with the resultant state of affairs, the protagonists of Aneeta's "fictional" stories grip us with their unfolding drama, the monumental clashes of religious and cultural conditioning and law. Her stories explore the resultant acute mental health crises and taboos, the kind which are often swept under the carpet in the unfair world we live in.'

—Datuk Ramli Ibrahim
Chairman, Sutra Foundation

'Mental health is the buzz word of today's world. What does it actually mean? When an employee says, "I suffer from anxiety," sometimes, there may be a deeper medical issue he is suffering from. When an aged parent stops eating, it may be a sign of depression in the elderly. When a parent or loved one dies, how you deal with the grief may be completely different from someone else.

After heavy rains, there are all forms of losses around and you feel you're losing your mind. Stories can be one of the most powerful ways for you to understand that you're not alone and seeking help is but one phone call away.

This is why I am very proud of Aneeta for putting together this collection of some of her award-winning short stories. The stories are heartfelt, funny in some instances, uplifting in a few and very real in all of them. It's a must-read and treasure for all.'

—Tan Sri Lee Lam Thye
Patron, Malaysian Psychiatric Association

'Be warned. Aneeta is dangerously addictive. She picks her material mostly from domestic vignettes. Aneeta's lawyerly training transmutes it into searing universal insights. We are astonished how similar the human condition is, everywhere. That explains why her stories win international awards.

Because time is scarce, we trade it warily. Aneeta's chosen medium of the short story is apt. She does not disappoint.'

—Cyril Pereira
Former Publisher, *Asia Magazine*

'"Say Hello to Yama" achieves a lot . . . A very dense and complex story enables the reader to reflect on the impacts of climate change on small communities.'

—Dr Marl'ene Edwin
Chair, Short Fiction Prize, Aesthetica
Creative Writing Award 2024

Tapestry of the Mind and Other Stories

Aneeta Sundararaj

PENGUIN BOOKS
An imprint of Penguin Random House

PENGUIN BOOKS

Penguin Books is an imprint of the Penguin Random House group of companies whose addresses can be found at global.penguinrandomhouse.com

Published by Penguin Random House SEA Pte Ltd
40 Penjuru Lane, #03-12, Block 2
Singapore 609216

First published in Penguin Books by Penguin Random House SEA 2024

10 9 8 7 6 5 4 3 2 1

This is a work of fiction. Names, characters, places and incidents are either the product of the author's imagination or are used fictitiously, and any resemblance to any actual person, living or dead, events or locales is entirely coincidental.

Tapestry of the Mind and Other Stories is a collection of short stories dealing with culturally and emotionally sensitive themes. The book includes elements that might not be suitable for some readers. Suicide, self harm, death, sex/masturbation, sexual violence, sexism, emotional abuse, addiction, violence, racism, and slurs, are present in the stories. Readers who may be sensitive to these elements please take note.

ISBN 9789815204773

Typeset in Garamond by MAP Systems, Bengaluru, India

www.penguin.sg

For Mano Maniam, Mr Rama, and Tan Gim Ean—my friends in need—and Emeritus Professor Malachi Edwin Vethamani and Elena Koshy

Contents

Author's Note

A few years ago, Tan Sri Dato' Seri Dr M. Mahadevan told me about his protégé, Professor (Adj.) Dato' Dr Andrew Mohanraj. In the course of my research on Dr Mohanraj, I learned about the remarkable and pioneering work he does. All of this resulted in me publishing a story about him called 'In the Shade of a Mango Tree'.

Dr Mohanraj served the Ministry of Health Malaysia for twelve years before taking up an international assignment after the Asian Tsunami of 2004. As a consultant psychiatrist and mental health development adviser, he has done pioneering work in the establishment of sustainable psychosocial rehabilitation services in Indonesia (post-disaster, post-conflict), the Philippines (post-disaster) and Timor Leste (post-conflict).

In 2012, Dr Mohanraj returned to Malaysia under the Return of the Expert Programme by Talent Corporation, a unit under the purview of the Prime Minister's Department. He subsequently joined Perdana University Graduate School of Medicine (in collaboration with Johns Hopkins Medical School, Baltimore) as associate professor in Psychiatry and its first director of clinical clerkship.

While he continues his consultancy work for local and international government and non-government organizations, Dr Mohanraj is also currently serving his third term as a member of the Mental Health Promotion Advisory Council to the Minister of Health Malaysia. In 2013, in recognition of Dr Mohanraj's international work in the promotion of the United Nations Convention on the Rights of Persons with Disabilities (UNCRPD), he was appointed as a member of the National Council for Persons with Disabilities, on which he served two terms consecutively.

Besides running his psychiatric practice in Mont Kiara, Kuala Lumpur, he is now engaged in a short-term consultancy to provide mental health services to refugees and asylum seekers whose intended destination is Australia. He is also actively involved in the mainstreaming of mental health issues in Malaysia as the president of the Malaysian Mental Health Association and, more recently, the Selangor Mental Health Association. He also serves as the treasurer/board member of the World Federation for Mental Health (WFMH).

Having completed a consultancy in Mental Health & Substance Abuse with the World Health Organization's Western Pacific Regional Office, he recently took up an academic position as professor, School of Liberal Arts and Sciences at Taylor's University, Malaysia.

Dr Mohanraj also publishes a monthly column called 'Matters of the Mind' in *The Star*. What he has written in this column, together with some of his other published pieces, have inspired the tales in *Tapestry of the Mind and Other Stories.*

—Aneeta Sundararaj
Kuala Lumpur, Malaysia
January 2024

Foreword

A fundamental beauty of storytelling is that it is simultaneously simple and complex.

Simple, because its elements are eternal: a proper plot and structure, great dialogue and interesting locations. These elements have determined the bones of a story since the beginning of time. Complex, because like any germ of an idea, each story grows differently according to the storyteller. The perfect example would, of course, be something like the Hindu epic, Mahabharat. This story has filtered down through the ages. But the success of the telling of it depends enormously on 'who' is doing the narrating.

This makes the growing of our stories—local, Malaysian, flavourful, and with contemporary dialogue—all the more noteworthy. It enhances the understanding of a multi-cultural, -lingual, -religious, and -racial society like ours. Most significant in this process are those who put their thoughts to paper. They've observed human frailties, absorbed their pain, and both sympathized and empathized with the suffering of others. They are our literary ambassadors. Prominent among them are both Andrew and Aneeta.

Here are two highly intelligent people I've known all their lives, but who have only known of each other in the last few years. It gives me an enormous sense of pride to state that Andrew is my protégé. He now writes a monthly column in *The Star* called 'Matters of the Mind' and has made great strides in the promotion of mental health issues in Malaysia and, indeed, the world over. Aneeta, of course, was instrumental in writing my autobiography.

It is now my pleasure to introduce this recounting of selected experiences of the various characters from *Tapestry of the Mind*. It is a book that does not proclaim the greatness of Andrew's work. Instead, Aneeta has used his published writing to craft extraordinary stories that expound on the mental health issues. She uses the elements of storytelling to highlight the problems many people face and corrects the many misconceptions about mental health. It is no surprise that many of the stories in this collection have won awards and have been highly commended by the literary fraternity. Indeed, the characters showcase that therapy and healing can be useful even in today's modern, urbanized world. They are ordinary individuals, like you and me, who find themselves in severe mental health crises and often don't want to turn to professionals for help. There are stories of women who cannot figure out how their marriages went wrong, men in loveless marriages, elder abuse, how the metaverse (and technology in general) can rob someone of all happiness, bullying that has its roots in sibling rivalry, spirituality gone horribly wrong, autism, and adoption. The one story that Aneeta excelled in is 'Say Hello to Yama'.

This was about the impact of an environmental disaster on a person's mental health and Andrew's particular expertise is in disaster psychiatry.

When internalizing our challenges, there is an awareness that everyone has a personal narrative. If that story is mentally unhealthy, how can the person who believes and lives it be mentally healthy? Ultimately, these stories serve to show its readers that if you're suffering from a mental health issue, you're not alone and help is always available. A person suffering from mental health issues can, more often than not, rewrite his or her personal narrative.

I pray that this collection of stories will help to transform lives.

—Tan Sri Dato' Seri Azlanni Dr M. Mahadevan
Kuala Lumpur, Malaysia
June 2023

Tapestry of the Mind

> The desire to provide a legacy that outlives us can be an excellent way to accomplish more in life. When we face a haunting reminder of our death, focusing on what we would like to leave behind could help us turn something terrifying into a positive motivational experience. Artists are the perfect example of this. Through their creative legacies, they live on and are never totally gone. Such legacies also help those who remain cope with their loss.
>
> —Professor (Adj.) Dato' Dr Andrew Mohanraj

All of Alor Setar's high society was abuzz with the news.

It wasn't that we'd have to turn up at Stadium Dato' Syed Omar on short notice. It was not that a celebrated dancer, who had returned home after an illustrious career in Australia, had chosen our tiny town in which to give his first live performance. It wasn't even the anticipation of wondering if this Malay–Muslim would publicly carry out the Hindu ritual of paying homage to both his guru and the gods before dancing. It certainly wasn't about a dance form that none of us had heard of. Mercifully, in a feature article published in the papers the day before he arrived, the dancer explained that Odissi was a sensuous and lyrical dance form which originated in eastern India.

The talk of the town was quite simply that Rosli Idris was coming to dance for us at the invitation of the Sultan.

I repeat.

At the invitation of the Sultan.

Imagine that!

This had never happened before or, for that matter, after Rosli's 'one-night-only' performance.

Seated between my parents, three rows behind the Sultan, I instinctively recited the Guru Mantra when Rosli, to the left of the stage, offered *aarti* in front of a brass sculpture of Ganpati, whom we believe removes all obstacles.

'See, Daddy,' I whispered every so often throughout that performance, 'that's Kuruma', or, 'that's Vamana'. I showed off my ability to interpret Rosli's depiction of the ten incarnations of Vishnu, one of the principal trinities of the Hindu gods. Vishnu descended into our world to restore peace and righteousness whenever humanity was threatened by chaos or evil.

Doubtless, Rosli's production that night called *Dasavatar* was an unforgettable event for the inhabitants of the town a mere hour or so south of the border with Thailand. After this magical evening on the second Sunday of August 1980, as the world hurtled towards the new millennium, Stadium Dato' Syed Omar was torn down, the Sultan's long and prosperous reign came to an end, and Rosli became a world-renowned dancer, showered with accolades, awards, titles, and much respect.

'But, darling, that was more that forty years ago!'

Such was Rosli's response, with one elbow resting on the shoulder of his principal male dancer, when I reminded him of his visit to Alor Setar.

'Ah well . . .' He walked towards the dining table of his house in suburban Petaling Jaya.

Ah well, indeed. Keeping in mind Rosli's multipronged oeuvre, the events of the past ten days were nothing short of unbelievable.

'See what they did.' He stretched his left leg from under him once seated.

I tilted my head. An electronic tag encircled his ankle.

'One step out of this house and, within seconds, sirens will be blaring.' Rosli reached for the jug of fresh lemonade and poured me a glass.

A week after Valentine's Day in 2023, Malaysians woke up to the following headlines: 'Iconic dancer arrested for alleged theft of a black diamond.' The report stated that Rosli and his dance troupe had agreed to an impromptu performance at a high-end luxury store. They were accompanied by a local artiste singing her heart out to Dame Shirley Bassey's 'Diamonds Are Forever'. The diamond stolen was worth 37 million dollars.

'Why are you giggling? What is so funny?'

'Rosli, you're an Odissi dancer.'

'So?'

'"Diamonds Are Forever"? How did you dance to that?'

'I can do other dance forms, you know.'

He had a point. The youngest of five children, after completing his studies at the elite Malay College of Kuala Kangsar, he'd pursued an engineering degree in Australia, after which he joined a ballet company. He also dabbled in contemporary dances before immersing himself in various Indian dance forms.

'But why? What was special about this black diamond?'

Sighing, he leaned back, 'I've been reading Jung lately. We are all going to die, you know.'

'Why, lah, so morbid?'

'No. No. No. I'm just thinking about my childhood. What is my legacy?'

'Hmmm . . .' I didn't know how else to respond. After four decades, Rosli had become synonymous with dance globally. It seemed inconceivable that a time would come when there was going to be no Rosli.

'What am I leaving behind? Has it all been for nothing? Is there zero purpose to all I've done?'

I recognized this lamentation of an artiste. Yes, our creative endeavours fed our souls. But at the heart of it was the desire that the life we breathed into our creations would live long after we gave up our mortal coils. That we, in some small way, touched another human being. That they, connected to us by blood or spirit, would hopefully find solace and comfort in our works if and when the need arose.

'But why do this, Rosli? The charge is stealing. I know you didn't do it. So, why?'

It's the way he looked at me. He neither smiled nor scowled. There was the faintest dilation of his pupils. He lifted his chin, challenged. 'What's the proof?'

'Errr . . .'

'That's what I mean. There is nothing to tie me to this. This is just another way for the authorities to stop me from dancing.'

'Huh?'

'Geeta, I am Malay. Right now, there are so many issues here. All those religious people, instead of serving the *rakyat*, they are forever being vigilantes and taking the holier than thou attitude to extremes.'

'But you've been doing this for years. Why should they bother you now?'

'Aiya. Now, we have a new lot. I've already been told I cannot teach Indian dance because it involves rituals. I expect to be arrested if I enter a temple or conduct the prayers with my students during Vijayadashami.'

He had a point.

'People think dance is just dance. It's not for me, you know. It's a passion. Actually, no. It's more than that. It's a calling.'

'I agree. You're so talented, Rosli.'

'That talent, Geeta, is a gift. It is a golden opportunity to fulfil one's reason for being. I love to quote Martha Graham who said, "I did not choose to dance. Dance chose me." That's it. Odissi chose me. Ballet chose me. I didn't choose them.'

During the ensuing silence, I wondered how I'd get him to reveal the location of the diamond or, at the very least, how he'd taken it from right under the noses of the authorities.

'Hypothetically speaking, Rosli . . .'

'Y-e-s?'

'Hypothetically speaking, how would you have done it?'

'Did you watch any of the videos posted online?'

'Well, sort of. I don't trust what I see.'

'Pity.'

'Huh?'

'Geeta, you're like so many of the children of the modern world. Your body is now weak and you're poorly coordinated.'

'Fine.'

'No. I'm not trying to insult you. Tell me, what did you do for fun when you were a child?'

'Play, I suppose.'

'Play what?'

'*Masak-masak*.'

'Masak-masak.' He hit his forehead with his palm. 'For God's sake! Did you run? Skip? Dance like there was no tomorrow?'

'No. I was in Alor Setar. We didn't have dancing schools like in KL. And, if I wanted to learn dance, I'd have to go to the temple. That wasn't what girls from good families did. We played piano. Other girls travelled to Penang to learn ballet.' I waved my hand. 'Bharatanatyam was out of the question.' I shuddered. 'And, all those priests? Huh! They would be staring at us.' Dropping my voice a few decibels, I added, 'Some didn't stop at staring, I tell you.'

'Hmmm . . . Okay. You're forgiven. But look at the ones in the city today. They are clumsy, sit like buffaloes, and look at their tablets all day. They can barely walk up the stairs without panting. They don't know what grass feels like under their feet.'

'They live in condos, Rosli.'

'Exactly! It's a real pity because Nature is the greatest teacher.'

'Okay, but that doesn't explain how . . . this . . . happened.'

'Well . . . actually, Geeta, do you know any Greek mythology?'

'Some. I mean, I know the major ones, like the Apollonian and Dionysian principles. Apollo and Dionysius were the sons of Zeus, no? Apollo represents order, predictability, and stability.

'Ah! So, you know something.'

'I studied it in school. Very basic. It's the idea of stability, no?'

He nodded. 'Sort of. With Apollonian, everything has to be symmetrical. With Dionysian, it's the opposite. Nothing is symmetrical. Dionysius is all about chaos, instability, and surprise. All my life, I've tried to create a balance between the two. That's what we did here. I created balance.'

I frowned. 'How?'

'I'm not going to tell you.' He had a twinkle in his eyes. 'I'll show you.'

I stared at him, trying to decipher his meaning.

'You brought your phone, yes? Put on the music and let me dance. Find something better than Shirley Bassey. Something Indian. I'll go change.'

In fifteen minutes, Rosli, dressed in a floaty white cotton *kurta*, walked onto his 'stage' in the lush garden of what, rumour had it, was going to become the archival centre of Indian dance in Malaysia. He winced when he stepped onto the sun-soaked slab of cement measuring some fifteen feet in diameter.

'There,' Rosli said, pointing to the middle of it, 'I put a piece of granite I brought back from the Annapurna Base Camp in Nepal. I was there on 9 September 1999.'

'Ah-so.'

'Music.'

As he began to dance to the tune of 'Lalitha Lavanga' by Sikkil Gurucharan and Anil Srinivasan, there was a sudden breeze. The palm fronds, leaves of the bougainvillea, and surrounding bushes all rustled, as though Mother Nature was appreciating this impromptu performance.

'The first avatar, as you know, is Matsya.'

Avatar? I took three deep breaths. Decades of yearning to see this particular performance and, now, under these strangest of circumstances, I would bear witness to it. I held my breath, afraid that the tiniest movement may make Rosli change his mind.

He moved his limbs to form a fish swimming in the waters. Similar to the myths of many a culture, Matsya forewarned the coming of a flood and ordered Man to preserve all the grains and living creatures in a boat while he retrieved the Vedas from the clutches of the demons.

'I,' Rosli said, 'wanted to preserve the goods from being taken by all the baddies.'

'Hmmm . . .' It was a rescue mission for the black diamond rather than its theft. That was how Rosli planned to plead, apparently.

'No man is an island like Mount Mandara.' Rosli opened his palm and stuck out his tongue. He was metaphorically tasting the mythical nectar of immortality, *amrit*. In this, the second incarnation, Vishnu was a tortoise. Acting as a pivot, the reptile stabilized the mountain for the task at hand.

'But I almost broke my back, lah, Geeta.'

'Why?'

'With so many people and things in the crowd, lah.' In a classic step familiar to thieves, Rosli moved his limbs, mimicking the act of avoiding an invisible, high-end handbag here, a string of Mikimoto pearls there, one fat Datin swinging her Louis Vuitton bag here, and the emcee there. 'Like Vasuki, the snake, churned the ocean, I moved around so much so that nobody would think that I stuck near where the diamond was.'

Taking a moment, he stood still. 'That Nagen dancing with me for incarnation number three was a huge mistake. It should have been Padmini. But she's busy with her parents right now.' Rosli then struck a pose to depict Varaha, the boar who raised Mother Earth from the bottom of the sea after the demon Hiranyaksha dragged her to its bottom. 'He was supposed to show that Bhoomidevi sat on the tip of Varaha's tusk, like a spot on the moon.' Shaking his head, he added, 'Instead, he was like a bull in a china shop. We missed our steps, almost knocking that whole pedestal with the diamond on it.'

I laughed, unable to help myself.

'Don't laugh, Geeta,' Rosli scolded from the stage. 'It was bad, okay? I had to do quick damage control.'

'Okay. Okay. Okay.' I pushed a lock of hair behind my right ear. 'What next?'

'Narasimha.'

For a moment, I wondered how this half-man-half-beast incarnation of Vishnu could possibly have aided Rosli's quest. When he bent his fingers to depict talons, I got it. This was a crime that had been committed neither by using tools nor exposed human fingers. Rosli wore gloves. The precious stone wasn't snatched under the cover of darkness or when the entire store was bathed in bright light. Its removal took place when the lights were dimmed and the focus was solely on the sinewy girls modelling various pieces of jewellery in the middle of the store.

'That almost worked, but, again . . .' He shook his head. 'Arrogance got the better of me.'

'What do you mean?'

'I miscalculated the number of steps to another dancer, Yogini. She is Nagen's younger sister. I was supposed to take only seven steps. But I needed ten to reach her.'

Ah! This meant the diamond had already been in Rosli's possession.

'If only I could have been like that Vamana.' The fifth avatar, this clever dwarf begged a king for all the land that he could cover in three large steps. The king granted his wish. Vamana then morphed into a giant who was able to cover earth, heaven, and all the space in between.

'Hmmm . . . If the steps were not enough then how did you do it?'

Patting the side of his nose with his forefinger, Rosli said, 'It's all in the timing, darling.'

'What does that even mean?'

'Remember how Parashurama wielded his axe to get rid of all those corrupt Kshatriyas? Well, I also began to twirl. The more I moved around, like I was wielding an axe, the more people had to make space for me. And that got me farther away from the . . . err . . . scene of the crime.'

'Okay. But this one thing I remember from all the videos online. You were not just moving around, Rosli. You stopped in front of so many people as though you were putting something in their hands.'

'Yes. That's what Rama did, isn't it? After he killed Ravana, he distributed the demon's ten heads to the presiding deities of the ten directions.'

'Huh?'

'I was making sure that as many people as possible were distracted from what I was about to do next.'

'Okay.'

'Like Arjuna in the Mahabharat, I let my Krishna, the eighth avatar, lead the way in the chariot.'

I frowned. Feeling like a real dum-dum, I asked, once again, 'What does that even mean?'

'Well, a charioteer guides the horses, no?'

'Yes.'

'He guides them off the battle field, no? Taking with him all that's in the chariot?'

'Ah-so.' Even if Rosli had been caught and searched at this stage, the diamond was already in the hands of dancers who left the stage altogether. 'Why did you continue dancing? All over, what?'

'I needed to change direction. Like with Balarama. The ninth avatar is said to have used his plough to change the course of the river Yamuna and save mankind.'

'I thought the ninth avatar was Buddha.'

'Aiya! It can be. But for my dance, it's Balarama, okay?'

'Okay. So, how?'

'Remember how Krishna danced off the stage? Well, I danced in the other direction and made sure that while my dancers left the store, all attention was on me. Then, I danced Kalki. I made the audience feel the *rasa*.'

Hearing Rosli's words, in my mind's eye, I went back in time to when I had been all of eight years old. My eyes were glued to the person on the stage at Stadium Dato' Syed Omar. All our surroundings—the sound of the music, the Sultan, my parents, the very air we breathed—became secondary to the dancer twirling, head raised to the skies. Round and round he danced with an unstoppable energy from within. Arms akimbo, he welcomed the energies flowing from on high. In the language of dance, Rosli was in communion with the Divine.

I exhaled.

Rosli did not bother to change out of his sweat-soaked kurta. Instead, he returned to the dining table and reached for the second jug of freshly made lemonade.

'I don't understand, Rosli.'

'What don't you understand now?'

'In that store, you danced to Shirley Bassey. Here, Indian dance. This doesn't gel.'

'A good dancer can dance to any tune. It can be dancing to tunes from Old Malaya to traditional dancing. Like you. A writer.'

'Huh?'

'A good writer can write books for papers and journal articles, no? Same here.'

'Ah.'

For a while, neither of us said anything. Then, I couldn't help myself. 'Where is it now, Rosli?'

There was that smile again.

He shifted in his seat. 'In dance, Geeta, we may learn what a *shloka* means. You know exactly the meaning of all the lyrics in *Dasavatar*. Nothing is more wonderful, however, than when these lyrics are imagined. So, imagine. Look around you.'

I did for close to a minute until I realized that Rosli's gaze was fixed in the direction of the cement platform with a series of concentric cicles carved into it.

Oooo . . .

What was that?

Hadn't he said that he'd placed something he brought back from the Himalayas there? Still, unprocessed rough granite didn't posses the power of reflectivity. As the light of the setting sun hit the very centre of Rosli's stage, light was not merely reflecting off the surface, but coming from within. It was quite simply sparkling.

Turning to the dancer, whose years on earth were close to threescore and ten, I shivered.

'R-o-s-l-i?'

We stared at each other for some moments. I knew the question in his eyes: 'What are you going to do now that you know the truth?'

I didn't dare say a word. And I knew I never would in this lifetime.

'I try not to be too specific about the future, Geeta.' Rubbing his chin, my idol for life added, 'Destiny will look after itself. If the endurability of your spirit deserves it—whatever the tapestry of your mind conceives it to be—it'll happen.'

Visitation Rights

> There are several phases of bereavement in children. First, there is the protest phase in which there is a strong desire to connect with the deceased parent. This leads to the despair phase which is characterised by hopelessness, withdrawal, crying spells, and apathy. Then the child undergoes a detachment phase in which emotional attachment to the dead is relinquished.
>
> —Professor (Adj.) Dato' Dr Andrew Mohanraj

'You promised. Remember?'

The voice in my ear was scratchy, as though the man was speaking for the first time after being extubated.

Jolted awake, I couldn't move. My chest felt heavy and I wondered if I would ever draw a breath again.

'Yes, I remember,' I whispered into the darkness.

Within seconds, I could breathe once more.

Why the hell was I still waking up in the middle of the night because of a man who'd been dead for five years?

* * *

Standing by the window of my high-rise flat, I stared out at the city bathed in ambient light. Even though the Klang Valley in Kuala Lumpur, Malaysia, seemed deathly quiet, I was certain that news reports from the night before were true. I strained to hear City Council officers trawling the dark alleyways to round up the homeless to prevent social ills.

What on earth were social ills? One drug-addled man having his way with a semi-comatose woman in her cardboard box under a bridge? Try as I might, I couldn't hear a thing at this hour before dawn.

These were all frivolous thoughts. A desperate attempt to shut out the more serious ones: Daddy's dementia's getting worse; Mummy's alone; so far, far away from them, will I ever sleep through the night again?

I shivered and mentally ran through my checklist for when the inevitable happened: ask my cousin to drive me home; call my editor to reassign the work she's given me; have a full petrol tank in the car.

What if I were overseas, though, when Daddy died? Must have enough money to buy a ticket home; must arrange for someone to help Mummy call the doctor, report the matter to the police, and do all the paperwork; Daddy must be taken to the mortuary by the time I was home; I have no brothers or husband so I must light my father's funeral pyre.

Such morbid thoughts. Still, I learned months ago that, in the dead of night, when worry and fear threaten to consume me, it was best to be practical and think of all that needed to be done. This mental activity was exhausting and shut out emotion; the body and mind eventually succumbed to sleep.

Even then, I knew that I'd lost my father two years before he actually died. He had suffered a severe bout of pneumonia and was hospitalized for two weeks in November 2014.

'Ma,' he had said, calling me by the Tamil term of endearment.

I had hurried to his bedside and helped him push away the sterile tubing with a continuous infusion of antibiotics before he said, 'When it's time, you let me go. Don't let me suffer. I don't want to lie in a bed all the time.'

Without hesitating, I had responded with, 'When your suffering to live becomes more than my suffering to let you go, I promise you, Daddy, I will let you go. For now, let me have the pleasure of looking after you.'

He had smiled brightly, held his hands below his chin, and closed his eyes.

Seated in the plastic chair, I'd watched my father sleep for the next hour and, thereby, heal from within. Daddy pulled through and was discharged on his birthday, 23 November. But he was never the same again.

Two things happened in the last months of Daddy's life that made me anxious. The first was the morning after I returned to the city for work. While I was at Village Grocers in Bangsar, the maid called and pleaded, 'Talk to your father. He has been crying all morning.'

Back in my flat, the moment I put away the groceries, I dialled the number for the landline in the house.

'Why are you crying, Daddy?'

'S-o-r-,' he choked on his words. I didn't need to hear the rest of his apology to understand that, in a moment of incredible lucidity, it had occurred to him that for the two weeks I was home in Alor Setar, he couldn't remember who I was. He tortured himself all morning assuming that I was upset.

'Daddy, don't cry any more. Don't worry about this. Please,' I begged, unable to bear my father's emotional pain.

'Promise me visitation rights. Okay? When I'm gone, you let me visit.'

'No,' I cried out. 'No such thing. If you keep coming back, the whole world will laugh at me. As though I didn't do all the proper prayers for you. No visitation rights.'

Daddy hung up on me. I knew he was angry, but there was no way I was going to make a promise that he could stay around with us in spirit form.

One morning, a few weeks later during my monthly visits home, Daddy called me to his room after he'd woken up.

'Say good morning, Ma.' Pointing to the end of his bed, he said, 'We have visitors.' Turning to look at me, he added, 'Later, when I visit, you give me coffee, ok. Promise?'

'Hmmm . . . Yes. Promise.' I didn't have energy left to argue. I'd already read stories that the dying will report visions of angels, deceased loved ones, or religious figures.

I will not let this happen.

I refused to be defeated by our visitors.

I guided Daddy to his spot at our dining table. After I poured the brewed coffee into his mug and was convinced that he was happy with his breakfast of boiled oats with berries and slices of papaya, I returned to his room to tidy it up. At the foot of his bed, I imagined that there was a person standing in front of me. In that moment, I decided to call him 'Someone'. Granted, it was an unimaginative name, but my world was falling apart and there were only so many grey cells I was willing to exercise at the time. Pretending to stare into Someone's eyes, I said, 'It's okay. You can be here for now. Keep Daddy safe. I know why you're here.' Wagging my finger at Someone, I implored, 'But you wait, please. A few weeks also can.'

At the threshold, I turned back to Someone and said, 'Actually, you can take longer. No need for you to hurry. Okay?'

I'd like to think that Someone listened to me because nothing happened for a long while, meaning that Daddy didn't mention the presence of visitors again. Instead, he continued to heal and our little nuclear family of three was happy in each other's company. Such was the improvement in his health that weeks later, Daddy was hale and hearty enough to make the five-hour car journey to my flat in Kuala Lumpur. I wanted medical experts in the city to assess him and made all the necessary appointments.

During the consultation, the cardiologist picked at a xanthoma peeping out of his shirt collar while he scanned Daddy's lab reports. After tension-filled minutes, he declared, 'Wah, Uncle. Your blood results are very good. Better than mine. You're doing very well.'

Next to me, Mummy exhaled, relieved.

When he then said, 'See you in six months, Uncle,' I heard a soft voice in my head say, *It ain't going to happen. We're never coming back here.*

Dismissing it, I helped Daddy with his wheelchair so that we could leave the medical specialist's room. Our next stop was the institute's pharmacy bursting at the seams with a cross section of Malaysia's obese and diabetic citizens suffering from all manner of heart ailments. Daddy came home that day with more than the requisite medication—he came home with a bug in his lungs.

Two nights later, when I was helping him get ready for bed, Daddy asked me, point blank: 'Who are you?'

I wanted to scream, 'I am your daughter, Padmini.' Instead, I smiled and continued to rub the night cream for his dry skin.

'See Appa! See Meneka!' he said, pointing to the end of the bed. 'She won't tell me who she is. But I have to let her touch me. So shame-shame.'

I held my breath, angry.

The visitors were here? In Kuala Lumpur?

They had the audacity to sit on the bed? My bed. Next to my father.

This was too much.

Logic dictated that this rage was unfounded. Clearly, Daddy's dementia had progressed to the extent where he no longer knew me, but he could name his childhood playmate and my grandfather who had been dead for more than forty years.

When my father was intubated and placed on life support five days later, I didn't dare bargain with God any more. A miracle had already taken place: I fulfilled Daddy's wish and brought him back home to Alor Setar. He was so frail that I feared he would die at the airport. But, like magic, everything fell into place and his final journey home went off without a hitch.

I knew that any medical intervention at this stage, such as kidney dialysis, could keep him alive but would render him bedridden. It was time I kept my promise. My task was not merely to let my eighty-six-year-old father go but to help him let us go as well. I steeled my nerves, let go of my selfish desire to keep my father alive at any cost, and silenced the voice of my sorrow.

I turned to friends and explained that for the last two years, my father had become a 'child'. I became his 'parent' and cared for and loved him. Now, as the finality of what was going to happen fast approached, I was worried. Would he be safe? Would he be cared for? I asked that they pray for me to have the strength to go through one of the hardest things ever. How kind they all were, regardless of colour, creed, and faith: Catholics recited the Rosary, Christians prayed, and Hindus chanted the mantras with me.

I can count on one hand the number of people I informed about Daddy's worsening and terminal condition. Yet, word spread fast. Uncles, aunts, and many friends dropped everything and rushed to be with us. The *makcik* who sat next to me on the plane during a quick dash to Kuala Lumpur to shut down my flat comforted me as I wept. My co-workers sent cards and comforting messages.

I held back tears when the nurses in the ICU told me that long after Mummy and I left the hospital to get some rest, consultants from other hospitals visited him. As a former medical superintendent in the government's health service in the 1970s, Daddy had once upon a time been their boss. They wanted to stay with him on those nights when he was alone with nothing more than a beeping monitor for company.

I chose to believe that in those last five days of his life, Daddy came back to us. Although physically helpless, he knew who I was and we learned to communicate without words. He smiled when I promised to look after Mummy. He squeezed my hand when I asked for his forgiveness for all my wrongs. Tears flowed from his eyes when I thanked him for giving me the honour of being his daughter. When I told him it was time to rest, he gave me a firm nod.

Finally, on the morning of 17 October, when there was no longer any cognitive function and Daddy was slipping away, we gathered by his side.

At one stage, I whispered in my father's ear, 'Daddy, if you can see, look around you. I'm here. Mummy is here . . .' and I continued to name all the people standing around his bed. I imagined that, like in the movies, Daddy's astral being would rise up and see us all.

'Daddy, pray to Amma,' I urged him. The word 'Amma' had a double meaning. For one, Amma was his *ishtadevam.* The name of his deity of choice was also what we called my grandmother, and I hoped that she would be a last-minute visitor to help Daddy in his hour of need.

Daddy opened his eyes and glanced at all of us. It was the validation I needed that he had heard me and knew that he wasn't alone. I looked into my father's eyes and whispered, 'Visitation rights, Daddy. You have them. Promise.'

When my father closed his eyes for eternity, I surrendered his body, heart, and soul into Amma's hands.

As Mummy and I got used to our new reality, and I told people about the perfection of my father's death, it was impossible to shed any tears. I had no right to cry when the entire sequence of events was a testament to the fact that every one of Daddy's wishes had been granted. He died peacefully, surrounded by the people who loved him body, heart, and soul, in a town where he'd earned enormous respect.

In time, my mother and I collected happier memories, such as my marriage to a Methodist man with whom I didn't share the details of my last words to my father. It wasn't that I was keeping secrets from my husband. I didn't think Daddy would hold me to a promise I made when he took his last breath.

Our son, Johnny, was three years old when my husband and I decided to move to our new home, a corner lot in a row of suburban terraced houses. The garden was large enough that we could plant a neem tree without worrying that its secondary roots could damage the foundations of what I was determined would be my family's sanctuary.

We converted one of the four bedrooms into a playroom for Johnny. A beautifully functional room, it opened out into our kitchen. This meant that while I was busy preparing our meals, I could still hear my infant's mostly garbled sounds as he joyfully played.

'What to do?' Johnny said, one day a few weeks ago. The mid-afternoon sun was way too hot for him to be playing outside. I put the air conditioner on in the playroom and my son seemed happy enough.

'No, cannot,' were my son's next words.

Something wasn't right. I turned the stove off and listened. After a while, it occurred to me that my son wasn't merely talking to himself. He was responding to someone talking to him. Could it be his imagination?

I walked to the bedroom and leaned against the doorframe to watch him. Johnny wasn't looking down at his toys when he spoke. Instead, his head was raised and eyes were wide open, as though he were looking into the face of someone seated on the floor playing with him.

'Who are you talking to, baby boy?'

He turned to me, dimples denting his cherubic cheeks. Pointing to nothing in front of him, he said. 'Someone.'

What?

I blinked.

Someone? Dear God, help me.

My breath grew laboured. Should I pick up my baby and run? But where to? Was my baby going to die? Was Someone here to take him away?

I blinked again and whispered, 'Who?'

My child turned back to this invisible being and, ever so politely asked, 'What is name, please?'

A moment later, he turned to me and said, 'Tata.'

I stood stock still.

Could it be?

Tata would have been the way Johnny addressed his Tamil grandfather had Daddy lived to meet his grandson.

Was it even possible that my son and Daddy were having a conversation?

I turned on my heel and walked away, stunned.

In the coming days, I said nothing. But every afternoon, in the kitchen, I sat with a mug of coffee in my hand and listened to this one-sided conversation my living, breathing child had with my seemingly dead, lifeless father.

Then, I made a huge mistake—I shared what had happened with my husband.

'What?' he practically shouted at me. 'Don't be ridiculous. I don't believe in all this hocus pocus, mumbo jumbo, bullshit.' Although I didn't mention 'Tata' again, my spooked husband called his family for a meeting and a unilateral decision was made to contact the Church elders the very next day. Pastor Michael was commissioned to come to our home and help us mere mortals.

I almost blurted out, 'He's my father. Not the Devil or a demon,' when I saw Pastor Michael gripping his wooden Methodist cross.

Who would have thought that Methodists were prone to following shamanic rituals? Here I was thinking that it was only 'my kind' (Pastor Michael's words, not mine) that made sacrificial offerings of slaughtered goats to Hindu gods and goddesses to appease them. Three nights in a row, Pastor Michael came to our house, garlic in one hand and the Bible in the other. With Johnny on my lap and my husband seated on the sofa next to me, we were given lessons from the Bible about our sins by a man who seemingly hadn't let go of his Hindu roots. On the fourth, fifth, and six nights, we slaughtered *kampung* chickens, mixed their blood with holy water and sprinkled it all around our house.

'So that the spirits don't take another life,' he explained.

The dead chickens, which we had to buy daily from the wet market so they were 'fresh', were taken away by Pastor Michael. I never dared to ask what he did with them. Maybe, the nuns in a nearby convent made chicken stew. Maybe, the school-going children in the Church-sponsored orphanage had fried chicken for dinner. Who knows . . .

On the seventh night, a time to rest, we hosted a dinner for Pastor Michael, a few parishioners, and my mother-in-law. 'It's all sorted,' he declared after he arranged his billowing robes and we bent down to kiss his ring. 'Everything will be fine from now on,' he insisted, comforting my mother-in-law as she lay a hand on her chest and sighed.

Within twelve hours of Pastor Michael's sort-of exorcism, I sat with a coffee mug in my hand and listened as my living son and dead father resumed their daily conversations. I vowed never to confess to my husband that all his family's efforts had been futile.

'Mummy,' my son appeared at the entrance to the kitchen and said, 'come, come.'

I put the mug down, took his outstretched hand and let him lead me to the playroom. He rushed to sit down on the straw mat and looked up at his invisible playmate.

'You tell her.'

'Tell me what, baby boy?'

'Tata said he's shame-shame to tell you.'

I smiled.

Shame-shame? Oh Daddy. Nothing's changed.

Oblivious, my son added, 'He said to say thank you.'

I swallowed. 'For what? Please ask Tata?'

A few seconds later, my son looked at me and said, 'For letting Tata visit.' He was about to turn back to play when he added, 'And my name, Mummy. Tata said thank you.'

Turning on my heel, I left my son alone and staggered back to the kitchen. Shaking from head to toe, I quickly pulled out a stool and sat down. I sobbed, for I was now aware that my father had known all along what I'd done.

When my child was born, I had insisted that he be given a Hindu name in addition to the Biblical one my mother-in-law had chosen for her first grandson.

'Please,' I'd begged my husband. Mercifully, he agreed.

'His name,' I'd said to Pastor Michael a month later, 'is John Sunder Pillay.' Watching the pastor pour water from the baptismal font over my child's head, I'd closed my eyes and silently added, 'With God as my witness, I will teach this baby to be deeply honoured to carry his grandfather's name, Dr Sunder Menon.'

The Obituary

> [Animal-assisted therapy] will further contribute towards improving the motivation of patients and indeed inspire those who require therapy via the bond that will be formed between the dog and the client, be it a special child or an adult.
>
> —Professor (Adj.) Dato' Dr Andrew Mohanraj

It is with a heavy heart that I announce the passing of Laddoo, our obsessively possessive dachshund. She lies in what my father once referred to, rather ungraciously I may add, as 'the dog cemetery'. In other words, Laddoo was buried in our garden.

Named after an Indian sweetmeat, Laddoo was the shortest lived of our family's numerous, neurotic, nomadic, four-legged babies. The average life span of our cohort was approximately twelve years. Laddoo was seven.

The notable exception was, of course, Gorby, who survived no more than a day after being dragged in from the cold by the cat. Within the week, he was joined by Lenin and Stalin, also dragged in more dead than alive by the cat. I defended our half blind Pinocchio by stating that at nineteen, the cat must have lost her sense of smell; she mistook these severely and terminally ill puppies for rats.

Hmmm . . .

My wife, Anjana, together with our sons, Adi and Akash, were predictably horrified. Nonetheless, we decided never to reprimand the poor old dame for complimenting us with the prey she caught.

We also kept absolutely quiet when our neighbour, a sexagenarian whose daughter was embroiled in a complicated matrimonial dispute, came enquiring if we'd seen said puppies. They had enough on their plate without having to be cautious when Pinocchio sauntered into their house for cuddles and general *manja.*

Another standout was Mandela, the giant Great Dane. He was so named because Adi took him on long walks to expend his energies. This imposed exercise also helped our son, who is on the autism spectrum, to come out of his shell, lose weight, and socialize with others. Tears fill my eyes at the memory of the inviolable bond between them. For all the protection he gave us by virtue of his size alone, the most peculiar thing about this dog was what petrified him. Of all the things that made him jump onto the sofa and not leave until he no longer saw or smelt their presence, were geckos. He would not enter a room if he so much as sensed the presence of even one of these reptiles a thousand sizes smaller than him. It's quite something to see a Great Dane quivering, much like Anjana when there was a cockroach in the house.

With such politically-inclined names our sons gave to our pets, it made sense, I suppose, that one was a career diplomat and the other, an aide to an MP.

I sort of bonded with Mandela. You see, ten years after Mandela's death (he was also seven), I still have what can only be described as a dent in my foot. It's where Mandela placed his paw while I studied my patient's case notes. Oh, I do miss Mandela's meaning of 'keeping in touch'.

'Now that your children have gone to university, why don't you get a smaller dog?' A thought was planted in our heads by the vet, no less, several years ago. 'A dachshund is good. Small, family friendly. And,' he wagged his forefinger, 'it's not a dog that sheds.'

All of it was true, of course. But no one warned us that a dachshund had to be walked every single day. Granted, Anjana and I lost ten kilogrammes between us within three months of this bundle of sunshine entering our lives. Honestly, though, if we skipped 'walkies' for a mere three days, the deterioration in Laddoo's mental health, and by extension ours, was palpable.

The whining. The pacing. The sad eyes. They were incessant.

Laddoo was, by far, the most privileged of our dogs. She had a stainless-steel bowl (others had plastic ones) and a custom-made bed to suit her extra-long body. For parties, Anjana dressed Laddoo up in a collar decorated with Swarovski crystals.

When she was diagnosed with congestive heart failure, my wife said, 'Ajay, you're a cardiologist. Can't you do something for the baby?'

I stared at her. She glared, clearly of the opinion that I would be able to treat patients with heart ailments no matter the species. Mercifully, she accepted the limitations of my expertise and Laddoo was referred to a vet in Brickfields who specialized in cardiac matters. It was too late, though. Laddoo was already in terminal stages of the disease. I did wonder, though, what would the treatment have entailed? An open bypass surgery? A cardiac stent? Would she have to be on beta blockers? Being the glutton that she was, I wouldn't have been surprised if the vet had said that she suffered from hyperlipidaemia or, possibly, *familial* hyperlipidaemia.

The routine after Laddoo's demise was bound to be the same morose one as for all our dogs. A square plot (rectangular in the case of Mandela and Laddoo) would be picked out within an hour of death. In the past, when a death occurred during the day, the funeral was over by nightfall. I dug the graves as my sons—the snowflakes—found it back-breaking work. Since Ladoo died at night, by eight in the morning, she was in her final resting place. Anjana cried uncontrollably during the solemn moments when I carried our dachshund to her grave.

I doubt anyone realized that the graves were becoming shallower. Surely the six-foot under rule applied only to humans, no?

I did have a recurring nightmare, though. On a dark and stormy night, I was in the middle of my garden with the carcasses of dead dogs floating all around me.

I have yet to break this sad news about Laddoo to the snowflakes. One is in Turkmenistan and the other is busy campaigning for his own seat in Sungai Kolok.

My back aches too much to type a personalized, comforting, and fatherly WhatsApp message to them. This bulletin will have to do.

Rest thee well, sweet Laddoo.

Metopia

> These days, even toddlers are given gadgets as a tool to distract them from throwing a tantrum. Some parents do this so that they can attend to their own gadgets. As the kids get older, their parents might want to limit their use of gadgets, video games or social media. However, parents who are themselves glued to their social media pages are not in a position to convince and advise their kids to control their use of gadgets.
>
> —Professor (Adj.) Dato' Dr Andrew Mohanraj

'Bullshit!'

This is my emphatic reaction to a paragraph of the *Leader* I'm reading. Honestly, it has to be a joke. According to the short piece, Malaysia upholds democratic principles and our political parties strive to protect the rights and freedoms of all its ethnic groups. The religious beliefs and values of a specific religion are never used to oppress others. Even though Islam is Malaysia's official religion, this does not make Malaysia a theocracy. Our democracy protects the rights of minorities who aren't treated as if their rights and opinions don't count.

Looking up from my mobile phone, for a moment, I debate between sneering and laughing out loud. I am Divya Shekar, a small-time Twitter celebrity. Still, it is more likely that a stranger would describe me as a middle-aged woman who begins unimpressively with a thinning hairline, titanium-rimmed glasses that have thicker lenses on the left, and what is regarded as an apple-shaped torso. Worse, I end disappointingly with a pair of legs squeezed into skinny jeans one size too small.

I read the rest of the *Leader.* No doubt, the piece is aimed at pacifying the citizenry into blissful ignorance about the fact that our leaders, especially the judiciary, often choose self-serving solutions as opposed to acting (if not practising) in a judicious manner. Indeed, because of the warped versions—yes, plural—of our judiciary, one court that has no jurisdiction over me allowed another that did to take away my child. Worse, they gave my child to the one man they shouldn't have—my husband.

If only our leaders could be wiser. They should emulate the likes of Sultan Suleiman the Magnificent of the Ottoman Empire. It's said that King Henry VIII of England commissioned a report about the Sultan's equitable judicial system when he embarked on reforms within his kingdom.

I move to the next link on Google and glance at a piece about technology's newest chapter in the internet world—metaverse. Maybe, the digital world is better. Maybe it won't recognize the difference between Muslim and non-Muslim, between democracy and theocracy, between mother and child.

Ping.

That was the phone telling me that the GrabCar I ordered is on its way. I move closer to the side of the kerb. When a Silver Proton Saga pulls up, I open the door and sit on the back passenger seat. I scan the laminated QR code the masked driver with bushy eyebrows is holding out. When he sees the screenshot that I've been fully vaccinated against Covid-19, he nods his thanks. I then lean back into the black PVC seat and try to relax for the drive to my former marital home. The face that's reflected back at me from the car's window is lined, marked with age spots at the top of the cheeks and has a hooked nose—it screams distrust of anyone and everyone.

I pull out a dog-eared copy of the 1992 edition of Neal Stephenson's *Snow Crash*. It's scheduled to be discussed at the book club next weekend. I gathered that it's a story where people escape from their world by putting on virtual reality goggles and earphones. Stephenson has conceived a world where the digital representations of people interact with each other. Recently, a newspaper columnist conjectured that we now live in such a world. It could be further enhanced by the metaverse where augmented reality would be a layer superimposed over the real world. In this version of the world, we would live inside the internet rather than merely accessing it. It's possible to fathom a utopia where technology narrows the gulf of inequality, where the rich and poor have the same experiences, and where no one is punished for the religion they profess. It may even be possible to go forwards and backwards in time at will, like in the movies. Instead of a man falling off the cliff, he'd be brought back up to the edge. If only I could do the same and reverse the events of the worst day of my life. It would be in fifteen frames.

The first would be when I closed the front door of my marital home.

When I glanced back at my child's ruined birthday party, a fat gecko was gunning for Barney's big toe.

The fifteen minutes before this were a blur.

In the arms of a stranger who followed my husband into our home, my distraught and tearful child cried out for me.

Above the deafening sound of toddlers wailing, my husband turned on his heel and walked out of my life.

'S-h-a-?'

'I converted. My name is Shamsir. Mohammed Shamsir bin Abdullah,' shaking his head, he was nonchalant.

The woman accompanying him pried my daughter's chubby hands away from my waist as a policewoman held my bony arms behind my back.

Other mothers huddled to protect their toddlers.

But the words made no sense.

Ah, he made it in time.

The voice was that of my husband's, Shekar's.

'Step away. The child is now mine. She is now Siti Zubaidah binti Shamsir.'

A wonder of the 2014 baking world, my daughter's birthday cake was a three-dimensional replica of Barney, the purple stuffed dinosaur my child adored.

I was about to strike the matchstick to light two candles on my daughter's birthday cake.

The end.

Actually, no. The beginning.

Sigh!

I can't read more of this novel. I put it back in my bag and let all the memories flow, beginning with a single question: How on earth has it come to this?

* * *

I was born at a time when a treat was going to watch a movie at the Rex Cinema. We watched what my father wanted to watch, which was the latest Tamil movie at midnight. They were always viewed through a thick wall of cigarette smoke, as the hall was full of patrons smoking their hearts out. My father was an engineer who trained in a relatively new field of intellectual property matters, but never reached his full potential professionally. He settled by becoming an expert that lawyers occasionally called upon for an opinion in motor-vehicle accidents. The irony of his death when I was nine years old wasn't lost on the reporter who published a story about it in the newspapers. On that rainy December morning, my father was on his way to our house in the respectable, upper middle-class satellite township of Petaling Jaya. He'd been in the city to conduct some business and was forced to stop on the emergency lane because of faulty brakes. The driver of a speeding trailer lost control and ploughed into my father's car, killing him instantly.

Where my sole parent was a widow, Shekar's was a widower who filled the lonely hours after his wife's death from uterine cancer by becoming a member of the association set up to manage the affairs of the Sri Sundaraja Perumal Temple in the royal town of Klang. A particular feature of this house of gods was the famous vegetarian dish made from faux meat called mutton varuval.

When the stars aligned ten years ago, or so the once-naïve me liked to think, I met Shekar at a wedding of a distant relative at this temple. When he sauntered in, the aunties' whispers spread like wildfire. Most of them were related to him by blood or marriage. Those who weren't fawned over him, nevertheless. 'He's an engineer, you know. Just came back from that Silicon Valley place, you know,' one of the aunties said. 'Must be so rich one, you know.'

Shekar announced to anyone willing to hear him that, actually, he wasn't meant to be at the wedding. The tone suggested that those present should be grateful that he'd condescended to attend this event at all. Anyway, he'd apparently taken a quick detour from a work trip to Singapore. At thirty-two years old, he was the youngest keynote speaker to present a paper called 'The Internet and Reality: Endless Possibilities' at a conference about the future of the internet in ASEAN.

One auntie, the sort of well-meaning lady whose muffin top hung over the waistband of her sari's underskirt and who played Cupid whenever and wherever she could, happened to glance at me. As though she was watching a tennis match, she looked at Shekar, then me, and repeated this several times. Behaving as though we were two of the most attractive people at the wedding, surpassing even the glowing and sparkling bridal couple decked in kilogrammes of gold and double-digit carats of diamonds, she made it her mission to introduce us to each other. To give her some leeway for a defence as the person who was instrumental in making what would become my disaster of a marriage, she was not to know then about Shekar's previous relationships. The first was with a colleague who had poured her heart and finances into helping him with his doctoral thesis. When he graduated and acquired the title of 'Dr Shekar Theophilus Stephan', he told her, 'I don't feel the need to share my life with you.' Three months later, he showed no remorse when he got wind that she'd slit her wrists. His priority then was to convince one of his graduate students, a girl whose father was the CEO of a technology company, to give up her coquettish ways and virginity to him. This, however, wasn't the sort of information that fell into the hands of the non-professional matchmaker aunties at weddings. It was enough that there were two people of marriageable age at the same place and time.

Introductions were made at the buffet table. Shekar gave me the treatment ingrained in the DNA of Indian men—to shamelessly stare at a woman. He watched as I piled on that special mutton varuval onto my plate and then walked me to one of the empty tables nearby. Once the 'boy and girl' smiled politely at each other, the beaming auntie withdrew.

'Do you always eat with such abandon?' Shekar scratched a pimple on his cheek.

'Of course. Doesn't everyone?'

With that simple exchange, we announced ourselves to the world, thereby giving hope to my mother, standing in one corner of the *kalyana mandap*, that I would soon be settled in a marriage.

The word to describe Shekar was 'controlled'. He was measured in his speech and chose what I called 'big-big words' like 'ostensible' and 'decompression' instead of the more common 'apparent' or 'relax'.

'Today,' he said in a deep baritone, 'if you want to go to a concert, you have to go to the concert hall. You never need to vacillate about which one to go to. One day, you won't have to. You can be in Carnegie Hall or Royal Albert Hall in seconds.'

'But doesn't that spoil the whole experience? I mean the joy is in actually being there, in London or New York, no?'

'Well, you could say that. Still, take dinosaurs or even fights in the Colosseum. Do you need to be there to experience what it's like? No. You don't need to create an actual dinosaur. We can experience anything we choose to when we make the internet and virtual reality part of our lives. We can create a perfect new world. Instead of just a brave one.'

'Ah-so. Aldous Huxley,' I said, sincerely appreciating his intelligence.

As we continued to flutter our brilliance at one another, for the first time in my thirty years, I was presenting to a suitor my best self—intense, passionate, and committed.

In the fine tradition of marriages among the South Indian diaspora, Shekar and I were 'engaged' within three months of first laying eyes on each other. Effectively, we were legally married, as we'd registered our marriage at the Department of Registrations (Marriage, Births, and Deaths) whereupon I took his first name as my surname. The surprise moment, for my mother most of all, was when Shekar didn't tick the box on the application form stating that he was a 'Christian'. 'Why should I tell anyone my religion?' he said to his new mother-in-law. 'It's not a condition of marriage for non-Muslims.'

Our wedding proper on 30 November 2011 was a low-key affair with 'family only' guests numbering no more than fifty people at a house Shekar bought in the upmarket suburb of

Damansara Heights. One look at the standout fifty-year-old leafy *angsana* tree in the middle of a vast, manicured lawn and, within the day, Shekar transferred RM250,000 cash as 'earnest deposit' into the astonished estate agent's bank account.

It is said that you never really know a person until you've lived with him or her for at least three weeks. Indeed, in less time than that, I discovered that my husband's public persona differed enormously from his private one. Desperate to be recognized for the brand he was creating for his newly incorporated company, he invited total strangers and certifiable sociopaths to our first Christmas party as a married couple. Regardless of colour, creed, or faith, these men enjoyed Shekar's hospitality and consumed crates of contraband alcohol. In the privacy of his journal, Shekar chronicled their misdemeanours, mercenary reputations, and patent dishonesty. To be blunt, he was creating a dossier of sorts on all these people. Fool of a new bride that I was, I chalked up this kind of hypocrisy as being preferable to the vices of other husbands in our social circle whose wives complained about being beaten black and blue after bouts of drinking or gambling. Lulled into a sense of security and marital bliss, within a year of our wedding, I gave birth to our only child, Stephanie (Stevie, for short).

* * *

'What are you doing?' my sexagenarian mother asked on 22 September 2014. It was five days since I walked out of my marital home and one hundred and twenty hours since I held Stevie in my arms. I ran my fingers through my uncombed, waist-long hair. The grease provided the necessary traction to turn the pages of the many newspapers of yesteryear strewn all over the floor.

'I have to find it,' I whispered, for once grateful that my mother was a hoarder.

'What?'

'Conversion case. From 2005, I think.'

'Ah . . .' She understood immediately. Putting aside other chores and tasks, we spent the next few hours combing through the newspapers and also trawling through the internet until we found every possible bit of information regarding cases of non-Muslims whose spouse converted to Islam and, without the consent of the person they married, converted their children as well.

'We must put all this on the internet, Divya-Baby,' my mother was halfway reading through her second article. I blinked several times, not wanting the tears to fall when she used my nickname. 'People must see your love for Stevie.'

'Why? No need for everyone to know my shame.'

Through gritted teeth, my mother said, 'No need for shame. You've done no wrong.'

I knew better than to argue and conceded with a weak, 'Okay.'

Within a week, my mother, who hitherto had no interest in the internet beyond scrolling through Google links, set up a Twitter account with the handle @swly. The letters marked the initials for 'Stevie, We Love You'. From five friends at the start, the number of followers ballooned to one thousand a week later and thousands more in three months.

The initial posts had photos of Stevie from the moment she was born until her ill-fated Barney-themed birthday were met with a lukewarm response. Out of the blue, in 2015, @aussieclean, a Malaysian who had emigrated to the Antipodes, shared a link to a YouTube video called 'Man in custody battle for beloved child', then proceeded to denigrate me for not fighting for my rights. Although incensed that such an unwarranted accusation could be made, I thought it wise to first watch the video.

'Mum, come and watch this.'

When I pressed play, my husband's face filled the frame. I reached out to grip my mother's hand. Next to him was a child dressed in a hoodie and dark glasses, and unrecognizable to the rest of the world. I saw the crooked little finger on her left hand, a miniature version of mine and held my breath. It was Stevie.

> Sorry. I had to bring my daughter.
> For protection. It's a battle right now.
> You know how it is. No one to look after.
> If I can't trust the mother, how to trust anyone?

I paused the video. 'Battle. Can't trust me. Protection. What is he talking about?'

'Ya. Ya. Ya. Just play. Let's see what other stupid things this man will say.'

In the next frame of the video, a blond man with a scratchy voice said, 'Fergal Cane. *Irish Times*. My question is for the child. Do you miss Mummy?'

I didn't blink for fear of missing my child's answer.

'Answer Uncle. He is asking you a question,' my husband prodded Stevie.

There was absolute silence.

The reporter tried with another question. 'What is your name, little one?'

The only sound that came through was the drone of the industrial air conditioner.

'Name?' The child looked down. In a voice replete with heartbreak she said, 'Don't know name, Papa.'

Through gritted teeth, my husband replied, 'Siti Zubaidah is your name.'

I stared at the screen, not aware of the hand that reached out quickly, clicked on the mouse and stopped the video. When the laptop was shut completely, my mother said, 'If he wants some stupid trial by media like this, I will give him a trial by media.'

In three days, my mother hired a virtual assistant, a student with the digital name of @tarastar undertaking a course in Mass Communication Studies at a local university. Her task was to filter and moderate all 'followers' and comments that came through the Twitter account. Through this exercise, a list of potential legal experts and media-savvy individuals or organizations were identified, then pared down to those willing to offer their services without a fee or at least a much-reduced one. As advised, @swly neither agreed nor disagreed with any views put forward. Instead, @swly vicariously told my story by telling the stories of others in similar situations.

The first was the tragic case of R. Subashini who, in 2007, lost her child when her husband converted their child without telling her. This kind of unilateral conversion of a child to Islam was permissible. No provision of our Federal Constitution was violated because the word 'parent' was used in Article 12(4); therefore, there was no need to procure the consent of both parents before her child was converted to Islam.

When the response was, 'What does this mean, actually?' the explanation from @swly in late 2016 was as follows: 'Since 2007, invariably, a non-Muslim parent in Malaysia in such cases has had no redress. So, effectively, I lost my Stevie and no court in Malaysia can help me.'

'What do you mean there is no court that can help you?' asked @agnessa. 'If he's now Muslim, then why don't you go to the Syariah court?'

I laughed. @swly, however, acted on the advice of her team and waited until the new year before publishing the following post:

> 'As a non-Muslim, I cannot go to the Syariah Court. That court doesn't have any jurisdiction over me. I can only go to the Civil Court, the relic of our colonial past. The day my husband—and he's still my husband—converted, our marriage became null and void. If I want to marry anyone else, I have to file for divorce. Now that he is a Muslim, he is subject to the rules and regulations of Syariah Law. Also, article 121 of our Federal Constitution says that the jurisdiction of the Syariah Court should not be disputed even though they are not constituted as superior courts. So, this means that I go to the Civil Courts and he goes to the Syariah Courts.'

It was a long while before @ruskilaw responded with, 'What does this mean? Why is the conversation such an issue in Malaysia? Can't you convert your child back? Are you saying that you're no longer the child's mother? No maternal grandmother either?'

Inserting a tearful emoji at the end of her reply, @swly wrote, 'She is now the child of God. I am not sure about my mother. What I know is that, in the eyes of the law, whatever that law is, we don't exist. The child has no choice in this. My child will be Muslim, for life. If she wants to renounce this, she becomes an apostate, which is not permissible by law. Everything, and I mean, everything, changes, from tax, inheritance, and so on.'

The 1,025 responses to this ranged from disbelief to discontent. The one that offered most comfort was a one by a former diplomat in a self-imposed exile now living in Adelaide, Australia, @harishamade: 'The Arabization of Islam in Malaysia is contrary to the concepts of secularism set up by the founding fathers of the Federation after Independence. It was written almost fifty years ago that in a multiracial and multireligious society like ours, the leaders of the country strove not to be too identified with any particular race or religion so that the various communities especially minority communities are assured that we will not allow their rights to be trampled underfoot.'

This brought about another three months of online discussions that centred on one issue: why did Shamsir convert to Islam in the first place? He had made it public knowledge that there was no third party involved in the breakdown of his marriage. When the Malaysian Twitterati suggested that Shamsir now stood a chance of obtaining the status of being a 'bumiputra', others begged for an explanation. So it was that when it was explained as 'affirmative action to help the Malays of the land' get the upper hand, it was the courageous @ruskilaw who asked the obvious question: 'Isn't that a discriminatory practice?'

Not one of the Malaysian Twitterati responded to this. Not even @swly. The reality of the situation, if ever it was put into writing, was farcical, at best. In this land of a thousand smiles, because I belonged to a minority race, I had few rights and almost zero access to any recourse when my child was taken away from me. In my land of birth, I was often referred to as a *pendatang* or an 'immigrant'.

While everyone online mulled over the conundrum I was in, time passed and, soon, it was 2018. There seemed to an upsurge of energy among @swly's nameless and faceless supporters when they read that, on 29 January, the apex court ruled that henceforth, in a civil marriage, the consent of both parents must be obtained before a Certificate of Conversion to Islam can be issued for a child. Although I was aware this was probably an act to pacify non-Muslim voters in an election year, @swly was caught up in collective clarion call to 'Go bring back our Stevie.'

@swly's online jubilation didn't quite translate offline. Outwardly, I regained eight of the ten kilogrammes I'd initially lost, the bald spots on my scalp were now filled with tufts of baby hair, and the nightly bouts of itching were confined to my upper arms. Crying myself to sleep every night, though, I filled the hollow in my heart with memories: Stevie sucking on her thumb, the first time Stevie said 'Changu' when her grandmother gave her the stuffed Barney, the special dress made for Stevie's birthday.

These were all in the past, though.

One day, in 2019, I began to fill that hollow with dreams of what my child could and would be in the future: a girl with ringlets down to her waist, a teenager with braces and pigtails, a young woman full of hope and optimism, an undergraduate throwing her mortarboard in the air upon receiving her scroll, a bride decked out in kilogrammes of gold. I drifted off to sleep each night with one thought: I will find my daughter.

'Forget the courts if you want to find our Stevie-Baby.' My mother declared one day in the third quarter of 2021 when the world was still grappling with the hardships from a global pandemic.

'Then how, Mama?'

'We hire a private investigator.'

The scrawny fellow had a stillness about him and a way of fixing his gaze that made you immediately aware that he didn't have a single iota of spontaneity or frivolity in him. His two-page report revealed surprises, the main one being that father and daughter never left town as assumed all those years ago. In fact, they were still settled in the house in Damansara Heights. Also, there was someone new in their lives named Versha.

* * *

When the GrabCar comes to a stop, I look around. Mumbling my thanks to the driver, I alight and stand outside what was once my home. Yes, the neighbours' houses are the same, notwithstanding the weather-worn spots of fungus peeping out from fissures in the walls. The smell of warm bread wafting from a home-based bakery business down the road evokes a sense of the familiar. Where there once was a rickety five-foot gate and overgrown hedge, there is now an eight-feet-high wall, plastered with white cement and ornate electric gates. Only the new shoots on top of the angsana tree are visible from outside. Peeping through the gaps, I can make out a whole lot of detached, individual, cauliflower-shaped cumulus clouds that mark fair weather conditions.

'Come inside,' a voice booms from nowhere. It is my husband's. But where did it come from? There is no speaker anywhere. Anyway, when the gates magically open, like Dorothy walking along the yellow brick road, each step I take fill me with dread and wonder in equal measure.

'You're here. Come inside.' He's uncharacteristically cordial when he opens the door. Showing me to a chair nearby, he says, 'Wait here.' He disappears behind an ornate oriental screen featuring a lilac phoenix and red-gold dragon soaring into a pale, yellow sky. This exquisite artwork renders it impossible to see the inside of what was once my home.

I remove my mask, reach into my bag, and pull out a smaller one that contains several gifts for Stevie: a new stuffed Barney, a pack of playing cards, a packet of sweets, my letters and birthday cards that were never sent for a lack of a postal address to use, etc. I sense a familiar presence and catch the doe-shaped eyes of a girl staring at me, unblinking. My Stevie appears to be spying on me from behind the screen.

Dropping everything, I run forward, fall to my knees, and gather her into my arms. It's as though with each kiss on the bony cheeks, I'm transmuting a memory to store in the hollow in my heart.

'Calm down,' my husband says. 'You'll scare her,' he adds and prises my hands away from the child. Regaining some decorum, I pull away and return to the chair.

'Come here.' I reach out to her.

The child, for she was still no more than that, looks up at my husband.

'Go,' he says and the child takes a few steps before she stands in front of me.

'Let me look at you.' I take in the short, choppy hairstyle with spiky and jagged edges. The skin is pale and the look, blank. It's as though the child doesn't know how to smile any more.

'Who are you?' The child's voice is soft.

I stare at her for a long while. Keeping my gaze intensely focused on my child, through gritted teeth, I ask, 'Did your Versha do this? Where is she?'

He smirks, not missing a beat. I recognize this immediately. He knows he has the upper hand and there's no harm in sharing information with her. Pointing backwards, he says, 'She was up all night with Siti Zubaidah. She's taking a break to recharge her batteries.'

I remember nothing of the remaining thirty minutes I spend with my child. No. Not my child. This zombie who is lifeless and finds the world around her strange.

That night, for the first time since I moved back in with my mother, I creep into her bed. In my mother's embrace, I weep for myself and the child who no longer knows that I'm the one who gave birth to her.

* * *

Meanwhile, in the house in Damansara Heights, Shamsir concluded that the events of the day proved that the success of his experiment had exceeded his expectations. As he put Siti Zubaidah to bed, he also helped her put on the custom-made goggles and plugged in the ear phones. When he switched it on, he could hear Versha's voice say, 'Hello baby girl. You've had a difficult day. It's time to sleep now.' The little girl stuck her thumb into her mouth and cuddled her new stuffed dinosaur for comfort. Shamsir walked to the plush master bedroom he had once shared with Divya, wearing a contented smile, and playing with his greying goatee. Seated at his desk, he opened his journal and, in his cursive longhand, wrote the following:

> Hypotheses proved. We don't need to bother with the byzantine bureaucracy of ideologies, governments, kingdoms, sultanates, or religions. The past must be forgotten to make virtual reality a complete success. In our lifetime, we didn't need to create an actual dinosaur to know what it would be like to see a dinosaur. We didn't need to rebuild the Colosseum to enjoy gladiators fighting. It was all possible with technology. Similarly, Siti Zubaidah no longer needs a mother. With the internet and virtual reality, she has forgotten the concept of an actual mother. The only mother she knows now is Versha. Ergo, metaverse is the **only** way forward for our brave new world. No. Not our brave new world. Our perfect new world. A Metopia.'

Minor Issues

> People who find themselves in an abusive relationship . . . may even still love the person who is abusing them . . . The victim may also be so psychologically vulnerable that they actually idealise their spouse and see only their good side, and make excuses for the abuse that occurs. This is especially as the person who carries out the abuse can often be charming and pleasant outside the periods of abuse.
>
> —Professor (Adj.) Dato' Dr Andrew Mohanraj

It was the darkest of gunpowder grey skies when we reached the toll plaza, perhaps an indication of what I should expect from making this journey. The lady in the booth shrugged when I asked if the traffic jam on the North-South Highway continued all the way to Bukit Mertajam.

'Find out for yourself, lah.' With a gloved hand, she handed me the change after topping up my Touch & Go card and slid shut the window.

We couldn't do anything else, I suppose. After all, we'd been driving north of Kuala Lumpur for close to five hours.

Shoving the RM5 into the breast pocket of my batik shirt, I put the gear into Drive when the barrier was raised. Our car moved ahead only to come to a standstill 100 metres away when the traffic was forced to merge into two lanes on this country road.

'I told you not to make a big issue about the delay,' Malini quipped. 'You knew, when we started that this was going to be a long drive. Luckily, I brought enough food so that we won't need to stop unnecessarily.'

If she hadn't delayed our departure by two hours because of the Zoom meeting with her staff that she'd forgotten to reschedule, we would have arrived at our destination much earlier. That was what I wanted to say. Instead, I replied with, 'Hmmm . . .'

Once we were back to following behind a BMW at no more twenty kilometres per hour, Malini reached for her phone. 'Anyway, I found out from Google that this St Anne's Church was founded in 1846 by French missionaries. It's now called . . . Wait, ah . . .' She swiped the screen of her handphone and said, 'It is now called the Minor Basilica of St Anne.'

'Yup. Like I sa—'

'Ya. Ya. Ya. No need to repeat,' Malini interrupted.

I sighed, silently recounting the family story anyway. In the nineteenth century, French missionaries decided to build a church, which we called 'The Old Church'. It was some four kilometres away from the centre of Bukit Mertajam, a town in the north of the Malay peninsula. By the 1950s, there was a need for a newer church. The site chosen was on the main road opposite Lorong Bukit Satu, where my grandparents lived. I was born in this tropical cottage, which we fondly called the 'BM House', located at the foot of a hill.

Papa used to tease me that if I wanted to lose weight, I should climb this hill and then 'seek God's help', since the Old Church had been built on the other side of it. My grandmother defended me by reminding Papa of his 'failures'. When he passed his medical exams in 1964, my enormously relieved grandmother donated funds to every religious establishment in town. Since then, every 26 July, those who rested at the BM House during the celebrations of the Feast of St Anne, were regaled with the unsubstantiated story that the source of the money for the cross mounted on the wall behind the altar was a devout Hindu.

This was the first time I was returning to the BM House after Papa sold it in the 1990s to fund a transfer to Kuala Lumpur and facilitate my grandmother's cancer treatment. I suspected that had we stayed in this bungalow and found another way to raise the necessary funds, my grandmother may have lived longer. City life, I was certain, hastened her demise within six months of our move to a semi-detached house in the heart of suburbia. The new owner of the BM House swiftly converted it into a homestay and promised us free food and board.

When we arrived, our portly host eyed my wife of eight years, as most folks do. He looked at her bare arms and shoulders, tiny waist and buxom chest, dressed in the hot pink bandeau dress. The caretaker makcik stared at me. I recognized the look. When I had tied the *thali* around Malini's neck on our wedding day, our guests were equally curious. The *lengha*-clad bride was unconcerned about baring her body from ribcage to pubic bone in a temple and the groom appeared to be struck dumb. The thing is, my feisty mother had long drummed it into me that to disapprove of a woman's attire wouldn't be viewed as trying to protect Malini but as imposing my will and misogyny. So, I learned to keep my thoughts about what the women in my life wore—or did not—to myself. Now, I held the makcik's gaze long enough to convey the message that I was still the man in this marriage, as though that explained everything. It worked, I suppose, because it seemed to be the catalyst for the makcik to pick up a tray and offer us a welcome drink each of iced lemongrass juice with honey.

An inky blue-black sky greeted us at the Old Church. A stranger agreed to take a photo of Malini and me with our arms around each other. With our backs to the centuries-old building, he was able to capture the majesty and antiquity of the Old Church in the background. Beggars from Rohingya lined either side of the steps leading up to the Old Church, capitalizing on their half-naked, wailing and malnourished infants. Ignoring them, Malini walked over to three women who stood on the top-most steps. Dressed in monotone saris, they kept their heads bent when my wife dropped several ringgit into the *dupattas* they held out.

'I honour their vow to beg,' Malini explained when I reached the top step.

We bought a foot-long candle each from a stall nearby and entered the Old Church. Walking up the aisle, I noted the emblem of the Catholic Church and a symbol of Papal authority of the crossed keys of St Peter on the furnishings. We lit our candles, held them up to the statue of the saintly matriarch who oversees the happiness of the family by ensuring the well-being of children and forging lasting marriages.

'It'll be placed near Mother until the flame burns out,' a volunteer informed us as she reached out to take our candles. Dressed in angelic white robes, she wore an intense look, as if she knew that we were lying even to God.

Outside, we walked around the Old Church, mimicking the circumambulation of a Hindu temple. Malini looked at a woman carrying a cherubic child in her arms, her yearning unmasked.

Oh, dear God! Please grant us this gift, which we've travelled all this way for.

I recalled what our doctor-cum-family friend had written in his referral letter to the consultant OB-GYN, Dr Suresh Thambyrajah: 'Thank you for agreeing to see this couple. They are desirous of their own issue to complete the family. I have assured them the best treatment under your care, such as the possibility of IVF.'

Back at the BM House, makcik served comfort food of rice, *kangkung* sambal, and pomfret curry. We then bid our hosts good night and retreated to the guestroom. When I looked at the queen-sized bed, my recurring worry that the truth about our marriage would become common knowledge assailed me. Perhaps, I'd accidentally blurt it out when drunk. It never happened because Malini's reminders were constant, like muttering the following at the Old Church prior to the photo being taken: 'Smile so that people think everything is okay.'

While Malini lathered the night cream for her face and neck, followed by body lotion, I scrolled through my iPad and checked my Twitter feed. Even my Twitter handle—@fattybombom—was a source of discontent for Malini. Sigh!

When I saw her screw the cap of the Nivea Milk back onto the bottle, I shut my mobile device. I turned to the woman I adored. There was a time, at the start of our eight-year marriage, when she adored me in return. I knew it in my very bones. For the past five years, though, she insisted that it was in my head that she wasn't reciprocating my emotions. Experts called this gaslighting, it seems. I wondered if it was still so when I'd already acquired proof of her infidelity.

I stopped breathing for a moment.

What was so wrong with me that Malini didn't love me?

No! Now was not the time to think about these issues.

Casting it and my self-worth aside, I reached out to touch her shoulder. 'Ready?'

Malini first checked to make sure that all the windows were closed, the latch on the door was in its proper place and switched off the lights. Only then did I hear the rustling sound of her removing her clothes. Once naked, she poked my chest and whispered, 'Like I said, we're not making love. I am allowing you to have sex with me to save twenty grand on IVF treatment.'

In that moment of utter despair before I gave in to our bodies, I choked back my tears. I once again begged the Almighty for a miracle so that my reality of unrequited love in a loveless marriage would pale into a minor issue if and when our baby was born.

Kumbavishaygam (An excerpt from *The Age of Smiling Secrets*)

> Power is intoxicating. The desire to control others releases dopamine, the feel-good neurotransmitter, in the same reward pathway in the brain that operates in addictions. That is why once power is tasted, it is often difficult to let it go, particularly when narcissistic qualities seep in . . . However, it can also lead to poor judgment, narcissism and subtle brutality in trying to be a 'no nonsense' leader.
>
> —Professor (Adj.) Dato' Dr Andrew Mohanraj

'What a joke!' Nandini stood inside the marquee and looked around her. The stalls were all set up for the 'Open Day' her mother, Kamini, was hosting. She glanced at Kamini's latest creation—a bedspread with a picture of a house by the side of a stream in the shape of a kidney bean. A mango-coloured ribbon pulled through the loops at the border added definition. A smile of recognition. She'd learned to swim in such a place.

Nandini looked up. Her mother's back was to her. This was her chance.

For the first time in seven years, the fifteen-year-old crossed the drain at the back of the Sungai Petani house and ventured deep into Foothills Estate. The further along she walked, the thicker the ground cover became. Unseen by the sun, the moss-covered roots of the rubber trees bulged. The living pillars, black and rough, extended high above the ground before they disappeared into a natural canopy of dark green leaves.

When Nandini turned the corner, there was a clearing and she saw a bridge. Across it, there was a motorbike outside the front door of a dwelling place. She recognized the red helmet on the seat. Karuppan's helmet.

What was he doing here?

'Karuppan?'

Karuppan stood by the window and looked out.

Kamini's child. Kamini's walk. Kamini's eyes. But the child's hair was wild. This was insane. If he turned down the volume of the TV, she would know he was avoiding her. If he allowed her inside, then . . .

What if she was like her father, Appa? He was the kind of person who called him that filthy name—estate boy.

Karuppan opened the front door.

'Nandini.'

Nandini looked up. Karuppan was standing with his legs apart and hands placed firmly on his hips. He was a tall man, at least six inches taller than her mother.

Imposing. Authoritative. Strong.

'What are you doing here?'

'I should be asking you that, Kanna.' He used her nickname on purpose. 'Shouldn't you be at your birthday party?'

'Huh! The party is not for me.'

Karuppan gave a broad smile and the muscles on his face relaxed.

Poor thing.

Within a few years of Kamini's enterprise, Jasmine Crochets, operating as a private limited company, she'd managed to build a substantial list of clients. To celebrate, every year, Kamini hosted an annual 'Open Day'. In the days before the celebrations, the Sungai Petani house teemed with people. From caterers preparing food to employees furiously crocheting items to be sold to the guests who would mill about, sipping cups of coffee or tea as they would chat among themselves. The one-off creation for the year would be auctioned and the proceeds would be divided among the workers to help fund their children's education. Then would come an intimate party to celebrate Nandini's birthday. Like a sentry guard, Papa Aunty, Kamini's houseguest who had outstayed her welcome, would stand near the buffet table and serve the food. She once told Kamini, 'Must stop these Chinkis who pile everything on their plates but don't eat anything.'

Karuppan invited Nandini into his home and she surveyed the place: the TV with an internal antenna, his sofa, kitchen, two pots, one pan, two plates, and a stove. At the threshold of his bedroom, she turned to face him. 'Sorry. Nosey.' Her one-sided smile showed her embarrassment.

'No problem,' he said. 'Sit down.' He waved his hand towards the dining table.

'Thank you. This place is beautiful.'

'Thank you.'

'You live here alone?' she asked, sitting down at the small dining table.

'Yes,' he answered, focusing on a spot on the wall above Nandini's head. When he returned from Kuala Lumpur five years ago, his inquiries at the Land Registry Office revealed that no one owned this place that he'd once named 'Kamini's Winter Palace'. He decided then to make it his. Metal beams were inserted in key places to fortify the structure. Slabs of asbestos and red tiles replaced the *attap* roof. Rainwater that collected in gutters was channelled into a pipe that led to the stream behind the house. The beams on the white walls were painted black—Karuppan's sanctuary was an English cottage in the heart of a tropical rubber estate.

'So, what brings you here?'

'Nothing,' Nandini shrugged. She twirled a lock of hair, then picked up a gardening magazine and flicked through the pages, paying zero attention to the articles.

Again, poor thing. Time to cheer her up once again.

'Do you know the story of this place?' Karuppan sat opposite Nandini.

She shook her head.

'It's called "The Legend of Nagakanna".'

* * *

Once upon a time, early in the twentieth century, the colonial managers of Foothills Estate picked up about fifty Tamil indentured labourers from Madras and brought them to tap rubber in the estate. They were given homes and a community developed as their numbers grew. In need of a place of worship, the Estate Elders commissioned a Hindu priest from Penang to help them locate a suitable place to build a temple. A party of six rubber tappers and the priest spent a month in June roaming the very depths of Foothills Estate.

On the day the Tamils call *pournami*, the day of the full moon, the exhausted priest decided to have a rest. He crouched down by the banks of a river, cupped his hands and scooped up some water to drink. His thirst quenched, he looked up and saw a jasmine tree in full bloom on the islet across the river. Next to the tree, a cobra raised its head and dilated the muscles of its neck to form a hood with a double chevron pattern. It started swaying from side to side.

A dancing snake.

The priest decided that this was a propitious moment and declared the spot a holy one. Everyone agreed that this would be the site of the new temple in Foothills Estate. Once the bridge was constructed, a temple with living quarters for the priest was built on that islet.

The consecration ceremony called *kumbavishaygam* was held soon after. People entered the temple's inner sanctum to place their hopes, prayers, dreams and offerings—gold coins, diamonds, or precious stones—in the hollow below a raised platform. The hollow was then sealed and an idol placed above this platform. The entire ceremony was accompanied by continuous recitations of Sanskrit mantras for three days. After this, the temple priest alone entered the inner sanctum. The *kumbavishaygam* was repeated every twelve years.

In the late 1920s, on a cold August morning, the priest heard a loud clanging sound coming from inside the temple. He rushed in to see a man squatting in the middle of the hall clutching his eyes and screaming. A crowbar lay next to him. The priest pulled the man's hands away. What the priest saw, in the light of the kerosene lamp, horrified him: there was blood streaming down the man's cheeks and the sockets of his eyes were empty.

The priest treated the man's wounds and made him rest. Then, he summoned the Estate Elders. When they arrived, the man confessed that he wanted to steal the jewels and gold in the temple. He had raised the crowbar to strike. Before he could bring it down on the idol, he had heard a hissing sound. The last words the man uttered were, 'I saw the cobra's fangs.'

There was worse to come because he began to run in circles, clutching his ears. He could no longer hear. No one knew his name or where he came from.

The Estate Elders gave the thief a Tamil name, Nagakanna: 'naga' meaning 'cobra' and 'kanna' meaning 'eyes'. He spent the remainder of his days in the temple grounds, and the people of Foothills Estate brought him milk and eggs to eat. Within a year, Nagakanna was dead. In spirit form, Nagakanna's sight and hearing were fully restored.

In time, the children of Foothills Estate grew up, left Sungai Petani and the temple crumbled. The priest's quarters remained but became dilapidated. And the story of Nagakanna became a frightful legend.

* * *

Round and round, the bow-legged ghost danced, overjoyed.

Having eavesdropped on Karuppan's narration, Nagakanna told a slimy baby iguana and a toad, 'I'm a legend, you know. A legend.'

He stopped dancing.

'How can this Nandini say that?' He put his hands on his hips, annoyed.

'But how, Karuppan? Not true, lah, this legend.' Nandini pouted.

'And why not?' asked Karuppan in his sing-song voice.

'Karuppan, the cobra's venom is a neurotoxin,' she said, rubbing her eyes.

'Wah! Where did you learn such a big word?'

'That's the new word Papa Aunty told us all about yesterday. It means a poison which acts on the nervous system,' Nandini answered.

'Oh,' he replied. 'Don't rub your eyes. They're the most important part of the body and the windows to your soul. If you rub them, you can even become blind. Then what? You'll be like Nagakanna—no one will know your name. Your life will be a complete secret.'

Nandini stopped rubbing her eyes but was quiet. 'I'm not blind. Still, I don't know what my real name is—Nandini or Nadia.'

Karuppan didn't know what to say. There was nothing he could do about the fact that Nandini's father had converted Nandini to Islam without Kamini's consent or knowledge. There was nothing he could do, either, about the fact that both Syariah and the Civil Law were practised concurrently in this, his land of birth. They—the authorities—had even changed Nandini's name to Nadia without anyone's consent.

He sighed.

'Come,' he said and took her hand. 'I have to take you back, birthday girl.'

Nandini sighed.

'I suppose so,' she said rubbing her nose.

'What? You don't want a ride on my new motorbike?' he asked.

Nandini's head shot up and she smiled brightly.

'That's better,' he said. With his hand on the doorknob, he turned to face her. 'You know, if you become blind, you'll become like this,' he stuck his neck out and opened his eyes so wide that they bulged.

Nandini burst out laughing.

'That's more like it, Kanna. Be happy,' Karuppan said and led her out the front door.

'Look at your mother. She looks so worried,' Karuppan said, when they turned into Jalan Sekerat ten minutes later.

Nandini leaned over his shoulder. Kamini stood at the front gates, wringing her hands and pacing. She turned her head when she heard the roar of the motorbike's engine.

'Nandini! Next time you go somewhere, at least tell me first.' Holding her hand out for Nandini, she added, 'Mama is waiting with your birthday cake.'

Nandini took her mother's hand and jumped off the motorbike. 'Thanks, Karuppan.'

He ran a fatherly hand down Nandini's cheek and caught her chin.

'Thanks.' Kamini echoed her child and asked his chin, 'You don't want to come in?'

Sixteen years. And she still won't look at me or say my name.

He looked at Kamini's long hair tied back in one loose plait down her back. Her shoulders in her sleeveless blouse glistened; the contours of her body were deeply attractive. She had become an exotic beauty before his very eyes. He cleared his throat. 'Sorry. I can't.'

Kamini nodded and slid her arm around Nandini's shoulders. Together, they turned, walked into the marquee. He could have stayed a moment longer to watch them and savour the smell of jasmine. Instead, he revved up the engine of his motorbike and rode away.

Ten minutes later, Karuppan threw his keys down on the plastic table at the *mamak* stall opposite the temple. While the hawker fried his mee goreng, Karuppan looked at the temple. A boy, with spindly arms and a thin moustache leaned a ladder against the wall. A girl with two plaits down her back stood next to him, holding on to a bunch of fairy lights. Karuppan hoped he didn't make the same mistake. He prayed the boy would say the right thing if the girl confessed her love for him. He looked up at the heavens above and whispered, 'The day she looks me in the eye, I will say I'm sorry.' Touching the scar on his left cheek, he added, 'And that I love her.'

* * *

Stretching her arms out, Kamini massaged the ache in the muscles at back of her neck. Uppermost was her angst at how difficult her daughter had become. It had been nearly three years since Nandini first ventured into Foothills Estate. Kamini wasn't opposed to Nandini's sense of adventure.

How could she stomach it if Karuppan one day told Nandini to get lost, too?

Sighing, Kamini put away her things and almost tripped over Max, the new puppy, as she walked out of her office. Once in the courtyard, she walked along the path by the side of maid's room. In front of the house, she sat down on the wide rim of the fountain, what she once called her Summer Palace. Shivering from head to toe, she looked at the elongated shadow of the crooked coconut trees on the outer walls of the Sungai Petani house. A lonely woman looking at her childhood home.

The leaves in the garden rustled in the wind; an owl hooted; tomcats meowed, poised for a fight; water gurgled in the fountain; toads croaked; crickets chirped.

Kamini couldn't think. It was so bloody noisy.

The street light outside the Sungai Petani house flickered.

What more was there to think about?

Kamini stood up. She ran from her Summer Palace, up the three steps, by the side of the house, past the Ashoka trees, past the maid's window, through the back gate, and across the drain. She chose to run to the left when the path bifurcated.

The wet stones and pebbles glowed in the light of the full moon. When she saw the light at the end the dark tunnel of row upon row of rubber trees, Kamini ran towards it.

Would he be there? He had to be.

Would he tell her stories? She loved his stories.

Would it be their story? She yearned for a happy ending with him.

She reached a clearing and stopped.

It was different. This was a garden. Clean and landscaped with shrubs. New roofing. A cement wall. Electricity. She took a few steps back. It was someone else's house.

The back of her legs hit something hard. She reached out to steady herself as she sank onto a rock. She'd lost him.

* * *

Nagakanna saw Kamini's return to her Winter Palace as his chance to direct the main characters in what he believed to be his own romantic drama. Even the setting was wonderful: in the light of nature's spotlight, Kamini's long and silky hair shone, a light breeze and the ferns rustled, fireflies danced all over the place. All the members of his current audience—furry rats, mongooses, the iguana, and chameleons—had taken their seats. He could not cajole the 'Queen' cobra away from her nest of eggs about to hatch. Feeling fat in her skin, she was eager for new fangs, eyes, and tongue tips. Apparently, humans called this process *ecdysis*.

* * *

Karuppan watched Kamini from inside his home. She remembered.

The confident walk.

Those almond-shaped eyes.

The hour-glass figure.

In the mirror on the wall by the door, Karuppan-in-the-mirror said, 'This is insane.'

From somewhere deep inside him, he heard, 'Hello! Can you hurry up? This is your only chance.' The voice was high-pitched and scratchy.

Karuppan opened the door and stepped out into the dark. He walked onto the grass planted a few months ago and crossed the small bridge. When an errant twig he stepped on snapped, she lifted her face. He saw the longing in her eyes.

Kamini watched him.

In that one infinitesimal moment, their senses were attuned to every nuance of change—the sound of leaves rustling faded away to be replaced by the sound of their hearts beating in unison, the smell of jasmine teased their shallow breaths, the curtain of an inky black sky excluded all others. The pain of past separation, the agony of a failed marriage, and the struggle for financial freedom were forgotten. Instead, a crackling energy drew them close.

Karuppan was dressed only in shorts. Kamini could see his muscular legs, black and gleaming—legs that were familiar with all of Foothills Estate. He reached his hands out.

She stood up.

He stood still.

For how long did they stand like this? Two hours. Two minutes. No one counted.

He rushed to her.

'Look at me.'

She looked.

Tenderly, he smiled back.

'I love you,' he said.

She smiled.

They kissed.

He took her by the hand and led her over the bridge, into the inner sanctum of their Winter Palace, where the keeper of hopes and dreams once lived. She went through the door first and looked around. He closed the door behind them and she turned to him.

Much later, when they woke up, both felt more alive than they'd ever been.

Throughout their affair, Kamini and Karuppan made a conscious effort not to talk about a future together, the Sungai Petani house, or Appa. How delighted they were with each new discovery. She scolded him for leaving the tap on while he brushed his teeth. He ironed his shirts before putting them on. She didn't draw the curtains to allow the moonlight to filter through. She liked lots of milk with her coffee. He drank his black and thick.

One night, Karuppan surprised Kamini when he prepared a special dish made from leftover vegetables. Bubbles formed when he added water to the hot pan and the vegetables squeaked when he stir-fried them. He called his dish 'Bubble and Squeak'.

Only once did they discuss Nandini. Karuppan told Kamini he suspected that the girl was planning to run away but said he did not know when, where, or how.

'What do you mean run away?' Kamini asked. 'Why? What's wrong?'

'I don't know. After that picnic you went on, she's been coming here during the day. She's even brought a bag with her. See?' he said, pointing to the corner of the bedroom. When he did not see it there, he turned to the other corner. 'Oh, it's there. Since you've come, I can't remember where things are. Everything is all over the place.'

Kamini started to cry.

Karuppan lifted her chin. 'Hey? What's wrong?'

Kamini looked down again. 'She wants to run away from me. I'm that bad a mother.'

Karuppan stayed silent for some time before replying. 'You know, it's nothing. She's a teenager.' He laughed. 'Didn't we all want to run away when we were that age?'

Kamini smiled. He didn't say she was a bad mother.

'I suppose you're right.' Kamini shook her head. 'Let's talk of happy things.' She narrated Max's latest prank: knowing how Papa Aunty hated her, the dog regularly urinated inside her shoes.

Once, Kamini brought a new bedspread featuring a design of two snakes mating. Karuppan demanded they imitate the scene. Another time, he said, 'Come, let's go to the main entrance of Foothills Estate. Let's go for a walkabout.'

'Walkabout? Where did you get that from?'

'I saw it on the television. Come,' Karuppan grinned, taking her hand.

'What? Isn't the path from my house the only way to get here?'

'No. That's the back way. There is a front way,' he said, smiling and leading her to the front door. He flicked a light switch. When he opened the door, Kamini looked out, clapped her hands, and gave a delighted laugh. There were little lights all along the pathway.

'This looks like an airport runway,' Kamini said.

When they returned, the jasmine tree was in full bloom. 'We have to plant another tree. This one looks so lonely,' he suggested, as she picked a flower and smelt it.

Kamini agreed. 'Yes, it will be our tree,' she said.

A month into their affair, Karuppan asked Kamini, 'Are you going to do something special for this year's Open Day?'

'What do you mean?'

'Well, it's Nandini's eighteenth birthday.'

Kamini bit her lip, for she had forgotten about it. A week later, she told Karuppan, 'I'll do something that reflects our Hindu culture. I'm going to have a *wayang kulit* show. We'll showcase the Ramayana.'

Karuppan was quiet. She had not expected this silence. She touched his hand and jerked her chin forward, as if to ask, 'What?'

'Wayang kulit is banned. Don't you think it will be dangerous?'

Kamini sat down next to him and held his hands. 'Nothing will happen. It's only for a select crowd. I'll make sure of it.'

Karuppan nodded. He refused to fight with her. He looked out of the window and, though it was still dark outside, he could hear the birds chirping. Like all mornings they were together, he wanted to watch her get dressed and leave. As she made her way back through Foothills Estate, she sometimes skipped and sometimes ran. All the time, she smiled.

* * *

'Well, what do you think? Will this all work out?' Nagakanna asked the agitated king cobra waiting for his 'Queen'—the one he'd left to guard their eggs. There was no reply.

'Hey!' Nagakanna shouted. 'Where do you think you're going?'

The king cobra had gone for a 'slitherabout'.

* * *

It was the night that Tamils call *ammavasai*, the night of the new moon and, possibly, one of the darkest ever. By about half past ten, the water in the drain behind the Sungai Petani house was overflowing. It carried a broken roof tile, screws belonging to hinges of gable-shaped canvas canopies, whole branches from coconut trees, and a red helmet. Abruptly, it stopped raining. Soon, even the drizzle ceased. The air was still.

A respite.

Karuppan was halfway to his sanctuary. Little light filtered through the gaps in the rubber trees. The ground cover cushioned his steps. When he stubbed his toe against a rock, his senses were jolted into awareness of everything inside and around him: the smell of rain mixed with unprocessed rubber, the stench of a decomposing rat, the voices in his head, and the look of disdain on the images of people in the movies in his mind. He had sheer contempt for his station in life.

Karuppan felt his way and sat down on the rock. He stared into the darkness around him and let his eyes become accustomed to the enveloping gloom. The intense interpretation of the ancient Ramayana during the shadow dance he'd watched half an hour ago stirred something deep in Karuppan. He understood the heroine's dejected state.

That image.

Kamini and her husband, Appa, with their daughter, Nandini standing in between them. A complete family unit. A couple celebrating their child's birthday. No. Not a child. A young lady of eighteen now.

He wasn't a part of any of it. He couldn't be. The laws of the land said so. He couldn't marry Kamini if he wanted to. Even though her husband had converted to Islam, Kamini, the non-Muslim party, had not. She remained Appa's wife.

It was as if Karuppan didn't exist.

What about the possibility of his family with Kamini?

Tears fell as he examined his dreams and effaced them, one by one. He no longer saw the faces of the children he and Kamini would bring into the world. He wanted two boys and two girls whose names began with the letter 'K'. Inheriting their best genes, they'd have Kamini's fair skin and almond eyes, but his kidney-shaped smile.

Maybe he'd been too hasty.

Maybe mad.

Yes, he was mad.

With his love for Kamini.

'She never once said that she loves me,' he whispered. He had to leave. Karuppan stood up and started to walk. He quickened his pace to a jog when it began to drizzle. With easy, fluid strides, it took him three minutes to emerge from the forest into the garden outside his home. He was as dark as the trees around him and his skin gleamed as subtly as that of the cobra's coiled next to a shovel nearby.

Once inside, Karuppan wasted no time. He changed into dry clothes. In his travel bag, he added his things—a toothbrush, shaving kit, and T-shirts. He zipped it and stood by his window to look out at the rain.

In the next instant, there was a loud knock on his door.

'Who is it?' he called out.

'Karuppan, it's me.' The voice had a hint of hysteria in it.

He flung open the door.

'What are you doing here, Nandini?' It was raining heavily again. 'Come,' he said, pulling her arm.

Once inside, Nandini reached into the pocket of her jacket and took out a folded serviette. 'Here,' she said, holding her hand out, offering him a piece of her birthday cake.

Karuppan stared at it for a long time. When he lifted his head, Nandini was a blurred image. He swallowed the lump in his throat and wiped his tears with the back of his hand.

When she nodded again, he reached out and accepted her gift.

Both of them saw the light coming from outside the window at the same time.

Loud footsteps on his wooden porch drowned the mating-call of the frogs.

Sensing trouble, he took Nandini by the elbow and guided her into the bedroom. 'Stay behind the door.'

* * *

In the soft light, Nandini noticed a framed collage of postcards of Malaysian beaches hanging, lopsided, on the light brown wall. A miniature statue of Lord Ganesh was mounted on another wall. An open toolbox, nails, a screwdriver, and a hammer sat on the floor. A blue, tattered, cotton blanket lay on top of a crocheted bedspread. The only trace of femininity in the room was the faint scent of jasmine.

'So, this is where you're hiding.'

Nandini recognized the patronizing voice. Through the crack between the bedroom door and its frame, she saw Appa holding a heavy torch.

'You know, it's easy to find this place. You've lit up the lane with those small lights. Quite pretty also,' Appa said.

Dhum-dhum-da-dhum.

Appa walked in a clockwise direction around Karuppan.

Nandini could not see his face but she heard every single word.

'Who do you think you are?'

Dhum-da-dhum-dhum.

'Like I said, an estate boy.'

Karuppan didn't move.

'She is still my wife. Did you think no one would know about your affair?'

Affair? Her mother and Karuppan?

'K-a-m-i-n-i.'

Through the crack between the door and its frame, Nandini saw Karuppan unclench his hands and take a step back. He bumped into the sofa and tripped.

Appa came behind the sofa, lifted his right hand and brought the torch down on Karuppan's head.

Nandini pushed her fist into her mouth to stop herself crying out. She watched her father drag Karuppan to the middle of the room and beat him over and over again.

Thud. Smash. Stamp.

The blood. The sweat. Mixing together.

The crack of bones. Bloodied earlobe. Nails pulled out.

Oh God. Stop.

Nandini heard the words Appa said without registering their meaning.

'Did you think people will listen to you? Estate boy?'

'And you go and touch Kamini? With your filthy hands? With these hands?'

'She is still my wife.'

'You are a nobody.'

The new pump Karuppan had installed in the kitchen of Kamini's Winter Palace drowned out any sound Appa might have heard as he washed the blood from his hands in the kitchen sink. Karuppan alone noticed Nandini crawling to the threshold of the bedroom, dragging the travel bag behind her. The bag? She wanted to run away? Now? He wanted to smile at her but he couldn't. He did not want to see the pity in her eyes but his right eye would not close; there was no eyelid. Too much pain.

'I will go and get help,' she mouthed to him. She rose to her feet, then ran out of Kamini's Winter Palace.

What was the point? Kamini wasn't going to help him. No one cared.

'I've done it, Papa.' Appa spoke into his mobile phone. 'Kamini will never know what happened. Papa.'

Papa?

Why was he talking to Papa Aunty?

In that moment, it dawned on Karuppan that Kamini hadn't betrayed him.

There was little this broken man could do. If the name of his lover was the last thing he uttered, the face of the girl he loved as his daughter was the last thing Karuppan saw.

Nandini ran into the sitting room of the Sungai Petani house.

'Mama,' Nandini said, dropping the travel bag to the floor.

Kamini turned to look at her. She dropped the cash box and stood up.

Nandini ran into her mother's open arms.

'What happened?' Kamini asked.

Nandini pulled away. She couldn't get the words out.

Kamini's shook her daughter's shoulders.

'What the hell happened, Nandini?'

The Interlude

> We need to normalise uncertainty by accepting it. This does not mean giving up. It only means grounding ourselves in the present and actively experiencing life with the sole purpose of moving forward. This allows us to build psychological flexibility and recognise factors that are outside our immediate control. It also makes us understand that the ultimate key to life is the focus on gratitude, empathy and mindfulness.
>
> —Professor (Adj.) Dato' Dr Andrew Mohanraj

Two husbands? Before thirty?

These were my thoughts every time I heard the waves hit the shore when I couldn't sleep in my sea-facing studio suite at the Holiday Villa. When I arrived in Cherating some two weeks ago, I had it in mind to inform anyone who enquired as to my whereabouts that I was on an assignment for the papers. I wanted to speak with the local people to discover stories about an ancient trans-land trade route between China and India, especially during the invasion of the Tamil Chola kings in 1025 AD. To prove my credentials, I'd whip out my mobile phone and access PDF versions of previously published articles. I'd scroll through photos that illustrated them such as the paddy fields of Kedah and the temples of Angkor.

Not a soul bothered.

In truth, I was running away from my second husband, the OB-GYN Peter Ponnudurai, and my first, the medico-legal lawyer Vikram Singh.

My time at the resort passed with me engaging in conversations that lasted no more than two sentences, excluding 'please' and 'thank you'.

Breakfast? Nasi lemak and black coffee.

Only *The Star* newspapers? No *New Straits Times*?

Fried sotong with sambal and rice for lunch.

A pre-dinner aperitif of gin and tonic with a light salad.

Red wine with spaghetti bolognese for dinner proper.

Chamomile tea before bed.

On day sixteen, when the hotel's capacity was at ninety-eight per cent, and since I was alone, a waiter in the Coffee House asked if wouldn't mind sharing my space with another. More statement than question, I had no choice but to nod in agreement.

Boy was he chatty, this young man whose facial hair was still soft and patchy. His name was Anand, and it took all of three minutes for him to reveal both his state of mind and life. Running his hand through a mop of shoulder-length curls that hadn't seen a barber's pair of scissors for months, this student from a nearby private medical college said that he was violently in love with one of his college mates. Unfortunately, the young woman in question was of both another race and faith—a Eurasian named Kylie. Her parents objected to this Malayalee Hindu boy. He'd retrieved his father's supplementary Platinum credit card and booked a room at the hotel 'to think things through'.

'I have to pass,' he said suddenly. 'If I fail, I have no future. In this country, especially.'

Since I simply stared at him, he made assumptions and further explained, 'People are not nice unless you have a title to your name. I must get that doctor title, no?' He lifted his chin that bit higher.

I'd seen that look once before, during breakfast at a buffet table of a city hotel.

Oh . . . the memory.

I blurted out, 'I'm here because I need to think about my failed marriages.' Then, I overexplained. 'I used to live in the north, then the south. Now, I'm trying to live here, in the east, for a while.'

My prayer that this would keep him quiet went unanswered.

'I think that people who are separated or divorced or even widowed are lucky.' He paused for dramatic effect. 'They know themselves. Or, if they don't, they know they don't. Because, when you live with someone else, they hold up a mirror to you. They tell you things about you that you didn't know. And once you know all that about you, you have a choice to correct what is wrong or make what is already good even better.'

For one so young, what he said was true. This conversation was teetering on being deep—exactly the kind that I was desperate to avoid. Petrified of my response, I smiled and called for the bill. Retreating to the sanctuary that was my room, I pondered the mess that was my past and the uncertainty of my future.

I met Vikram when we were both fifteen and studying for a primer for legal studies. Seven years later, two newly-minted law graduates got engaged. It was another twenty-one months before we became Mr and Mrs Vikram Singh Khanna. He not only personified the stereotype of a Sikh man in his looks, for he was tall and sported a full beard but also in practice. Ever ready to argue, Vikram soon stood out for consistently being successful in pleading his clients' causes by finding obscure legal dicta to support his suppositions and arguments. He was happiest whenever we visited the *gurdwara* and fed the masses during the *langar*. No one asked, any more, why I didn't join my husband's legal practice for word had gone round that the reply would be an acerbic 'I don't want to be damaged like all of you who joined your husbands at work.' Honestly, though, lacking Vikram's voracious appetite for legalese, I pursued, instead, a hitherto rather mediocre career as a freelance writer.

Shortly after our fifth wedding anniversary, I joined Vikram when he was travelled to the city for a medico-legal conference in Kuala Lumpur. As the newest legal advisor to a Malaysian-based medical defence union, he was 'making the rounds' to introduce himself to potential clients. The very first night we arrived, I dressed up in a sari, donned a dazzling pair of diamond earrings my husband had bought me as a birthday gift, and schmoozed with the who's who of the medico-legal fraternity in the opulent ballroom of the Istana Hotel.

The next morning, I lazed in bed until I simply had to get up or risk missing the buffet breakfast altogether. Being one of those days when I could intuit a warning of danger ahead, I chose a table by the ceiling-to-floor window even though there was an intense glare filtering through. I was deciding whether or not to abandon my resolve to be vegan and indulge in a breakfast of slices of beef ham (no pork was served in this halal-certified restaurant), with eggs on toast, when I sensed someone standing next to me and staring. My intention was to be rude in return. I did stare, but in awe, and he lifted his chin that bit higher. When he noticed that the waiters were already clearing the other tables, he asked if he could join me. I nodded.

Over coffee, Peter told me that his lecture that day would be an overview of the abortion laws of Malaysia. He was tired, though, having had to deal with a tricky case of dilation and curettage the night before. Unexpectedly, he asked me what I thought of the institution of marriage. I shrugged my shoulders and said, 'It's okay, I suppose.'

'That doesn't seem very promising.'

'Why?' I asked, a small smile developing on my face. 'Are you running towards or away from one?'

He threw his head back and laughed.

Who would have thought that I could evoke such a response?

Hmmm . . .

In that moment, I couldn't remember a single time when Vikram had laughed at anything, let alone something I'd said.

'It's my sister,' Peter replied. 'She's thinking of getting married to a Swiss man. She's scared of moving so far away from us.'

'Ah,' I responded, saying nothing more.

In so many ways, he was the first man other than Vikram—discounting relatives, of course—with whom I'd had a proper conversation since my marriage. We agreed to meet for breakfast over the next few days. He told me about his recent trips to far-flung places like Hawaii, Mozambique, and Bhubaneshwar. Not that he saw any of the sites in these places, for he was more acquainted with the insides of conference centres. Unlike Vikram and his family, who loved to travel in big noisy groups, his travels were solitary and educational.

On the final morning of the conference, there was a hurried air about our breakfast. Unsurprisingly, there was a collision of crockery between us. With his lecture and presentation due in less than an hour, I hurried Peter into my room to clean up the mess of orange juice and coffee on his shirt. When I went into the bathroom to rinse out the stains on his shirt, he followed me. He pulled my arm, I turned into his chest and in seconds, I committed adultery on the very same hotel bed I'd shared with my husband for the last three nights.

You see, this was no affair, for the word implied that there was a continuity in what we did. After all, it was no more than five minutes in another man's arms. At least that's what I told myself. In fact, the very night we returned home, I made sure to fulfil my wifely duties with such vigour and enthusiasm that Vikram was astonished. I wanted to wipe out the memory of what I'd done. Or, more like the knowledge that I—who had loved no other man except my husband, slept only with him, and cherished him—was capable of being intimate with another. I was not the principled woman that I'd been proud of. Then again, it takes two people to be intimate, no? Peter had to take some of the blame here. He could have waited outside while I cleaned his shirt. Why did Peter follow me? Why did an almost stranger follow another almost stranger? It was all his fault.

A month later, I received a WhatsApp message from Peter: 'When can we meet?' I didn't reply. Instead, I confessed everything to Vikram. To my eternal surprise, he'd anticipated my infidelity, as he always felt that I was too good for him. This lack of self-esteem was unattractive. I should have felt some gratitude for the all the time we spent together, but I was too in lust to think straight.

'Okay, Simran. You go now,' he said. 'But we are meant to be.' He kissed my forehead and walked out of the master bedroom of the single storey home we'd built together.

I married Peter out of a sense of propriety three weeks after my divorce from Vikram came through. 'To make an honest woman of myself,' I said. I thought it would make certain that Peter would stay faithful to me even though at the back of my mind was the thought that it was adultery that brought us together in the first place. One year to the day, I checked into the hotel in Cherating.

Every week, Vikram sent me a message. Punctuated with news of his successes and failures in court, they were more filled with the anguish of missing me. Peter, on the other hand, sent nothing. Two months, three weeks and three days after I first stepped into the hotel, I received a WhatsApp message with a PDF file attached to it from my husband's brother, the other lawyer in the family. I was given notice that Peter was divorcing me on the grounds of that catch all phrase, 'irreconcilable differences'.

It was time to stop existing and start living.

Right or wrong, I accepted that what I presumed to be sexual satisfaction with a man in whose arms I wasn't supposed to be, was a sense of guilt that I'd compromised my own principles. In the process, I'd found nothing but an emptiness in my soul. No amount of reading, writing, or conversing could erase the fact that I'd let something that should have never happened get so out of hand.

Maybe, with all the uncertainties in my life, I felt there was zero purpose to it.

Maybe it was because I was nothing more than a harlot.

Maybe it was because I was lonely.

I wrote a message to Vikram and asked him to forgive me. He wrote, within the minute to say: 'I will always love you.' We agreed to meet in Kuala Terengganu a week later. A city at the north-eastern tip of the Malay peninsula, it was unfamiliar to both of us and, therefore, the perfect way to start all over again.

The day before I left, Anand, now back at university and in arms of Kylie, became both my tour guide and driver. We crossed state borders and came to the one-street, seaside town of Chukai. The townsfolk watched us as a cagey lion watches its prey. A smile came upon them only when we walked into the *kopitiam* and asked if we could order some lunch. The local fare—which were the base dishes of fried chicken, fish, or seafood throughout the peninsula—was made distinct by the accompanying sambal or mix of sauces. In Alor Setar, there was the distinct lemongrass flavour because of its geographical proximity to southern Thailand. Here, it was all hot, sweet, and aromatic, with the peppery Szechuan flavour.

Much later, when it was cooler, we sat by the sea.

'Think about it,' I said to Anand, 'Chukai can be *cukai*, no? The Malay word for tax.' I'd looked it up and this was indeed where taxes and levies were imposed on riverine traffic and could have been part of the trans-land trade route between China and India in times gone by.

'Suppose so,' with the same kind of interest that an aged dog shows a gregarious puppy.

'Imagine,' I said waving my hand at the vast expanse of water. 'There's the South China Sea, full of money. $3 trillion to be precise. There's crude oil, natural gas, rights to fish and explore for minerals. China, Taiwan, the Philippines, Brunei, Indonesia, and us . . . all want a piece of that pie.'

'Err . . . Okay . . .' Anand nodded. 'Speaking of China,' he said, pivoting the conversation to his favourite topic. He whipped out his phone to show me a recent photo he'd taken of Kylie. 'She is lovely. Classical with a hint of Europe,' he said. I took it to be a simplistic term youthful romantics use but had to admit that he was only being accurate. With hair that was thick, dead straight and black, it framed a face that was round and smooth.

'I cannot bear to watch her sleeping. It's such an intimate thing, a solitary act, one which I can never be a part of. It's sad that for one third of our lives together, if we finally do end up together, we'll have to be apart.'

I stared straight ahead.

'Don't you think?'

In that moment, I felt that the only appropriate response would be to strangle him for his innocence. How I longed for my hotel room, the one place I felt safe, except when I was with Vikram whom I now felt I didn't deserve.

Instead, I sighed.

The clouds above slowly turned from bright blue to grey.

I sighed again, then felt a pang of something strange—tenderness, I suppose. A need to protect Anand in the way a mother would her child. That's what happens when you venture out into the world alone. Mostly, you discover parts of yourself that could break that you never knew existed; you hurt in ways that seemed improbable; you discover the capacity and multitudes of love, including a protective kind for an almost stranger. Mystics like to find words that explain this—a soul connection, they call it.

Someday, this interlude would be a memory. Like Peter. Throughout our tumultuous relationship, we hadn't taken a single photo of each other or one together. As though we knew that our marriage was a temporary matter.

How lucky he was, this Anand. Love was simple to him. Boy meets girl, boy loves girl, boy waits for girl, they marry and live happily ever after. I had met boy one, married him, divorced him, met boy two, divorced boy one, married boy two, now was being divorced by boy two, returning to boy one, and no longer believing in the myth of happily ever after.

I felt a tug at my sleeve. I turned to look, and Anand handed me a crumpled paper and said, 'It's for Kylie, but you can have it.'

With neat writing, so unlike a doctor-to-be, he'd written:

My Love,

I must share this moment with you. As the day turns into night, it hits me that we will always be as close as two people can ever be. I think of you with every breath I take. This is a beautiful moment.

Your Love.

Spoonful of Blood

> '[A]part from the abolishment, another aspect that should be highlighted is how the authorities should deal with those who intend to resort to suicide . . . As far as the application of Section 309 is concerned, we need to understand that the country's judicial system has always t[e]mpered justice with mercy, as it was hardly ever used, previously, when it comes to suicide attempts.'
>
> —Professor (Adj.) Dato' Dr Andrew Mohanraj

To the world, William Copperwood was a career diplomat who told stories about his travels to erstwhile islands from Nauru and Tuvalu to Mozambique and Mauritius. To the inhabitants of Taman Proton, who called him Willy, he was more often than not 'Marigold's father'.

At dinner parties, Willy sat at the head of the table and issued instructions. 'Make a drink for me,' he'd say to his son, expecting the ten-year-old boy to know precise quantities of whisky and soda to make the perfect aperitif. 'Serve me,' he'd say to his wife, Bettina, as she stood by his side and ladled out his favourite murungakkai dhal onto a mound of steaming rice on his plate. 'Bring the acar,' he'd say to Marigold and watch his copper-colour-haired daughter retrieve a bottle of Acha's Mango Pickles from the refrigerator.

To those in the know, the real power in the household belonged to Bettina. All of Alor Setar society nodded politely, but sniggered behind their backs, when an inebriated Willy put his arm around her and said, 'My beautiful and fair wife.' Bettina was no beauty. In fact, the word neighbours whispered among each other to describe her was 'tedious'. Certainly, she was fairer than her husband. Rumour had it that there was 'a spoonful of Indian blood' (Willy's words) on his father's side. His great, great grandfather was an English man. Unfortunately, he had made the mistake of succumbing to the attentions of a particularly alluring daughter of a merchant from the Malabar coast in Kerala. She died in childbirth and their ever-so-dark son had been deemed legitimate the moment he was baptized and accepted Christ as his saviour upon his father's death. The traumatized Anglo-Indian teenager had also promised never to stray from the Church's teachings in exchange for boarding, food, and clothing. His descendent, Willy, inherited the dominant melanin pigment.

'Luckily my Mari got my colour lah, Savitri,' Bettina would tell her immediate neighbour. Fanning herself, in the guise of having averted a catastrophe, she added, 'Or else, don't know how, lah. She will be a darkie like her father.'

Savitri smiled politely. In fact, Willy's skin tone was no darker than a latte.

'They are all harmless statements,' Savitri said to her husband, while walking back home after yet another dinner party at Willy's house. 'Marigold's father is dark. Marigold's father is not dark. That's all a matter of opinion.' Shaking her head, she added, 'What is difficult is when they say something that is obviously a lie. Worse, if I point it out, they won't even understand what I'm saying.'

'Ya,' her husband replied, aware of the topic his wife was referring to. A month ago, Bettina and Willy had discovered from mutual friends in Kuala Lumpur that Savitri's sister had emigrated to Pune, India, to marry a native of the city. Keeping this in mind, during the dinner, Willy let Savitri in on a family secret—apparently, the Malabari woman who had sullied his side of the family with her Indian blood was, in fact, a Marathi. Willy concluded that he, therefore, had the blood of a superior caste running through his veins.

'How to tell him that Marathi is the language?' Savitri asked her husband. 'That he actually means to say that he's probably a Maratha? A Kshatriya. And how on earth do I tell Marigold's father that I know these distinctions because I'm full Brahmin?'

Her husband's warning was swift and immediate: 'Don't bring up our caste. You know what all these people are like. They became Christians or Muslims because they want to get away from the caste issues. Then, when they want to get married, the first thing they'll look at is the other side's caste. It's part of their culture, it seems.'

Savitri rubbed his arm, 'Eh, calm down.'

'I just get so tired of people being ashamed of their Indian heritage.'

'Hmmm . . .'

'What hmmm? Is there something more?'

'Not nice, lah, to talk about it.'

'Savitri,' her husband stopped, pulling his wife's arm, 'we're out here in the open. We can say what we like. No one is going to hear us. Tell me now.'

'Okay. That same person who told Willy about my sister called me a few days ago, she told me about Bettina's side. Until now, you know how Bettina made it sound like only Willy's side had messed up blood?' When her husband nodded, Savitri said, 'Actually, her side is also all messed up.'

'What do you mean?'

'You see how Bettina has all that copper-coloured hair? Same-same like Marigold?'

'Yes?'

'That came from some white man ancestor. Where Willy's ancestor fooled around with an Indian, this side fooled around with a Chinese. That's why Bettina looks a little Chinese.'

'Oh . . . okay. Why such a big secret? They'll be proud of this, isn't it? Our Indians will also love the Chinese blood. It's having Indian blood that people hate. You know those politicians who hate the Chinese and Indians. Just you wait. They'll also start saying that they are also fully this or that. And, shamelessly give press conferences about it.'

'No, lah. This is something else.'

'Haiya. Then why tell me this?'

'Wait, lah. Don't be so impatient,' Savitri said, shaking her head. 'It seems, that the white man in Bettina's family, he was a little . . .' Savitri closed her fist, extending her index finger and circling it around her temple for several seconds, 'you know . . . *gila*. He committed suicide. So, there is this crazy disease in their family. They're all a bit mental.'

'Oh . . . I see . . .' her husband said, letting his words trail off.

'That's why she always says they were from a poor family. When he committed suicide, all that money the white man made for the family was confiscated by the Church.'

Her husband's eyes widened. 'Huh?'

'Ya. You know what, how suicide is a sin and all. The Church will be the first, before even the court, to punish the living for anyone's sin. So, they took all the man's possessions because he committed the sin of murdering his own body.'

'Murder? How'

'Aiya. That Ten Commandments say, "Thou shalt not kill," yes? Here, when he committed suicide, he killed his own body. So, he broke the commandment. And, when you break a commandment, the Church punishes you. Simple.'

'Oh . . . quite clever also.'

They'd arrived home and their conversation seemingly came to its natural end. Although not a word about either of these issues passed between them after this, Savitri and her husband understood each other's instinct to be cautious in all future interactions with Willy, Bettina, and their children. Each time their children played with Marigold or her brother, either Savitri or her husband made it a point to be in the room, in case either child tipped into becoming mentally unhinged at the drop of a hat.

Among the wider Catholic community, though, such awareness of his 'tainted pedigree' (again, Willy's words) and her supposed genetic abnormality made people wonder how Willy and Bettina ever got married. It was fated, the Church elders once said. Bettina, the sixth of nine siblings and third daughter, met Willy at a three-day theological camp sometime after World War II. For both of them, it was curiosity, rather than love (certainly not lust), at first sight. The elders refused to let go of the chance to join in matrimony two people in their congregation. Banns were posted and, voila, Bettina and Willy were married within six months of leaving the camp.

Beyond saying, 'You know what happens, yes?' Bettina's mother had explained nothing about what to expect on her wedding night. Blushing profusely, Bettina nodded, unable to bring herself to confess to having read all her sisters' *Mills & Boons* and knowing exactly what to expect. She already imagined the blurb should a story be written about them:

> It's Bettina's first time travelling overseas and she is excited by the sounds and smells of new lands. As a diplomat's wife, she promises to love, honour, and become the source of pride for him. William is impressed by this feisty beauty and promises to fulfil her heart's desire, which, to his amusement, is to become the proud owner of an authentic Persian carpet. Can the commanding and caring man contain his exuberant wife as they enjoy wild and passionate nights together?

Such were Bettina's imaginings in the bridal chamber of her new home. She had to wait, though, because Willy was being plied with alcohol 'to give him courage,' her mother-in-law said, closing the door behind her.

Courage?

Now that wasn't a word that any handsome landowner, count, or prince from her *Mills & Boons* needed. They were strong, never wavered and were sure of themselves in every possible way. The promise from those stories was an entire night of unbridled passion and that was what Bettina was looking forward to. She expected it, in fact. She kept her head lowered when the handle of the door finally turned and in stepped her husband. And that's the moment all her dreams crumbled. He stumbled towards her, slurred his words and removed her clothes with the finesse of a racing rhinoceros.

When he rolled off her, he left Bettina with her shattered dreams and the smell of sweat and sex, not love. They were certainly together for the rest of their wedding night, but while he snored, Bettina spent it awake with a single repeating thought: 'What the hell just happened?'

In the 'aftermath' (Bettina's word) of her wedding night, she learned to acknowledge that something horrible had come to pass, but to tell it the way that others wanted to hear it. It wasn't the truth of how, when, or where something happened, but simply that it happened. Meaning that when her sister, eager to hear all about Bettina's first sexual experience with none other than the brother-in-law everyone in Bettina's family loved, the new bride described losing her virginity using precisely three words: Yes, it happened.

Making such a statement meant that there was nothing more to add, infer, or conjecture and the conversation ended. Never in a million years would Bettina admit, even unto herself, how extraordinarily boring sex was with her husband. Bettina experienced the excitement of sex, or as was more delicately described by her favourite writers as 'love-making', vicariously through her one guilty pleasure—every two weeks she bought the latest *Mills & Boons.*

Bettina did share one thing with her husband, though. She, too, wanted a big family. When their son was born exactly nine months after they said their marriage vows, to the minute almost, Willy believed he was the most blessed man in Church.

To rival a famed Eurasian family in Sungai Petani that boasted ten sons, Willy wanted as many children as possible. When year upon year passed yielding no offspring after the birth of his son, a sadness descended on the family. For eight consecutive years, Bettina became pregnant, but never carried any of the foetuses to term. With each involuntary termination of her pregnancy, it seemed to her that an invisible higher power was removing part of her body together with the dead foetus, like a child hacking away at the limbs of plastic doll. One time, when they were in bed, she looked deeply into her husband's black eyes. With her thoughts alone, she suggested he find another woman to be more of a mother than she ever could. His anger at the very suggestion was evident in his stare. She blinked, smiled, and turned on her side. He turned on his and within seconds, she heard him snore. That's when Bettina allowed her quiet tears to fall down her cheeks, making sure to avoid waking up her husband. These were not tears of rage or sadness. They were tears that she'd given up hope and no longer had faith. She knew that she needed to be grateful that at the very least she had one child and that it was a sin to be greedy. Her son was certainly her pride, but she wanted a daughter to be her joy.

When she became pregnant again, she swore that with this ninth pregnancy, the only thing left in her was her heart—lose this baby and there would be nothing left of Bettina to give to the next one. The heart, the Catholic priest told her during her weekly confessionals, was all she needed to sustain the pregnancy and that God was merciful.

From the time she was three months old and cradled in her mother's arms, Marigold absorbed the lesson about how to project the best image of a situation, even if the reality was patently untrue. A perfect example was when her paternal grandfather had died. All of six years old at the time, Marigold observed everyone in the Catholic Church in Penang with much interest. Those who offered her parents their condolences kept their heads bowed and held on to Bettina and Willy's hands a bit longer as though they believed that Willy was an exceptional son and, by extension, Bettina a good daughter-in-law. Indeed, Marigold's brother said so in his eulogy, praising his parents for looking after his grandfather. Her mother, wearing a black hair net and matching lace gloves, had tears full of sorrow. These, however, Marigold knew were crocodile tears and was far removed from reality.

And, pray tell, what was the reality here?

To the outside world, Willy was the most filial of sons because within a month of Marigold's birth, Willy's father, a widower for over five years, became a part of Willy's household. Whenever the family had to relocate as part of Willy's work, it was always a condition of his transfer that he be allowed to bring along his increasingly infirm father.

Only, once Willy left for work at 8.30 a.m., the door to the room where her bedridden grandfather was confined stayed closed so that the horrid smell when he soiled himself wouldn't permeate the entire living space. Her mother, meanwhile, spent the hours her father was away fussing over Marigold, cooking, gossiping with her neighbours, and reading the newspapers cover-to-cover. Lunch was a tray of food that mostly landed on his upper body because multiple strokes had rendered his arms close to being useless.

A half hour before Willy was scheduled to return from work, Bettina would summon the maid to give her starving and wilting father-in-law his bath and feed him an early dinner. Willy, seeing his father's talcum-powdered face, would openly praise his wife for caring for someone who wasn't technically her blood. In moments of marital bickering, though, Bettina would let slip that she despised caring for her father-in-law. When Marigold was five years old, she heard the one and only time her exasperated father shouted back at Bettina: 'You can leave if you want. I will look after my father myself.'

Bettina never said a word of complaint about Marigold's grandfather from that moment on. However, Marigold saw Bettina mix chilli in his porridge to make him purge unnecessarily; whenever Willy was overseas, Bettina gave Marigold's grandfather pineapples precisely because he was allergic to them; and, she added sugar to his coffee knowing full well that he was a chronic diabetic.

'I'm making it delicious for him,' she would say to Marigold and smile.

Marigold never mentioned to a single soul, not even to the priest during the weekly confessions, that she believed that her mother gradually made her grandfather's life so miserable that death was preferable to life.

Three months after the dust had settled on her father-in-law's grave in the overcrowded plot of consecrated land on Penang Island reserved for Catholics, Bettina arranged for her daughter's first holy communion. It was custom among local folk that this was when a child's names were confirmed. For Willy, having had a great grandmother whose name was Lily, a grandmother who was Jasmine, and sisters who were Petunia and Petal, it only made sense to choose to name his daughter after a flower. His first choice had been Tulip, but Petal had already given that name to her daughter and Willy wished to avoid the confusion of first cousins having the same name. Since his favourite colour was orange, he chanced on Marigold and read that the flower's unique and beautiful scent made it a much sought-after companion plant. Bettina agreed. During the ceremony for holy communion, she requested that another name be added, as she felt it necessary to honour God in some way. In the Church's hundred-year-old registry, Bettina and Willy's daughter's name was noted down as 'Marigold Mercy Copperwood'. Such pretty names, full of faith, hope, and love for a child.

It was a gargantuan error of judgement.

When Marigold's brother became the victim of a trio of sinners—a seductress who demanded luxuries in return for sexual favours, a loan shark from whom he borrowed money to pay for the said luxuries, a thug who beat him to a pulp for no reason—she convinced him that the voices inside his head were right. His life was of no use and he was a burden unto his family. As such, the only way for her brother to get out of his misery was for him to end his life. Marigold bought him a box of five individually wrapped stainless-steel double edged razor blades. Those who cause hurt, people say, are hurting themselves. Perhaps, when Willy refused to consent to Marigold's choice of her husband because he wasn't a Catholic, the hurt stayed with Marigold. Or so Savitri and the rest of the people in Taman Proton conjectured. It was, therefore, one hundred per cent of a surprise to all when Marigold's brother pushed a razor blade into his veins on the eve of 2019, careful that not a spoonful of his blood fell onto Marigold's new Persian carpet.

During the next Spring Equinox, seated in a wheelchair, an emaciated Bettina put her thumbprint to a document transferring all her property to the only child she had left. After all, Willy, too, had died five years before. As she urinated into the adult diapers, she looked up into her daughter's face and said, 'I wonder what *paraquat* tastes like.'

Marigold smiled knowingly at her mother.

An hour later, Marigold walked into her mother's room carrying a vintage mahogany tray she'd brought back from one of her many travels around the world. On it, there was a mug of blue liquid. Having stirred copious amounts of sugar into the mug to camouflage the noticeably pungent smell, she handed the mug to her mother.

Everything happened all at once.

When Bettina began to gag, her daughter held the mug to her mouth so that she'd continue drinking the contents of the glass. At that very moment, they heard a gasp from the window and when they turned to look, it was their nosey neighbour, the widow Savitri. Marigold rushed to the front door, flung it open and ran towards her neighbour's house. It was a miscalculation. The widow had run in the opposite direction, to the recently erected guardhouse and sought assistance from the security guards hired by the housing association to protect the inhabitants of Taman Proton.

While Bettina died in the hospital a day later, Marigold was placed under observation in a psychiatric inpatient unit. After two weeks, with no witness reports and hardly any evidence collected to try her for a crime under section 309 of the Penal Code, the district police officer, Supt Abdul Majid Mohd Puad, decided to show the elderly woman some mercy. It made no sense to keep in a person with mental illness in the same lockup as those who'd committed heinous crimes like buggery, murder, and drug possession. There was no point making an effort to gather evidence to convict her of a crime let alone punish her. Therefore, he released her without charge.

That was the official version of what happened. Unofficially, her freedom was granted the very moment Marigold transferred, anonymously of course, RM100,000 to the police retirement fund.

Back at Taman Proton, as they watched Marigold step out of the police vehicle and walk into her home, Savitri and her neighbours came to the same conclusion: Marigold, named after a flower with delicate petals, had emerged from the entire drama smelling like roses.

Lolita

> [Victims of bullying] are more likely to experience depression and anxiety, which may persist into adulthood. Other ways in which bullying impacts a victim [. . .] includes suicidal thoughts, engaging in suicidal behaviour, and skipping or dropping out of school. In some instances, a bullied victim may already have a pre-existing condition such as depression or problems at home, in which case . . . bullying inadvertently becomes a tipping point for suicide.
>
> —Professor (Adj.) Dato' Dr Andrew Mohanraj

June 1977.

'Are we there yet?' The four-and-a-half-year-old Tara leaned into the gap between the two front seats.

'Not yet,' Mummy said through her smile. Turning to gently push the child back onto the back seat, she said, 'Why don't you go to sleep. I will wake you up when we arrive.'

From the back seat of her father's Mercedes Benz, Tara looked out the window at the moving clouds, consigned to guessing what each one of them looked like. There was a chariot before it pulled away and changed into a peacock.

Next to it was a hibiscus that morphed into a huge leaf. It split in the middle, down the vein, into two little humans facing each other and holding hands. This solitary game continued until she heard, 'We're here.'

Daddy had turned the car from the main road onto a straight, tree-lined driveway that led to a small fountain around which the car had to go before coming to a full stop in the covered porch. Two large wooden doors opened into an expansive hallway. To the right of it was a sitting room where her grandmother watched the television and entertained guests. To the left was the dining room where little ones sat on stools brought in from the kitchen because the table could only accommodate six adults at any given time. On the first floor, there was a wide balcony that went all the way round. Many nights, while the adults turned over sausages and meat patties sizzling away on a coal-fired barbecue, Tara leaned against the cement balustrade and gazed at the mass of earth in the distance.

On either side of the closed stairs were inbuilt nooks. In each one, her grandmother had placed a doll—hand-me-downs from her grandmother's siblings and extended family. Heirlooms, Mummy called them. Stuffed with lightweight coconut husks, it was the miniature saris—Kasavu, Chiffon, Benaras, Kanjeepuram, Mysore Silk, Nauvari, and Paithani—they wore that set them apart. While these were fascinating to Tara, none captured her attention more than the doll that was placed in one corner of the sitting room. Three times the size of these yesteryear Indian Barbie-dolls, that doll was a pink, plastic one which sat on top of a giant speaker. Her name was Lolita.

* * *

'Don't touch,' all the elders would say if Tara so much as glanced in the doll's direction. Take a step towards it and she'd be yanked back by the collar. The closest she was allowed to get to the doll was to stand on a spot in the corner of the carpet three feet away from Lolita. Standing, with hands clasped behind her back, a child with big eyes, bigger cheeks and no chin stared at a doll with pink cheeks, long hair, and plump hands, sharing a secret

Lolita, you see, was special.

Mummy explained that Lolita was a gift for Sitara from Aunty Sheela and came from that far away Eng-ga-land. Tara had been barely a year old when, in 1973, Aunty Sheela and her husband, Bhaskar Uncle, had gone to the UK to complete their postgraduate medical studies. The couple left their young children with Aji and Grandpa, giving them the joy of looking after their grandchildren. Tara grew up believing that Sitara, technically her first cousin, was her elder sister.

Lolita was given to Sitara in 1974, during what the elders called 'Sheela's quick dash home to Bidong' to see that all was well with her children. She didn't wish to leave Bhaskar Uncle alone for too long in London. Lolita was meant to keep Sitara company. At night, like Babushka dolls, their grandmother would hold Sitara in her arms and lull her to sleep. Likewise, Sitara would cuddle Lolita and assure the doll that she wasn't lonely.

Upon completion of their course, Aunty Sheela and her husband first returned to his hometown in India to set up a medical practice and buy a new home. Six months before Tara's fourth birthday, Dipak and Sitara were uprooted from Aji's House in Bidong and went to live with their parents.

Lolita was left behind under the pretext of keeping their grandmother company.

Staring at Lolita, Tara was begging to be the replacement granddaughter in Aji's bed. If she hugged Lolita then Aji was bound to hug her as well. There was no doubting that via Lolita, that inanimate giver of affection, Tara would gain access to that bubble of love created between grandmother and elder granddaughter.

What if those hugs from her grandmother never came, though?

Therefore, little Tara watched the doll the way a woman watches the man she loves adore an unworthy rival—with an outward persona that everything is as it should be, but a silent and raging impatience for the inevitable downfall of the couple's union.

* * *

The day had arrived.

'Here Tara,' their grandmother said within the hour of Tara stepping into the Bidong house. 'Your sister doesn't want the doll any more. She is sharing Lolita with you. Sisters always share-share, no?'

Big eyes became bigger than ever.

Lolita was hers.

Still, Tara was so used to the waiting that now that it was over, she was a little confused. Stepping into her grandmother's house, going straight to the living room, standing by the edge of the carpet, and staring at Lolita had become a routine that it occurred to Tara that, henceforth, she'd have nothing to do.

When Aji picked up Lolita by her legs and placed the doll, head down, in Tara's open and chubby arms, the little girl blinked several times. She couldn't believe it. The doll was finally hers. Tara turned it so that the doll's head was tucked under her chin. She looked into her grandmother's face and smiled brightly.

Mummy, seated on the sofa, lifted her eyebrows and spoke up, 'What do you say, Tara?'

'Chan-gu,' the little girl whispered.

Her grandmother smiled back and gently pinched Tara's chin, which was beginning to make an appearance.

Tara turned then and saw Sitara seated on the floor, her knees tucked under her and head lowered. She was 'reading'; at least that's what Tara had heard the elders say.

'See how clever Sitara is. She can read a whole storybook on her own,' Aunty Sheela said, bringing the attention of everyone else in the sitting room—Mummy, Daddy, Bhaskar Uncle and Dipak—to the little girl with cute ringlets coming down to her shoulders.

'Sitara, what do you want to be when you grow up?' This was the third time that evening they'd asked the girl the same question. No one paid attention to the boy lying down on the sofa with his legs dangling over the backrest and an open copy of the latest National Geographic magazine bent in his hands. His profession was decided the moment he had been a fully-formed embryo. The elders were flexible, of course. They didn't mind if Dipak, three years older to Sitara, chose to become an endocrinologist, pathologist, dermatologist, or anything else with an 'ist' at the end of the specialty. As long as he became a doctor first.

'Maybe you want to become a nurse,' their grandmother said to Sitara. 'Like me. I became a midwife and could help Grandpa during the War years.'

Sitara dropped the book and turned her head towards her grandmother. Miss Angricks, the moniker she'd acquired during this trip because it seemed as though Sitara was perpetually angry, frowned and her lips became blade thin. 'Not nurse. I will be a doctor.'

'Ooooo . . .' Aunty Sheela laughed. Turning Sitara's shoulders so the child faced her, she said, 'Yes, *shonu*. You'll become a doctor. No nurse-wurse for you. Smile for everyone Dr Sitara? Smile?'

Although her cousin sister did not look at Tara, the four-year-old sensed that even if she did, Sitara wouldn't be smiling at all. After Lolita was placed in her hands, Tara sank down onto the carpet. She stroked the doll's hair and ran her forefinger along its chubby hand. Surprisingly, Lolita was sticky all over. Her skin wasn't smooth like Mummy's and she couldn't pinch Lolita's forearm. When she pressed its skin, nothing happened. She used her nail to scratch the doll, but Lolita didn't make a single sound.

It was most frustrating, indeed. Wasn't this what she'd seen others in the kindergarten do? They pinched each other until all the children cried. If that didn't work, they pulled ponytails.

Lolita was absolutely silent.

Something had to be done.

Anything.

At 3 o'clock in the afternoon, while everyone in Aji's House enjoyed their siesta, dragging Lolita along the floor by her hair, Tara made her way to the one place she'd find what she needed most—Aji's art studio. The last room on the right, it had ceiling-to-floor glass windows, and was cluttered with easels, canvases, half-completed paintings of fruit bowls, trees, sunsets, and houses. With single-minded determination, Tara went straight to the drawer in the only table there. Reaching inside, she took out a pair of scissors. She sat down on the floor and set about her task.

So focused was she on her task of provoking a response from Lolita that little Tara didn't hear the door creak as it was pushed open.

'Tara! What are you doing?'

Tara dropped the scissors and stared ahead, momentarily transfixed by the reflection of her grandmother in the glass window, searching for clues about what was going to happen. Her grandmother turned on her heel and her reflection disappeared. Tara picked up the scissors and continued her task.

Moments later, Mummy appeared at the door followed by Aunty Sheela. Last of all was their grandmother and her elder sister.

'What are you doing, baby girl?' Mummy's voice was softer, but no less firm.

Tara turned her head to look up at her mother standing behind her. At the same time, she heard her mother's gasp. Why was everyone so shocked?

'Oh my God!' Aunty Sheela said. 'How can she destroy this?'

'She's only four, Sheela. She doesn't know what she's doing,' Mummy replied.

Suddenly, all the elders were speaking at once and Tara couldn't comprehend the words. Big-big words and phrases like 'learn to share,' 'not destroy,' and 'it's a matter of principle'.

The only one who didn't say a word but ran her eyes over all that was splayed out on the floor was Sitara. Two little girls then stared at each other. The younger one smiled, hoping her elder sister would now play with her. Instead, the elder one's gaze hardened and Tara couldn't fathom what the look meant.

Tara turned back to assess her handiwork. There, in front of her lay a dismembered Lolita. A punctured right arm on one side. Stripped naked, the doll with alopecia areata and three intact limbs was on the other. The white dress with ruffles and embroidered little roses had been cut right down the front. Gouged out eyes mixed with mounds of faux hair lay all around Tara, like a black halo around a little star.

'See, Mummy,' Tara said. 'Nice?'

Mummy continued to stare at her.

'Nice?' This shriek, almost, was from Aunty Sheela.

Something was wrong. Everyone was becoming angrier.

But why?

All these years of waiting.

No more share-share.

This was now Tara's doll.

Tara looked at her elder sister. Sitara wasn't there any more. Miss Angricks was. But it was the strangest thing. Not only was her elder sister angry, there were tears in her eyes. It was the first time Tara saw someone be angry and cry at the same time.

'Let it go, baby,' Aji said, but not to Tara. Almost whispering, she said to her elder granddaughter, 'She is not the same. Not like us. Our blood doesn't run in her veins.'

The next thing Tara knew, Mummy reached down and put her hands under Tara's armpits. Tara dropped the scissors when she was hauled up into her mother's arms.

'Up-see-daisy,' Mummy said, but she wasn't smiling like she usually did. Instead, she quickly turned on her heel and pushed past her sister and mother. Tara reached, but the three women who had the same blood running through their veins had crowded around the remains of her doll.

Tara never saw Lolita again.

* * *

A memory.

Two little girls with the same name, stood next to each other at the one and only photo studio in Alor Setar. Dressed in identical red dresses with a Peter Pan collar and yellow daisies, smiling brightly into the lens.

'Sitara and Tara, you were such good-good girls at the studio,' Mummy said later, when she was tucking the girls into bed. With one child on either side, she asked, 'So, what story do you want me to tell you?'

Two little girls looked at each other, then at the adult, then at each other again. Tara said softly, 'Princess?'

'A princess one?' Searching her mind, she said, 'Which princess?' Before the girls could reply, she quickly cautioned, 'And none of this Cinderella-Binderella story. Choose an Indian one. We have so many.'

'Meerabai, Mummy. Tell Meerabai story.'

'Good choice,' Mummy said, and tweaked her nose. 'She was about the same age as you, Tara baby, when she found her lord and master.'

With one child curled into her either side of her, Mummy narrated the story of the Rajput princess born in the fifteenth century who devoted her life to singing the glory of Lord

Krishna. At one point, when she was frustrated with life, holding the idol of Lord Krishna in her hands, Meerabai went to the river to commit suicide. She was about to jump in when someone came from behind and put his hand around her shoulder. She turned around and fainted when she recognized her saviour.

'When Meerabai opened her eyes, Krishna said to her, "Your old life is over. You now belong to me. Go to Vrindavan and live there in peace."'

When Mummy looked down, two little girls, dressed in identical pyjamas, were holding hands over her waist. Slowly, Mummy pulled the tiny hands apart, slid down the bed and then turned to look at the girls. Even in deep slumber, they'd known to move close to each other, searching for warmth and love, and wrapping tiny hands around each other's bodies.

Mummy crossed her hands over her heart and sighed.

Ah! Sister hugs.

The foundation was there for these two cousin sisters—no, sisters—to remain friends for life.

* * *

In the bedroom Mummy, Daddy, and Tara were given for the duration of their afternoon visit, Tara was plonked on the bed and Daddy was woken up. Mummy and he had a heated debated before Daddy pulled Tara close.

'Let it go, Savitri. You and I know that she's ours. Let it go.'

'But we must tell her. And tell her now.'

'Okay.'

Mummy and Daddy sat Tara between them. 'I want to tell you something.'

Tara stared at her mother and blinked, her way of saying, 'Yes?'

'This is our secret. You cannot tell others. But you must know. Do you promise not to tell anyone?'

'Promise,' Tara said instantly.

'Sitara is fully Brahmin. I am, but Daddy is not. So, you're a half-caste child. That is why my mother said their blood doesn't run in your veins.' Her voice rising in tempo and cadence, she looked at Daddy and said, 'My sister thinks that her children are better than mine because they are full Brahmin.'

Daddy shook his head. 'I don't understand. She is your sister. Why would she be like this?'

'Because Daddy—my Daddy—always thought that she's better than me.'

'But why? I mean you are sisters.'

'Yes. We're sisters. But we're not friends. And my father was always friends with Sheela. He thought I was funny.'

'Funny?'

'Yes. Funny. As in odd.'

'Why?'

'You sound like Tara, asking why all the time,' Mummy teased.

Daddy rolled his eyes.

'I think that Daddy liked Sheela more was because he probably thought that I was joining a cult.'

'Oh, you mean that thing you were involved in when you were in London?'

'Yes. My father was so scared that I would give them all my money. So, he gave it all to Sheela.'

'Hmmm . . . Makes me happy that I have no brothers and sisters,' Daddy sighed, his ability to immediately let go of unnecessary hurts an instant balm on his wife's wound.

Daddy sighed. 'No more children, okay? Our little princess is enough.'

'Really?'

'Yes. Let our Tara be a happy child. We are all the family she needs. Blood is thicker than water, yes. But Tara is the child of our spirit. And spirit trumps blood.'

'Hmmm . . .'

'It's the right thing, I am telling you. No need to worry about what anyone else thinks,' Daddy responded and turned to lie on his back. 'You are now gazetted as a specialist and that will give us more mon—'

Tara wasn't listening any more. When her parents turned to face each other on the bed, like nyctinastic plants that fold their flowers and leaves to protect themselves from nighttime nectar thieves, Tara was safely cocooned in their loving embrace. Slowly, she closed her eyes. Sucking her thumb, the memory of her sister's anger faded. In her dream, Sitara was not crying, but using a machete to hack away at Lolita's remaining limbs. While Tara watched perplexed at the destruction being caused, all the elders consoled her weeping sister, crying in unison: 'It's okay, Sitara. Remember this: our blood does not run in her veins. She is not family. It's a matter of principle.'

Exchange Marriage

> Stigma is defined as a set of negative beliefs that a group or society holds about a topic or group of people . . . Stigma is rarely based on facts but rather on assumptions, preconceptions and generalisations. Hence, its negative impact can be prevented or lessened only through education and in some situations, by legal mandate.
>
> —Professor (Adj.) Dato' Dr Andrew Mohanraj

'I'm taking the plunge, Dato. Celia's the one,' Yogi insisted, the day he told his best friend that he had found the woman with whom he wanted to spend the rest of his life.

The corners of Dato's mouth straightened.

Yogi didn't think that Dato would be upset. Not this upset, anyway. Sure, things wouldn't be the same again after this, but they were good friends. They had known each other all their lives. They had gone to school and played football together. They'd got laid for the first time at the same brothel in a border town between Malaysia and Thailand called Dannok. They regularly got drunk and pawned their souls by exchanging whores or, as their favourite half-Chinese-half-Thai ones were called, 'guest relations officers'. They knew that they'd redeem their souls when their mothers found them 'fresh girls from good families to marry' (their mothers' words).

'You know you've just destroyed an exchange marriage, yes?'

'What on earth is an exchange marriage?'

'It's what the Ceylonese like to do. Celia was supposed to marry her brother's wife's brother to keep the dowry in the family. Now she's marrying you, the money won't come back into Celia's family. It'll remain at her sister-in-law's.'

'Dowry? I don't care about all that rubbish.'

'Neither does Celia, obviously. She loves you. And now, it's your family that will get the money.'

'I told you. I don't want the money. I am a lawyer and I can make my own.'

'Ya. Ya. Ya. I know all that. I'm just telling you that it's the principle that will matter most. And what you're up against.'

'Okay. But I really love her,' Yogi said, shaking with the intensity of his feelings. 'There's something about her that's different . . .'

Celia came from a Tamil Lutheran family. Her parents were the kind who signed up for a tour of South India but made sure never to get off the tour bus because they couldn't bear to look at a Hindu temple (or in their words, 'the house of Satan'), let alone step into one. The magnificence of the architecture and seemingly indestructible nature of these houses of worship—like the Meenakshi Amman, Brihadishvara, and Venkateswara temples—were completely lost on them. They only consented to the marriage when Yogi promised them that any future children Celia and he had would be baptized and confirmed as Lutherans. He was determined to do anything to see Celia smile the way she did for him alone. Besides, the more important celebration of his marriage would take place inside the ballroom of the new PJ Hilton off the Federal Highway, not at the Evangelical Lutheran Church in Brickfields.

The wedding dinner on Boxing Day in 1965 was all he had expected it to be. Hosted by his new father-in-law, eighty per cent of the guests were from the 'bride's side'. Naturally, they were all Lutherans. The Hindus, his side, were relegated to two tables on the periphery of the wedding hall lest their presence contaminate the preferred ones.

Yogi was oblivious to this apparent slight to his family for his sole focus was on his bride and her dazzling smile. Seated next to her, he could barely contain himself. Celia looked stunning in her bridal finery. To honour her family's side, she wore a wedding gown rather than a sari. To please her new mother-in-law, Celia added colour to her attire. Not wanting to offend the Church elders entirely by wearing red (the ubiquitous colour for any Hindu bride), she chose pink—a mix of both white and red. The entire congregation was stunned but couldn't say a word, for the bride was absolutely glowing from within.

To her new husband, the perfume of jasmine was intoxicating. Her skin was luminescent and he sensed that her hormones were running wild. The bridesmaids were hovering around her, making sure every strand of her wavy hair was in place for the photos. He couldn't wait to get her all to himself. When he finally did, Dato strolled across the parquet dance floor and put his hands on the back of

Yogi's chair. Although his gait was steady, when he spoke, the alcohol-laced speech signalled to Yogi that Dato was quite drunk.

'Remember what I said about common touch?' Dato stood with his back to Celia, thereby, excluding her from their conversation.

'Huh? What?'

'Move with kings, but never lose the common touch. Or something like that.'

'Yes,' Yogi said, recognizing Kipling's famed poem that his friend had all but butchered.

'Well, that's what you're doing here. You're losing the common touch.'

'What are you talking about?'

'They say that once you marry, you'll lose it forever. Do you think you can do all that doggy style the Thai girls showed you with Celia?'

Yogi searched his mind and then he remembered. On a sticky day in Songkhla, southern Thailand many moons ago, Dato had given him a birthday treat of entry to a special kind of club off a backstreet. For the first time in his life, Yogi witnessed what he'd only read about in the naughty magazines found under the mattress of his paternal uncle's home. In a case of art imitating life or, in this case, nature, couples were mating like dogs or, as it was called in ancient Rome, *coitus more ferarum*, which roughly translated to, 'sexy time like wild animals'. When three nubile girls with alabaster-smooth, hairless skin beckoned Yogi into their fold, they whispered into his ears, 'Doggy style.'

'Hey! This is my wedding.' Yogi was unable to hide his blush. 'Don't be so crass. And who is this "they"?'

'I don't know. And I never will because I'll never marry. I will always only move with kings.'

Yogi was half tempted to offer a banal reply like, 'Yeah, right. Your kings are going to be okay with all that doggy style.' Instead, unsure of his friend's motives, he said, 'O-k-a-y.' Then, he looked beyond Dato's shoulder, at the companion that Dato had abandoned. 'Go back to the lady, Dato. She's looking this way.'

Dato glanced over his shoulder and then back at Yogi. Sighing, he straightened his shoulders and said, 'Goodnight.'

Later that night, when he was spent, lying on his back and holding his wife close, Yogi thought how wrong his friend had been. In the moment when he had consummated his marriage, Yogi knew grace beyond compare. Celia was all he'd dreamed her to be—energetic, sexually inventive, and beyond desirable.

When their son made his debut, the family gave him the pet name Raj because everyone's world quite simply revolved around this new king of the family. One miscarriage and another pregnancy followed in quick succession. Secretly, Yogi was happiest when he had Celia's body all to himself. He never told a soul that there were times he begrudged the creatures they'd made together taking over his wife's body. With each pregnancy, and a move from the city centre to the suburbs, Celia became bigger than ever. Worse, she was clumsy and caressing her belly was more like massaging cottage cheese. Sore nipples, purple stretchmarks everywhere and sex was as smooth as rubbing himself against a cement wall.

It irritated him that Celia was content letting a baby and toddler, rather than her husband, fondle her breasts or be the recipients of her look of love. In the privacy of their home, chores, errands she had to run and the needs of the children were of paramount importance. In the presence of society—the all-important congregation during Sunday mass—they held hands, a show of what a perfect family with Christ and the Lutheran Church at its centre, should be. They stopped having sex regularly and Celia didn't seem to mind.

Perhaps, I should never have married, thought Yogi, on his tenth wedding anniversary. Gone was the prospect of sexual adventures and entanglements with women he would never meet again. His mind raced to remember what it was like to have no necessity for seduction, romance, or love. A quick tryst and that was it. It was money well-spent. Drunken parties, the touch of experience rather than convenience, doggy style . . . all things of the past. He should have left things well alone.

'What happened to you, my friend?' Dato patted Yogi's midlife paunch on his fifteenth wedding anniversary.

Yogi laughed, hiding his smarting ego.

The still buff Dato had turned up at their single-storey bungalow in the satellite town of Klang an hour earlier. This newly-minted psychiatrist looked spiffy. He was in town to collect the United Nations (UN) Congo medal in recognition of his services at the UN Operation in the Congo (ONUC) in support of the postcolonial government.

'Why don't you join me tomorrow evening? A few of my friends are getting together and we can have dinner. Bring your son along.'

Yogi looked at Celia. She nodded, more focused on picking out weevils from the uncooked rice in her rattan winnowing fan.

'Let me get you a drink,' Yogi said, walking to the piece of furniture that was his pride and joy—a custom-made teakwood bar in one corner of their suburban living room.

As he mixed the whisky with water, Yogi knew what to anticipate if he went out with Dato. It would be to revisit the past and he knew the order in which everything would pan out. They would meet up with two or three others at a hawker stall where, seated on plastic stools, they'd use their fingers to eat off a banana leaf. This time though, with Raj in tow, this was where Yogi's involvement would have to end. He wasn't yet prepared to introduce his son to more adult adjournments such as a bar—the seedier the better—and a brothel.

'I know what you are expecting.'

Yogi slapped his friend on the arm. 'No lah. You think you know. I'm married now.'

'Married?' He burst out laughing. 'You don't fool me. I know you longer than Celia. I told you. You'll miss the common touch.'

Yogi rolled his eyes.

'Tell you what? I'll take you somewhere else okay. Something different. Fine drinks and men. No hanky-panky. Somewhere the boy can come as well.'

'Are you sure we should bring him?'

'Of course. Give your wife a break. Make this a boys' night out.'

'Okay.'

That night, Yogi tried to make love to Celia. It had been several weeks and he desperately needed his needs fulfilled. It was no good though. Both of them had bellies that overhung their thighs and got in the way. He closed his eyes, trying to remember his wedding night when her body had been taut, when her desire for him was strong, and when she looked into his eyes the moment he whispered, 'I really love you.' In the present moment, neither of them said a word. Soon, she began to cry.

'I'm nothing now. Not beautiful. Not sexy. My body is ugly to you. You can't even get it up for me.' She moved to the other side of the bed, as far away from Yogi as possible. She pulled a bedsheet over her nakedness, to hide her body's unsightliness from her husband.

'No,' he said, reaching out to her. 'I must be tired.'

Celia didn't respond with words. In the light beam that filtered through the open window, Yogi saw his wife's body shake.

'Please Celia,' he all but begged. 'Don't cry.' When he touched her shoulders, she pulled away. He spent a long while in the nude, watching the blades of the ceiling fan rotate clockwise. With one palm on the top of his belly and the back of the other resting on his forehead, he sighed.

How had they come to this? This wasn't how it was meant to be.

Her sobs were relentless. Blaming him. Blaming her.

Both of them had changed beyond recognition.

The next night, Yogi, accompanied by Raj, turned up at the swankiest hotel in town—an old establishment recently bought over and refurbished by the Hilton group. They announced themselves at the reception and were told to wait for a bit. A manager turned up and ushered them to the lifts. Inside, they were not going up. Instead, he inserted a key into a slot, turned it, and a secret panel opened up. He winked at Raj then pressed the 'Down' button. When the doors opened, he said, 'Welcome to 'Sultan's Lounge".'

Goggle-eyed, Yogi put his hands on his son's shoulders and pushed him out. The women who paraded in front of them balanced tankards of beer on trays and were dressed in nothing more than bikini bottoms and tasselled stickers to cover their nipples. On the stage, more athletic ones defied gravity by balancing their bodies on a shiny pole. At the roulette table, a man was whispering into his cupped hands and, a moment later, he rolled the dice. It was Dato.

As though sensing Yogi's presence, he turned and his smile became broader. 'Ah! You're here. Come. Come.'

Yogi and Raj walked to him.

'What is this, Dato? The boy . . .' Yogi whispered his annoyance into his friend's ears.

'The boy? He's no boy. He's almost fifteen, for God's sake. Better he is with us for this first taste of the common touch, no?' Ignoring Yogi, Dato turned to Raj and said, 'Go, boy. Have a look around. See, but no touch, okay.' Dato winked, then added, 'Not yet at least. There's time for you to learn all about the common touch.'

'You're a young man now. Go and walk around a bit. There are some interesting things in that hall. Go have a look. I want some time alone with your father. I have something to ask him.'

Yogi clicked his lips, an attempt to hold on to his firstborn's innocence, but to no avail. The boy had already turned his back on the two men.

'Come my friend. Forget your son for a while. Have a drink. I need your help. It's about my Madhu and that land in Merbok, lah. My family's property.'

* * *

There was no other way to say it—Dato resembled a monkey. It was more accurate since his actual name was Hanuman, after the monkey god in the Hindu epic, the Ramayana. Hanuman Pradhan was a fair fellow, but stocky and balding with a distended neck. His mate, Madhuri Roy, on the other hand, was dark, but with a body like a song: a stunning beauty with silken skin and coily hair.

Why didn't they simply marry each other?

Well, they believed wholeheartedly in whatever their mothers said; and, their mothers, in turn, believed wholeheartedly in the word of astrologers, those human intermediaries with the Hindu gods. Actually, it was an insult to shamans to refer to these half-naked men as such. Instead, they were mostly high on *ganja* and could no more predict the future of a marriage with any more certainty than a weatherman could predict an approaching thunderstorm. Nonetheless, the couple's mothers trusted the readings of no less than three astrologers who said the same thing. In most cases, in that *pavitra rishta* of marriage—the purest of bonds sanctified before a sacred fire—the union was supposed to lead a couple to *moksha* and liberation from the cycle of rebirth. In the case of Dato and Madhuri, however, the couple was doomed. Should they marry, they would generate such negative karma that they would be reborn as lesser beings, such as dogs or, worse, amoebae.

The reality, however, was that theirs was a love of open secrets—the world knew they were a couple in the biblical sense but no one said it to their faces. They attended all the same events but made sure never to be caught holding each other's hands, lest there be photographic evidence of their union. They secretly exchanged unmentionables in the master bedroom of his sprawling bungalow in

Merbok in the north of Peninsular Malaysia. If ever they were queried (which never happened), their ready answer was that she was merely a tenant looking after his aged mother. To the world, Madhuri Roy occupied the guest bedroom downstairs.

* * *

'You have to help me,' Dato said, a hint of desperation in his whisky-laced voice.

'How? Why?'

'I need the money, lah. To start a practice here. I have so many problems and I need your help to create an exchange marriage here.' The two men then focused on how to create a reciprocal exchange of spouses between them when none of the parties involved were related by marriage or blood. In the past, Dato had transferred ownership of the land and house in Merbok to Madhuri. She agreed to mortgage this asset to get much-needed funds for Dato. He'd recently found out from agents managing his properties that Madhuri, now older and more spiritually inclined, had appeared on the radar of a new organization called Saptarishi Spiritual Centre. They were on the lookout for a large piece of land to build their ashram and had Madhuri's land in Merbok in mind. Dato was petrified that they would manipulate Madhuri's vulnerabilities for their benefit and he'd lose the property altogether. The plan Dato conceived was a pseudo exchange marriage. It was simple—Yogi would be given a Power of Attorney over Madhuri's ownership of this particular property, and both he and Dato would make sworn declarations that they were siblings. In this way, Yogi would be obliged to see to it that

Dato would one day be back in possession of the property. Yogi would effectively commit to spending all his energies and resources to fight to get the property back, even if it took the rest of his life to do so.

A quarter of an hour later, Dato raised his hand to call for a waitress. Once she was close, he said, 'My friend here is a married man. But he's . . . errr . . . hungry. Anyone interested?'

Seated on a bar stool, Yogi crossed his arms on top of his beer belly. He noticed the girl's small but well-shaped breasts. He missed those—the kind with pointy nipples. Although the girl's smile remained intact, there was a fleeting moment of hesitation when her eyes became wide. It was all Yogi needed to become aware that she was physically repulsed. He took a deep breath and reached out to take the tankard of beer Dato had ordered for him. After swallowing half its contents in one go, he slapped Dato on the shoulder and said, 'I have to go look for my son.'

'Okay. Okay. Okay,' Dato said, putting his arms around the waitress and pulling her onto his lap instead.

Yogi found Raj standing at the entrance of a hall. He was observing couples in all manner of inebriation, gyrating their bodies to what Yogi now recognized as 'boom-boom' music. He shook his head. Dato had, to all intents and purposes, brought them to an upper-class strip club.

A moment later, Dato stood on the other side of his son.

'There you are, Uncle. Nice place.'

'Don't call me Uncle. Call me Dato.'

'Okay, Dato.' Looking up at the older man, Raj smiled. 'This one is boring,' he said, pointing to the scene of debauchery in front of them. 'That side,' he said, using his chin to point at a narrow corridor, 'is more interesting.'

Dato smiled. 'Really?'

'Yes. Come, I show you.'

So it was that a young man accompanied by two middle-aged ones found themselves standing at the entrance of a room without a door. The row of hanging beads strung from the doorframe was meant to maintain the privacy of what the couple were up to behind this apology of curtain.

'They're mating. I saw a programme on television,' the youth whispered.

'Raj!' Yogi cautioned.

'What?' Raj said, not looking at his father, but maintaining his gaze on the couple. 'It's all natural.'

Turning to Dato, Raj said, 'It was interesting, you know. After they finish, they stick to each other for a while. Like those two inside. It's called doggy style, no?'

Yogi saw Dato's eyes widen and hid his smile. He could tell that for the first time in his life, Dato was stumped by the comments of a precocious teenager. For Yogi, though, Raj's comment ignited a feeling that was altogether different, and it made him forever look at his son with a simultaneous layer of curiosity and reluctance to find out the truth. He followed the lines of Raj's body and saw that it was well-shaped. Chiselled, hard, and ready for the muscles that would soon line it and hair that would cover his skin. The eyes he'd inherited from Celia were bright and wide; the flared nostrils from him and the full lips, an actual combination of both Yogi and Celia. It was his smile, though, that intrigued Yogi—a genuine show of joy coupled with interest at what was possible. You see, Raj had just witnessed two humans of the same gender copulating.

He didn't push his hands into his trouser pockets.

He didn't look away.

Raj, his son, the fruit of his loins, was enjoying the show.

How on earth was Yogi ever going to explain his suspicions to Celia? What would he say to her? If she then confided in the parish priest, the stigma would stay with Raj for the rest of his life. Yogi was certain that their son would be subjected to conversion therapy to ensure that Satan and evil were chased out of his little one's heart. Worse, Celia already had her eyes set on a suitable daughter-in-law for a possible exchange marriage in fifteen years.

Dato interrupted his thoughts, sensing the need for distraction.

'This name of yours, Raj, it's your house name, no?' Dato said. 'Like your father and me. We're Yogi and Dato to the common man. But, actually, we're Rajendran and Hanuman. I've never known your actual name. What is it, boy?'

'My name is Matthew Luke John.'

'Ah-ha,' Dato replied.

Yogi rolled his eyes when he saw Dato's smirk, desperate to hide his amusement that two of his son's names couldn't have been more Christian.

Having summoned a waitress, Dato then handed the boy his first glass of whisky, put his arm around the young man's shoulders and said, 'Welcome to the world of adults, doggies, and the common touch, Matthew Luke John Rajendran.'

My Final *Tapasya*

> Mental health disorders may be treated with the help of spirituality through a psychotherapeutic method called Spiritually Augmented Behaviour Therapy . . . It focuses on four key areas which are acceptance, hope, achieving meaning or purpose, and forgiveness. At the community level, research suggests that religiosity reduces suicide rates, alcoholism and drug use . . . However, on the flip side, some irresponsible people may take advantage of emotionally vulnerable individuals ostensibly supporting their spirituality. If we are emotionally susceptible, we can be more easily convinced to take part in unhealthy activities and be instigated to display intolerant behaviours.
>
> —Professor (Adj.) Dato' Dr Andrew Mohanraj

What utter codswallop!

The professor's words were endlessly spinning inside my head when I picked up a rusty razor blade. I ran the two-inch piece of metal over the scab on my thinning hairline.

Acceptance, hope, achieving meaning or purpose . . .

At that moment, a push notification triggered an alert that my message had been sent at 1.53 a.m. The text that friends and family would see on the screens of their mobile devices would read: 'I'm sorry. Nisha.'

I stopped scratching the welt and put the razor blade down on the mattress.

Sticking out my tongue, I enjoyed the taste of salt on my fingers. A few seconds, that was all it would take for this, and every single pain I'd endured, to be over.

What would my other family—the spiritual one—think of me now? All of them would be sleeping, cosy in the arms of their partners. And here I was, alone in the master bedroom of a bungalow in the heart of a housing estate in an older part of Alor Setar.

One of the neighbour's dogs began to bark. Could it have sensed the dumpster truck making it rounds to collect rubbish? That green, metallic giant on wheels that stank and made me turn my face into a pillow. Why did they collect the rubbish before dawn? It probably made sense for a spiritually-inclined person, though. The hour before the sun rose was propitious because it was the divine hour when Hindus did everything from getting married and making a baby to praying or taking a dip in the Ganges.

Sigh . . .

All those years of regularly sitting in a lotus position to undergo tapasya; all in the belief that such penances would ensure the well-being of my chakras. Apparently, the simple act of breathing activated these subtle energy centres and made them spin in a clockwise fashion. This aided in ensuring that I was in control of my life. My ultimate aim was to attain moksha, the elusive liberation from the cycle of rebirth to which all Hindus aspire. At least that's what my spiritual guru once said.

My spiritual guru . . .

* * *

Was this man for real?

Barely ten minutes had passed since we met for the first time on a warm evening in mid-November 2015. Standing in the reception of the Saptarishi Spiritual Centre (7S for short), he was dressed in office clothes, complete with a necktie befitting one who held a senior position in the financial services industry. Now, the man in this windowless room at the back of a dingy shoplot in suburban Kuala Lumpur was seated on a brown faux leather sofa lined with a faux tiger skin, which had a furry tail hanging over one armrest. His leg was tucked under him, presumably on the tiger's head. With a yellow scarf draped over one shoulder, a liberal amount of white ash smeared on his forehead, and sandalwood rosary beads dangling from his hand, he'd transformed into someone whose persona was far removed from the corporate world.

'Come,' he said, inviting me to sit on a plastic chair in front of him.

So as not to continue staring, I hurried to make myself comfortable.

'Your name is Nisha, yes?' When I nodded, he said, 'You can call me Guruji.'

Perhaps, sensing my barely concealed hostility, he changed the subject and we had a pleasant enough conversation about life in general. Finally, he came to the crux of the whole matter and asked, 'So, what do you need help with?'

'Well, two things, really. My father's health isn't great and I need help with this marriage issue. I'm already forty-three and my parents are worried.' The same sentences, with the only variable being my age, had rolled off my tongue whenever I met with astrologers and matchmakers in the past six years.

I scanned the room. There were images stuck on the back wall, as though forming a halo above Guruji's head. I recognized those of Amma the Hugging Saint, and the celestial family of the Hindus, Shiva, Durga, Murugan, and Ganesh. There was one flapping in the gentle breeze of the ceiling fan. It was an image of Kriya Baba.

'Careful.' I put my hand out to warn Guruji when the image dislodged and was about to fall to the floor.

Guruji twisted his body and reached out behind him to straighten the image and press one corner of it into a lump of Blu Tak.

'I've met him,' he said, flippant.

I held my breath.

This man had met Kriya Baba?

Growing up, I'd read a classic spiritual treatise about the one many called the 'Deathless Guru'. Only enlightened beings were allowed to meet Kriya Baba. It was inconceivable that a mere mortal—one I'd assumed was no more than a charlatan making baseless predictions for a fee—had met a spiritually exalted being.

'I've also met Agastya Rishi. That's why we call this place 7S. It's named after the *saptarishi.* The seven sages.' Smiling, he said, 'You can close your mouth.'

I shook my head and swallowed, embarrassed.

'Don't worry about your father,' Guruji said, nonchalant, reminding me of the reason for my visit in the first place. He shook the handheld brass bell on his side table and, within seconds, Ruben, the young man who manned the reception of 7S, appeared at the door.

'Give her five bottles of blessed water,' he instructed. Turning back to me, he said, 'Make your father drink one bottle a day. He must finish all five bottles. He'll be fine.'

'Thank you, Guruji,' I said, taking the canvas tote bag from Ruben.

'And, you must meditate more. You know how, right?'

'Yes and yes Guruji,' I said. I had been initiated into a meditation practice twenty years ago, when I was still reading Law in London. Since then, I'd been reciting a one-syllable mantra for ten minutes every day.

'When you come back to KL, you must join our meditation. Ours is better. You can go faster on the spiritual path,' Guruji added.

I nodded. That's the moment when, like a moth that comes out of hiding and angles its body to a source of light, I started to spiral towards Guruji's all-consuming spiritual flame.

Ruben then said, 'Do namaskar now.'

'Namaskar?'

When he waved his hand downwards, as though he were petting an invisible dog, I realized he expected me to bend down and touch the Guruji's feet to seek his blessings. Unable to look either of them in the eye, I said, 'I can't do this.'

I could feel Ruben's laser-focused fury targeted at me.

'No. No. No.' I put my hand up, an indication that they'd misunderstood. 'I can't do all this going down and up on my knees. If I do, I don't think I can come back up. These jeans are way too tight.'

I looked at a midway point between the two men, an empty spot on the back wall. I wondered what Guruji's response would be? Anger, perhaps. Would the blessed water now not work? I stole a glance from under my lashes. Guruji's eyes were dancing. He was amused and I was intrigued. I left 7S that night with a sense in my being that I'd met someone extraordinary.

On a humid afternoon eleven months later, an undertaker carried a body wrapped in white cloth into our house in Alor Setar. No. Not a body. It was Daddy. Someone I could still hold, touch, and feel. How I envied those who buried their dead because they would always have a grave to visit. In less than twenty-four hours, Daddy would be reduced to ashes in a state-of-the-art electric crematorium outside town. From 18 October 2016, my father would be nothing more than a memory.

By evening, the number of mourners swelled. The scent from the garlands and wreathes of daisies, jasmine, and tuber roses placed in and around the coffin just about camouflaged the odour of embalming fluids. The continuous recitation of melodic Sanskrit mantras for the dead in the background offered comfort.

Close to midnight, I pulled out a bundle of '555' notebooks. I no longer needed this evidence of yet another tapasya. It had become another form of meditation that strengthened my connection with Guruji. You see, in November 2015, seated next to Daddy's hospital bed,

I'd not only ensured that he'd drunk the five bottles of blessed water, but I had bargained with the Divine Mother:

Let Daddy come home and I'll write Your name 108,000 times.

Let him recover and I'll turn vegetarian.

Let him live and I'll recite the Mahamrityunjaya mantra 108 times for 48 days.

Now, with these little notebooks full of the word 'Amma' in my cursive penmanship, I knew that the Divine Mother had kept Her word. There was no more bargaining to do. I shed no tears.

'Go be with the Divine Mother, Daddy,' I whispered and placed the notebooks inside the casket at my father's feet.

In the next instant, there was an alert on my mobile phone. Guruji had sent a message to the group chat he'd set up on WhatsApp for those who were now regularly meditating: 'Nisha's father is in Her hands. The Divine Mother will look after him. All will be well.'

I exhaled in the knowledge that my connection with Guruji was inviolable. I put my palms together, a sign of gratitude for Divine benevolence, unaware that my tapasya had not yet been served in full.

Towards the end of November 2016, I was summoned to 7S. The newest recruit to Guruji's Inner Circle, I took my place next to Ruben. Poor fellow. As the second of six boys, the twenty-two-year-old man often complained about being overlooked by his parents at their modest semi-detached home in Petaling Jaya. At 7S, Ruben was the first to accept Guruji as his true guru and become a *shishya.* This disciple was, therefore, beyond special and touted to hold a significant place in Guruji's heart.

Guruji spread an A1-sized paper on the marble table top and five of us in 7S's Inner Circle studied the drawing of what appeared to be a temple.

'This is our new ashram. Its name is Rishipuram. I've already been there,' Guruji declared in his high-pitched voice.

Already been there? How?

Ruben leaned in and whispered, 'Guruji can travel through time.' I later learned that Guruji, having practised months of intense meditation, had been granted the ability to dissolve the dimension of time by gaining access to the astral plane. For years now, he had been able to perceive the past, present, future, and all that's in between. Through his divination, Guruji had determined that Rishipuram would be located on a twelve-thousand-square-feet piece of land with a split-level bungalow built on a slope. The cement-flattened backyard had something special—a concealed fire pit. During religious *homas,* a raging fire acted as an energetic vehicle to carry the dreams of mere mortals to the angels, spirits, and gods watching from on high.

In the following days, impatient for Guruji's divination to become manifest, Ruben drove around neighbouring residential areas in search of this promised ashram. One evening, when the traffic lights turned green, Ruben stepped on the accelerator with minimum regard to the slippery conditions of the road after a storm. In seconds, he was a victim of a broadside collision.

Listed as 'ICE' in Ruben's mobile phone, Guruji was the first to be informed that his disciple's bloodied body was in an ambulance and on its way to the nearest hospital. When Guruji and I walked into the Emergency Room ten minutes later, we were in time to hear a medical officer's verbal report—Ruben had a five per cent chance of survival.

Ruben's mother, who'd arrived moments earlier, turned to Guruji. In Tamil, she said, '*Eṉ makaṉiṉ vāḻkkai uṅkaḷ kaiyil.*'

I held my breath, astounded she'd placed her son's life in Guruji's hands.

Guruji patted her shoulders, comforting the distraught woman. Taking broad strides, following in the footsteps of the doctor, he turned to me and said, 'Follow me.'

That day in the ICU, I was the sole witness to the man that Guruji was, rather than the persona of an exalted spiritual being he projected to all at 7S. First, he assumed the *shambhavi mudra* and gazed inward at his mystical third eye. Then, to my utter surprise, tears streamed down his cheeks.

An hour later, Guruji and I were a roadside stall. He poured steaming coffee into a saucer and, Indian style, slurped the brew from the saucer. He swallowed before he said, 'Ah! I needed that.' Putting the saucer down he said, 'I'm exhausted. I had to go see Amma just now.'

I raised an eyebrow, perplexed.

He clicked his lips and said, 'Aiya. I had to go do namaskar to her, lah. I decided Ruben must continue to live and I wanted her to listen to me.'

The half cup of coffee churned in my stomach. It was quite something to become aware that I was in the presence of one who was empowered to intercede with the Divine Mother and demand, almost, that a fellow human being's life be prolonged.

When we returned to 7S, Guruji decreed that none of us were allowed to visit Ruben for fear that our negativity would deplete what little energy Ruben had. Instead, preparations were to be made for continuous prayers to celebrate the Divine Mother. A week later, Guruji proclaimed (I can think of no better word) to all those in the wider 7S family that the spiritual balance was restored and Ruben would henceforth heal. Within the hour, Ruben's vitals improved and, in no time at all, he was transferred to a rehabilitation centre.

Excluding Guruji, Ruben's parents and those in the Inner Circle were the only ones privy to the Divine Mother's actual fee for granting Guruji's demand that Ruben be permitted to live. In the hour before dawn on the first night Ruben spent in the ICU, Guruji presided over a *datta homa* during which Ruben's parents voluntarily surrendered their child, body, heart and soul, into the hands of Guruji. Also, for the next 108 days, under a divine embargo to stay away from Ruben, Guruji underwent a concentrated practice of spiritual austerity. He also demanded that all in his Inner Circle donate RM21 per day to 7S's coffers.

On the 109th day, an emaciated Guruji, boasting a full beard, hosted a thanksgiving ceremony during which he was reunited with his 'son', a now-mobile Ruben. When it was all over, the Inner Circle remained at 7S, not merely to clean up but also to have a private audience with Guruji. During that august meeting, the sum total of monies we in the Inner Circle had collected, cash amounting to RM9,072, was placed on an ever-silver tray and presented to Guruji as a gift. He touched his fingers to the tray, careful not make physical contact with the cash itself. The scriptures, Guruji explained, didn't allow for enlightened beings to do so, lest they be corrupted by the sin of avarice.

'I'll decide what to do with the money later. Maybe during Guru Purnima in July,' Guruji said, pushing back the tray of this *guru dakshina.* 'But,' he added, 'the Divine Mother gave me a download just now.'

A download? I hid my smile at Guruji's use of such a techie jargon.

'She said that in some previous lives, I was successful spiritually but poor. In some others, I was successful materially but poor spiritually. This life, she wants me to be both. You will never meet another Swamiji like me—I will be spiritually enlightened but rich also. Living life to the fullest. Being happy all the time, right?'

No one around that table said a word. Indeed, what was there to say? Like the others, I placed my palms together, a sign of gratitude at having heard the words spoken by one whom we were instructed to henceforth acknowledge as the manifestation of the Divine Mother on earth. Looking directly at me, Guruji then said, 'I want you to write about this.'

'Yes, Guruji.'

'No. Swamiji,' he instructed. 'Explain my tapasya. You must show that, from now on, I am the guiding light for all true seekers.'

Within a month, I created an online newsletter called 'The Prism' and it was to be disseminated to over 5,000 members of 7S via social media. For the first-ever 'Letter from the Editor', I wrote:

Progression
by Nisha Sagadevan

7S's visitors are usually absolutely quiet. You can see the many questions in their eyes, though, the main one being, 'Why is the guru's name so long?' The answer can be distilled into one word: progression.

> It begins with the name given to our guru at birth—Yogendran. As his father's name was Sundralingam, throughout his childhood and young adulthood, he was known as Yogendran Sundralingam.
>
> In February 2009, he began his spiritual journey. Within a month and a half, Kriya Babaji, one who is believed to be more than a thousand years old, appeared before him. During this august meeting, Kriya Baba accepted our guru as his disciple and permitted him to use the name Shishyakriya.
>
> By November 2013, such was his continued devotion to the spiritual masters that, in no time at all, Lord Shiva (the Adi Guru) appeared before him. During that majestic audience in the astral plane, our guru was bestowed the title of Guruji. Additionally, it is said that the Adi Guru has five 'faces'. The title a disciple acquires is based on which face accepts a flower when it's offered in obeisance. In our guru's case, it was 'Agama'. With that, he was permitted to add Agama Shiva to his name.
>
> As it is with all journeys, when one ends, another begins. In the first quarter of 2017, he received a command from on high to embark on a special set of prayers, which took 108 days to complete. At the end of it, our guru was allowed to insert the words 'Maha Lakshami SwamiRama' in his title.
>
> Put it all together and this is the full name, replete with the meaning of our guru: HH Maha Lakshami SwamiRama Sri Shishyakriya Yogendran Agama Shiva.

Reading the published work, I rejoiced at the emergence of a hitherto missing spark of happiness from within. I'd created something my guru deemed relevant. I wholeheartedly believed that SwamiRama was a spiritual being who would never betray me. Especially when SwamiRama approved of the man of my dreams—Ivan Nagalingam—who appeared in my three-dimensional world in the most unexpected way.

* * *

He's an idiot!

I freely criticized Ivan, thought to be the top psychiatrist in the city. Ruben had come under his care, as the young man was suspected of suffering from PTSD owing to the fact that he was still suffering from nightmares and intermittent insomnia. In the course of their conversations, Ivan mentioned that he was looking for a writer with whom to collaborate to create a collection of stories based on people with all sorts of mental health issues. My name was put forward and that's how we met one balmy evening in the second half of 2017.

Perhaps, he wasn't an idiot. An obtuse ass, maybe.

I mean, he didn't have the book-opening etiquette I expected from someone of his stature. I did not like that he placed my most recent non-fiction work, *All Number Nine*, on the table and opened it until the spine was crushed. How on earth could I collaborate with such an uncouth man?

When he lifted both ends of the book, snapped them shut, and whistled, I stood up, picked up the book and put it into my leather satchel. He stopped whistling.

'Thank you for seeing me,' I said and turned to leave.

'No. No. No,' he cried out. Standing up, he pleaded, 'Please don't go, Ms Nisha. You're the writer I've been looking for.'

I stared at him. 'Really?'

'Yes.' Opening his palm and inviting me to sit, he added, 'Please, sit down. If I sound flippant, it's because I'm already familiar with your work.'

He then rattled off some of my best-selling titles, like the biography of a cardiologist and a collection of short stories about a sweet dachshund. He explained that he wanted to model his book on the work of another psychiatrist, Brian Weiss, who'd become a leading expert in regression therapy. Ivan was practically bubbling with delight, removing his glasses and rubbing the rim between his fingers. I found myself charmed, by the man and his vision for his book.

That's how it began.

To ensure that we were not distracted, I agreed to meet Ivan at a café, rather than his clinic, once a week. Where he provided the medical jargon, my task was to dumb down the complex theories, conditions, and treatments, then create stories to illustrate everything.

When I was working alone at home, though, I analysed everything connected to him: my sense of yearning, his every word and message to me, and what he wore to our meetings. That's the sort of blinkered view a woman gets in unrequited love. With each memory, I would turn it over and play games. What if I changed his tailor-made, short-sleeved red shirt to a blue, polo neck pullover? Would that make Ivan more common and, therefore, accessible to me? In any event, with each word I wrote for *How Are You?* it was as if I were paying homage to this vision I had of the man rather than the reality of who he was.

Was I in love with Ivan, though?

Well, I'll tell you who I was in love with once upon a time. The man was a hotelier named Julian Nair. The memory of what we had—mostly sadness and longing on my part—haunted me like a bad fairy-tale.

We met when a former front office manager complained about being unfairly dismissed. I was tasked with observing the hotel's in-house proceedings and reporting back to the partners of the legal firm I worked at. I couldn't bring myself to ever call Julian–Nisha a relationship for it seemed to be over before it began when I moved to the city four weeks after submitting my final report. Julian promised to follow suit, as it was his dream to open a restaurant in the city. 'In big neon lights. NISHA. That's the name I want,' he said, looking through the space he created when he brought together his thumbs and forefingers, as though he were framing an imagined signboard.

In the eight years we were supposedly together, there was always an excuse for his absence—his ailing mother, ex-wife, financially ruined brothers, and estranged daughter needed him. I wasn't ever allowed to need him. He never moved to Kuala Lumpur. And his fine dining establishment that served authentic Kerala cuisine never materialized. I spent a long time giving myself permission to grieve before actually grieving for what I didn't have with Julian. The latter took a day, but the former had taken years. I learned that time doesn't heal all wounds. Instead, it generates a need to be creative with the circumstances presented which, for me, meant writing non-stop.

What was also exquisite about this exercise was that to the outside world, I seemed fine and my career flourished. At the same time, there was no one to interfere, edit, guide, or suggest changes to the internal narrative I'd created alongside the written pieces. Like the time I wrote a review for *Salmon*

Fishing in the Yemen by Paul Torday. I could relive the curiosity with which I tried fresh salmon for the first time when Julian called in a favour with one of his suppliers and had them flown fresh from Norway. While preparing a feature article for the papers based on an interview with a woman who yearned for a child, no one saw me weep when I recalled the time Julian sent me a text saying: 'I will marry you, but never touch you because I know your greatest desire is for a child.' Hiding behind the cloak of words I had created gave me the privacy I craved.

One fine day, I read that every time you remember what was and try to imagine what could have been, a miniscule number of the cells inside you die. When these necrotic cells become a mass, you either excise it from your body or it takes hold and disease sets in. To preserve my health, I decided to remember only the good about Julian and that's the day I allowed my grieving to happen. Like the time I picked him up from the train station. I saw his reflection in the rear-view mirror and it was as though a Bollywood actor was walking towards my car. Soon, I forgot the ache of not having seen him in years. Indeed, recalling my memories of Julian became yet another kind of calming meditation practice to which I retreated when my outer world threatened to disintegrate.

That was until I met SwamiRama.

After the head of 7S tied a saffron-coloured string around my right wrist in July 2017—a sign that I was on the first step to accepting him as my guru—he said, 'You must meditate on your chakras every day. You will become more balanced and be able to align with others who are the same as you.'

Even during that intense moment, I had but a single thought: Could I meditate myself into Ivan's heart?

This was precisely the question I asked SwamiRama in April 2018 when I finally plucked up the courage to share all the details of my love life with him. Yes, I was aware that I sounded confused mentioning Ivan and Julian in the same conversation, but my guru didn't see it that way. That was his gift—to sift through my thoughts and choose only what was real.

'You're learning the art of letting go,' he replied, playing with a golden pendant. Called Gowri-Shankar, it was the guru dakshina that we in the Inner Circle had commissioned a goldsmith from India to create. 'It's like you've embraced the guru within.'

If I hadn't thought it facetious at the time, I'd have responded with this: Does this mean that I've embraced you? Are you my guru within?

Instead, at that moment, Ruben walked into the centre. When he noticed SwamiRama, he rushed to bend and touch his guru's feet with the fingertips of his right hand.

'Careful.' SwamiRama put his arm out, preventing the boiling-hot, vegetarian hokkien mee from tipping out of the opaque plastic bag Ruben was holding in his left.

'Sorry. Sorry. Sorry, Swamiji,' Ruben said, quickly reaching out to hold the base of the bag, stabilizing the contents therein.

'Go. Go. Go. Put it in a bowl in the kitchen and bring back for me,' SwamiRama said, waving him away.

'So,' SwamiRama said, turning his attention back to me, 'when do you plan to do namaskars to me?'

'SwamiRama, I can touch your feet, but I won't do the bowing, scraping, and so on. With my bottom in the air,' I said. 'I know everyone else does it. I still can't.'

Smiling, he said, 'They do it because I'm like a father to them. They love me. You would have done it for your father when he was alive, right?' SwamiRama misunderstood my silence as me answering him in the affirmative. 'I'm like your father now, right? So, you will soon do the same, right?'

I didn't say a word.

Love him?

Revere him, respect him, seek his counsel, yes.

But love him?

'About this Ivan fellow. Leave him to me. I will make the impossible possible. For now, you learn as much as you can about him. And meditate more.'

It was the way he said it. There was a force, a certainty that brooked no opposition. Once again, I put my palms together, a sign of gratitude, but this time for SwamiRama's benevolence. Once again, I was unaware that my tapasya had not yet been served in full.

Surprisingly, Ivan had a distinct interest in all things spiritual. Although he refused participation in the retreats 7S organized as luxuries for which he didn't have the time, he admitted to having read varied works from Ouspensky and Jung to Nisargadatta Maharaj and Osho. He quoted from their texts, but I always got the impression that they were nothing more than noise in the background of his mind. In this, we were diametrically opposed, for if I learned a particular teaching, I embodied it wholeheartedly. For example, soon after hearing about 'embracing the guru within', I made it a point to study this concept in some detail. In no time at all, I began to talk to the guru within and share with it (I couldn't decide if it was male or female) all my thoughts, ideas, and stories. Like the fact that even though I knew that post Julian–Nisha, he had taken up a job in Brunei. Where, exactly, in the oil-rich nation, I no longer cared to find out. When he sent me a photograph of himself behind the wheel of a company-issued Mercedes Benz, I understood that he'd achieved his dream of becoming a member of the upper management within the hospitality industry. It was like reading the news on the television where zero emotion was attached to the facts being imparted. I never replied because I was past indifference—I didn't want him to fail, but I couldn't be bothered if he succeeded either. The day came when I told my guru within that I was grateful Julian–Nisha didn't work because if it had, I may never have met Ivan.

Although it was impossible yet to accept that I was in love with Ivan, the more we worked on *How Are You?* the more enchanted I was.

Out of the blue, Ivan insisted that I include a poem he'd created in the manuscript. And like everything that happens without warning, it was also the moment when my emotions tipped from admiring Ivan's innate intelligence into something new and exciting.

'You know how,' he said while crossing his arms, 'you open a book and there are all those pages in the front? What are they called?'

Once I explained the details of the frontmatter of a book to him, he showed me the poem he'd composed. It was hopeless—the syntax was wonky, the words didn't rhyme, and the cadence was erratic. I didn't have the heart to tell him that including it could damage the quality of our work, especially when he acknowledged its failings by singing the lyrics from one of the most famous Bollywood movies of all time: 'Mai Shayar Toh Nahi'. Roughly, this translated to, 'I'm no poet.'

Ivan's poem was called 'The Divine's Embrace'. I guessed that it was his attempt to convey the idea that when two people truly loved each other, it had nothing to do with them, but was the work of the Divine. The last stanza was particularly awful:

> When he sees her in all and sees all in her,
> It is then they don't leave the other.
> Having a human experience is the Divine's purpose,
> Let the light of the Divine be upon us.
> Though we be far, we seek the lovers' embrace.

The worst you could say of Ivan was that he worried silly about the details of his outer world. He craved adulation from those who had even a whiff of a title to their name and showed them more respect than they deserved. It seemed strange for someone who was so well-accomplished. I mean, if I so much as sat next to him, instead of opposite him at the café, he would make sure to lean away from me, making me wonder if I was that physically repulsive. In photographs published by the media of events he attended, you could see the glow in him as he stood next to a vacuous princess staring at her with puppy-dog eyes. When he was appointed to a UN post, naturally, congratulatory messages poured in. He responded to those from the *orang kenamaan* with profuse, verbose texts. To my heartfelt one, he sent 'Thanks, kind regards,' via WhatsApp.

Even in his choice of attire, where I saw a jacket, he knew the difference between a sports jacket and a peacoat. For me, the all-purpose chiffon sari my mother had given me years ago was suitable for all events, whether it be a gala fund-raising festival hosted by an Odissi dancer or the launch of a book by desperate-to-be-woke junior member of one of Malaysia's nine royal families. For Ivan, though, it mattered that he wore a batik shirt to one and a suit to the other.

This sort of compartmentalization in his outer world was a reflection of the inner workings of his mind. For *How Are You?,* it was as if he opened one drawer in his brain, took out the information there, put it into words, and that was it. Such was his concentration that what he wrote didn't warrant much editing.

I, on the other hand, would write one paragraph of a story, let it percolate in my psyche for a few days, then write a revised outline for the said story. The next day, I would take bits out and add dialogue I'd overheard in the train the day before. Together, the work we produced was the perfect match. Where he added the factual bits of a story, I added all the drama and emotion. Where I was sympathetic when what we created wasn't up to the mark, he was overly hard on himself. We were a perfect match.

Still, I expected that, in time, my feelings would plateau or taper altogether. I didn't anticipate that they would deepen. When I became aware that he was the first person I thought of when I woke up, I studied him more than ever.

The night we received the first edition hardcover copy of *How Are You?,* we went out for dinner to celebrate. It was to a Japanese restaurant that had opened to much fanfare in October 2019. Hours later, instead of dropping me off, he parked his car in the underground carpark of my condominium complex. Still somewhat tipsy from all the sake, we made our way to the now-closed poolside area and, cloaked in semi-darkness, he took both my hands in his. For a full two minutes, we stared into each other's eyes. Try as I might, I found it impossible to look away and the intensity of his gaze scared me silly. A while later, when the spell broke, he walked me to my sixth-floor flat. We stood for a few moments outside my front door. Quite suddenly, he nodded and turned to leave.

'Are you walking away from me?' I asked him, horrified.

He stopped, mid-stride, turned, and walked back to me. Gathering me into his arms, he patted my shoulders, as though he were comforting a dog with separation anxiety.

When he let me go and turned away, I blurted out, 'Is that all?'

He didn't stop this time.

'Next time, I want more,' I said to his back as he entered the lift.

Love, even if it is analysed through a rose-tinted veneer of my mind's eye, is an enjoyable process. That night, I pictured keeping him company while he worked. I would sit in his leather chair with my feet tucked in and book in hand while he typed away on his laptop at his desk. From time to time, we would venture to the balcony. Arms around each other, we'd look out at the stunning garden created by the landscape artist we'd hired. We'd make plans for a dinner we were going to host to celebrate *How Are You?* winning a prestigious award, thereby making us both award-winning writers.

It took courage to dream like this. Until now, I'd always been on the outside looking in at other couples' happiness, observing how they lived their lives, and thinking, *Wouldn't it be nice to be exactly like that?* When it becomes a habit to question one thing in your life, soon, you find that you begin to question everything else as well. Why did a cat turn up out of nowhere in the flat? What's the meaning of finding cigarette butts outside your front door?

Things don't take me by surprise. They stun me. Like the fact that I never saw Ivan again. I heard from him, yes, but not a word passed between us in person. Instead, I received messages via WhatsApp, the last one being as follows:

> 7.34 a.m., 4 December 2019
>
> Hi Nisha.
>
> Thank you very much for your all your help. I am really sorry that nothing worked out between us. I think we should not prolong this even further. It is not fair to you. Once again, thank you very much Nisha for all your help. You are a good person. I wish you all the very best in life. I shall always think of you very fondly. I don't want more. Good bye.
>
> Ivan

I forwarded the text to SwamiRama and requested a meeting with him to seek his counsel. I expected solace, comfort and, at the very least, kindness.

'I believe you were told that this will not work,' he said when I was seated opposite him at 7S.

I stared at SwamiRama, reeling from this metaphorical slap in the face.

I was told it wouldn't work?

By whom?

Wasn't it his voice I heard inside my head every night before bed saying, 'I will make the impossible, possible? Trust me.'

'You pushed him away with your intensity and need to know what happens. You're at fault that he left you. Now, you move on.' SwamiRama then threw down the fountain pen, a gift that Mummy and I had presented him as a token of our appreciation for his prayers when Daddy was dying. 'For God's sake, you're always fighting my advice with emotional justifications.' Looking straight at me, he said, 'Your energies have been negative from the day you stepped into 7S. You are not meditating enough.'

'But, Swamiji, I thought- . . .'

'What? What think–think?' Pointing at my head, he yelled, 'You are irrelevant. I will tell you what to think. You just meditate more.'

So it was that after the demise of a non-starter of a relationship with Ivan, I retreated into my shell, as I did after Julian–Nisha. Only, this time, instead of writing, I followed the strictures of one who was several steps closer to becoming a permanent presence in my life—I poured all my sorrows to the guru within.

And then my mother fell ill and was admitted to the ICU.

Three years and four months to the day after Daddy died, I sat before SwamiRama in the same room where he'd first shown us the plans for Rishipuram. I'd flown into the city to beg in person to my guru.

'Swamiji, please help me. Help my mother.'

He stroked the new piece of jewellery that hung from his neck. He'd informed us at the start of 2020 that he'd had a download from the Divine Mother. It had been her wish that the disciples of 7S donate RM101 per day for 108 days. The sum of RM54,540 collected had been used to commission this much larger Gowri-Shankar pendant and a smaller one as a reserve in case of theft. Both pieces of jewellery had been presented as guru dakshina for all the Divine Mother's son had done for us.

'What's your problem now?'

'SwamiRama, she's developed the same pneumonia as Daddy. I'm frightened.'

With eyes as hard as the *rudraksha* prayer beads strung around his neck, SwamiRama looked me in the eye and said, 'You are toxic in mind, mouth, and mood.'

In that infinitesimal moment, I didn't hear the chatter of new recruits to 7S, I didn't feel the cold air blowing on to my face, I didn't taste the blood on my lip as I bit into it.

'Toxic?' I whispered. 'That means poison. Are you saying that I'm poison?'

SwamiRama stared at the gecko on the wall before looking into my eyes. 'Yes. That's why your mother is in the ICU right now. Because of me, she is still alive. You are going to kill your mother with your negative energies.'

I left 7S that day, wondering what thoughts go through the mind of a moth, should it have one, when it makes a kamikaze dive into a raging flame.

On 16 May 2022, after I lit the funeral pyre for Mummy, I stopped communicating with SwamiRama in both the astral and physical plane. Instead, after I'd completed the ceremonial bath upon returning from the same crematorium where I'd said my final goodbye to Daddy, I sat for hours on the edge of the double bed in what used to be my parents' bedroom.

The cacophony of all ten dogs barking at once was the disturbance to my reverie. I looked up at the clock. There was about an hour and half before the *azan* from the state mosque. At that time, the dogs wouldn't bark but would howl.

Far away, in the paddy fields, farmers would be waking up. Instead of getting the bulls ready for the day's ploughing or even tractor oiled up to collect a harvest, I guessed that they would be charging batteries with USB ports and cables. Having embraced technology, obese farmers now stood in the shadiest corner of their lots and moved their fingers to control the drones that sprayed pesticides on the harvest. It was life hurtling into the future, leaving me behind.

I picked up the newspaper again and read the professor's words: 'It focuses on four key areas, which are acceptance, hope, achieving meaning or purpose, and forgiveness.'

'Bullshit!' I threw the paper aside.

Forgiveness, the professor wrote.

Whose forgiveness should I seek for what happened to my mother? After what he said, there was no compassion to be sought from SwamiRama. And Ivan wasn't going to answer any of my calls. And which friend was going to believe that it was the words of a spiritual master and a psychiatrist that had given me zero hope? Indeed, I no longer had the desire to search for a purpose to my life. I had to have one last bit of strength, though, for nothing was more horrifying than surviving suicide in Malaysia. The police would call a psychiatrist. Knowing my luck, it would be Ivan and he'd have all the power under the law to lock me up for attempting suicide. He would laugh at me.

I took a deep breath. The rubbish collectors would be wise to come after I'd finished my task. That way, the maid could scoop up all the mess I was about to create and it would all be clean again. A mess. That was all I was now—an awful mess.

I scratched my scalp, wincing when my nails dug into an open welt that ran parallel to my right ear. Rubbing gritty bits of skin between my fingers, there was a distinct smell of iron in the air.

I was toxic. Poisonous.

Full of negative energies.

I killed Mummy.

That's what SwamiRama had said.

Perhaps, there was another way to end this pain.

'N-i-s-h-a.'

Startled, I looked around.

Who was that?

Suddenly, my space was infused with light. When I looked around, the source was neither inside the master bedroom nor out of it. It was everywhere. Through the prism of an intense, clear light, I looked within. Every spinning chakra of my subtle being came to a complete stop. A moment later, they started to spin again, but anticlockwise. I sensed the words with every fibre of my being: 'Come into the light. Be happy.'

I picked up the razor blade, poised to push its rusty end into the veins of my left wrist.

My final tapasya.

Unchartered Waters

Parents of children with autism have one common dream for their children: for them to live in a world where they are not only accepted, but also understood, welcomed and appreciated . . . Whether it's learning more about those living with autism among us or offering support to someone we know who is living with autism, there are many things we can do as individuals, including sailing in unchartered waters, to build a more inclusive world. I am reminded of what another parent of a child with autism said about their child: 'I wouldn't change you for the world, but I would change the world for you.'

—Professor (Adj.) Dato' Dr Andrew Mohanraj

Miss Sumitra Suppiah
5 Jalan Tempinis
Bangsar
Kuala Lumpur
15 March 2000

I am very glad to have met you. I feel that my baby will be safe with you until I can come back for him. His name is Raj Lim and he is of both Chinese and Indian parentage. His father, James Lim, died in a motor vehicle accident before we could be married. We were supposed to be married six months ago at the registry office. I am now alone. I delivered the baby at a clinic and left the day after, as I could not afford to stay longer than necessary. Still, I was lucky because I was able to get the clinic to certify that this child was born there. That's the piece of paper I have left with you. As I explained to your staff, after two weeks, my milk has dried up and I have no money to buy formula. He cries so much and I've been lucky that the girls at the halfway home have been generous in donating some food. But rice with bits of fish and vegetable are not right for a newborn. He has diarrhoea and I have now given up changing his nappy at a moment's notice. I wait until it's soaked and this is not good for the baby either. The other girls said that giving Raj to you and throwing myself at the mercy of your Kuala Lumpur Baby Hatch may be the best idea for now. Please be kind to him and do not think that I neglect my child. Please feed him for now and give me time to find a way to make ends meet. With luck, this is only a temporary measure and I'll soon return for my baby.

God bless you!

Miss Sumitra Suppiah
67, Taman Golf,
Alor Setar, Kedah
15 May 2000

Thank you for all your goodness. I hope that Raj has not given you any more trouble. However, he is only less than three months old. I must admit that I am relieved knowing that at this very moment, Raj is in the best place that he can be. You say that he has a crib assigned to him and a place at the dining table to eat. Since I doubt he'll be able to sit on his own, I assume he has a carer to help him. I am glad that you have asked a Hindu temple priest, Mr Govindan, to keep an eye on him. If it's okay with you, I will write periodically to ask after Raj. I cannot, as yet, travel to Kuala Lumpur. I returned to my parents' home at the start of this month. They do not know about my relationship or pregnancy. James and I were both students at a college. He studied accounting and I was undertaking a diploma in psychology. Our plan was to get married and then tell our families. I pray that you'll keep him a while longer. I have enclosed the form you sent to me so you have proper papers for Raj.

God bless you!

> I, Sumitra a/p Suppiah, of 67 Taman Golf, Alor Setar, Kedah, am the biological mother of a baby boy born on 28 February 2000 at Kelinik Petaling Jaya, 721, Jalan Professor Khoo Khay Kim, Selangor. I hereby freely and of my own will agree that Kuala Lumpur Baby Hatch will provide a home for my baby until a time when I am able to collect my baby once more. I hereby promise not to interfere in the care that will be provided for my baby.

Mrs Sumitra Panikar
78 Jalan Bendahara
Alor Setar, Kedah
10 December 2000

I have thought very hard about what you wrote. I understand that there is a couple who would like to look after him. True, it would be great for him to stay in a house instead of an institution. Do you get paid to give him to a family? I fear that my child will become an innocent pawn in a baby-selling racket. That is not what I want to happen to him at all.

I planned to take him back by now. However, my circumstances have changed somewhat. As you can see, I am now a married woman. My husband, however, doesn't know of the existence of Raj and I write this to you in secret. I need some time to break the news to him and I will then endeavour to bring Raj back to me. I trust that you will continue looking after him for a while more. Please do not, as yet, give my child away to a family, however desperate they are for a child. Raj is still very much a baby, is he not? I recall the document I signed a while ago. I understood that it was only meant as a protection for all of us and not to be used as something to force my hand. Please do not take this as me being ungrateful. I just need a little more time.

God bless you!

Tong Chin
Ipoh
15 December 2000

My wife and I lost our only living child—a girl of five—two months ago. My wife's pregnancy was very difficult and we've been advised by the doctors that her life will be in danger if she becomes pregnant again. I have lost my daughter. I cannot risk losing my wife as well. Other than the physical loss of a child, there is the mental problem. Pearly cries non-stop. It isn't one tear. It's a whole ocean she cries. Imagine crying that hard.

Still, we are desirous of having a child, but one young enough to have absolutely no memory of the past. If it was possible to choose, we'd prefer a little boy this time so that no comparisons can ever be made. It matters not to us if the child is an orphan or illegitimate. In fact, it would be better if there were no relations.

I understand that there is a fee to be paid which accounts for the care of the child so far. This, I understand, amounts to RM20,000 and you require cash. The money has also got to be paid in advance and full before the child is in our custody.

My wife and I are agreeable to all these terms (for want of a better word). We trust that the birth papers of this child will also be handed to us when we pick up the child.

I must share that it was our lawyer who suggested that we contact the Kuala Lumpur Baby Hatch. If all goes well, which I hope it will, please ensure that the little boy is looked after well until we come to pick him up.

Tong Chin
Ipoh
7 March 2001

My wife and I would like to thank you for the delight that is this little boy. As my wife is also of Indian origin, he has fit in well with our interracial family. He now answers to the name Paul. We are arranging for him to be baptized in our Gospel faith.

Our lawyers are in the process of preparing the papers to ensure that we will be able to formally adopt the boy as our child. I thank you, and God, for all the assistance you've provided us thus far.

Mrs Sumitra Panikar
78 Jalan Bendahara
Alor Setar, Kedah
20 April 2001

Oh dear!

I am troubled to know that Raj has been given, seemingly permanently, to a family without my consent. I understand that it was becoming too much to look after him without any financial contribution from me. But I had hoped to be able to raise some funds and send them to you.

Unfortunately, my husband is not keen to bring up a child that is not his own. I am hoping to convince him otherwise, especially since I am now pregnant with his child. It was my hope that once our child is born, he would allow me to bring Raj back. Now that you tell me Raj has been given to this new family, my dream of seeing him again seems to be fading.

Can you please assure me that the people who have taken Raj will not change his name and let him know that I am coming to collect him soon? Please tell them not to start the process to legally adopt him. I am coming. Soon.

Tong Chin
Ipoh
25 April 2001

I write in a moment of some distress. We took the birth registration document for our Paul to the Registration Department. We wanted a birth certificate to be issued so that we could begin the adoption process. To our absolute horror, when we provided the birth mother's identity card number, her religion is listed as Islam. This is in spite of the fact that her name is clearly Indian in nature. Please help us to rectify this as soon as possible. I have succeeded in stalling the matter with the officers of the Registration Department. However, if this is not corrected immediately, they have informed me that they have every right, under the law, to take our Paul away from us. If a baby is born to a Muslim woman, that child cannot be adopted by non-Muslims.

Please do not advertise this matter either. Our lawyers have made it clear that under the Adoption Act of 1952, it's an offence for any advertisement to be published indicating that we are desirous of causing the child to be adopted.

I assume that you have the birth mother's contact details. Perhaps, a phone call to her will be good enough to inform her to make the necessary corrections.

Please help us!

Mrs Sumitra Panikar
78 Jalan Bendahara
Alor Setar, Kedah
30 April 2001

Thank you for letting me know about the error in my NRIC. I can confirm that I have made the corrections. May I ask, how did you come to know about this error in the first place? I would have thought that it would be the Registration Department who would inform me of this.

My husband is still not agreeable to me bringing Raj back to stay with us. Please look after my child for a while more. I promise, the day will come when I will be able to bring him back with me.

Tong Chin
Ipoh
23 December 2002

I write to inform you that, with delight, we have been approved for adoption. The investigations by the Department of Social Services were indeed very thorough. But we were very lucky, as we had the support of our lawyer, friends, and family. All the paperwork seems to have gone through without a hitch either. We are now, officially, our Paul's foster parents. It will take another year or two before the formal adoption can take place. Our Paul's birth certificate has been issued and, for now, we do not plan to take him out of the country. It will be tedious, I feel, to have to apply for a passport right now. In any case, we're not concerned, as we are delighted that he's with us.

Our Paul's third birthday will be coming up soon. No doubt he's an active child. However, we've noticed that he likes very much to play on his own. At the kindergarten, he doesn't seem to mix well with other children. Nonetheless, he's our world, our joy, and our love.

Mrs Sumitra Jones
149B Baker's Street
Sydney
Australia
20 April 2006

As you can see, I've not only changed my name, but my address. As it happens, my ex-husband was abusive. I was severely injured when he beat me. I lost our baby when I was seven months pregnant. He was arrested for domestic violence and I filed for a divorce. It was a tough two years before I got back on my feet. Then, I met Michael and, like a real whirlwind romance, we got married and moved to Sydney. He fully accepts my past and is very supportive of my desire to bring Raj back to Australia. I shall be contacting you shortly with my travel plans.

Tong Chin
Ipoh
25 April 2006

I am absolutely horrified to know that the birth mother wants to be in contact. Please convey our objection and the fact that we are now, legally, our Paul's parents.

I appreciate that the bond between a biological mother and child will remain forever, but our Paul is now ours. We have taken very good care of him. Indeed, we have given him the best medical care, especially when we realized that there was something not quite right with his milestones. We took him to a specialist who diagnosed our Paul as having Asperger's Syndrome. He needs proper care and attention, which we are giving him. We have been in contact with the Malaysian National Autism Society and the staff have provided invaluable assistance.

At the centre, our Paul comes out of his shell and interacts openly with the other children. He's a joy to us.

Can you please assure us that our address will never begiven to the biological mother? I have heard of stories where a biological mother abandons her child, then turns up at the home where the child has been adopted and creates a scene. If this issue is not addressed, I will seek legal advice, if necessary, and take appropriate action.

Tong Chin
Ipoh
30 May 2006

Thank you for your letters. I do apologize if my previous letter sounded harsh. Only, my wife has been ill, and sometimes, I feel it's as though we'll never be left in peace with our boy.

I note what you say that it would be good to inform our Paul that he is adopted. And that his mother wishes to take him away. I beg your pardon, but you fail to comprehend two things. Our Paul is on the autism spectrum. Yes, his is a mild case. Nonetheless, children with autism cannot have their world disturbed. Even the slightest of disturbances can lead to much heartache for him. So, no, I will not agree to enter into any kind of correspondence with the biological mother nor will I consent to her meeting our Paul. The fact that she intends to come here and take him away alarms me no end. I have not told my wife of this new development so as not to further weaken her position.

I do wonder, though, why does the biological mother think she still has a right to claim her child? Is she not aware that we've legally adopted him?

Our Paul is so much part of our family. Now, when I think of what it was like before he came into our lives, I can see how empty it was. He's filled us with so much joy. He is now fully baptized and has joined the choir in Church.

He is growing up healthy and very happy. I will not change our Paul for the world, but I promise you, I will change the world for him.

Tong Chin
Ipoh
2 June 2006

It occurs to me that I should forward to you a copy of the adoption certificate. I never sent it before because I figured that our business was done and dusted years ago. However, now with the threat of his biological mother wanting to remove him from us, I feel it would be wise to share this with you. If you're minded to forward it to the biological mother then you have my permission to do so. I hope that this will put a stop to her near constant request to not only meet with our Paul but to take him away from us too.

In the matter of Paul,
an infant to be known hereafter as Paul Tong Ching
26th day of January 2003

ORDER

UPON READING the petition of Tong Ching and Pearly Ching, dated the 26th day of March 2003, the affidavit affirmed by Tong Ching and Pearly Ching, and the exhibits thereto filed herein on the 20th day of January 2003, and the report of Mr G. Palanisamy, Pegawai Kebajikan Masyarakat, Ipoh, Perak, dated 14th day of November 2002 filed herein in the court being satisfied that the allegations in the said Petition are true and being also satisfied with the undertaking of the said Tong Ching and Pearly Ching as to the provision to made for the abovenamed child and being further satisfied that it is for the benefit of the said child, Paul Tong Ching, should be adopted by the said Tong Ching and Pearly Ching jointly and all the requirements of the Adoption Ordinance have been complied with. THIS COURT DOTH ORDER that the said Tong Ching and Pearly Ching be authorized to adopt the said child.

Mrs Sumitra Jones
149B Baker's Street
Sydney
Australia
20 September 2006

I am alarmed reading your last letter. I cannot believe that Raj was formally adopted by his 'parents'. I am his mother. As I believed it at the time, I was only placing my child in your care for a temporary period of time until I could get back on my feet. Still, my husband has advised me to do all that is necessary and I am going to seek the advice of lawyers here in Australia.

Mrs Sumitra Jones
149B Baker's Street
Sydney
Australia
30 September 2006

I write further to my previous letter to you. At the insistence of our lawyers, we hired a private investigator in Malaysia to track down this child. I am now given to understand that Raj is an autistic child. I did not know this. Moreover, he is being cared for, very well, by the couple who taking care of him. I refuse to call them Raj's parents as I am his mother. I've always been his mother. You say his name is now Paul. I will never use that name. He is Raj to me and always will be.

However, I am also advised by my lawyers here that to bring an autistic child into Australia, and one that has already been legally adopted, will probably not be feasible.

I have to tell you that this breaks my heart enormously. It seems to me that I have no luck where children are concerned. Raj was taken away from me, my baby from my previous husband died before it was born. From the injuries he inflicted on me, the doctors here say that I probably cannot have any children. I feel like killing myself.

I will call what happened to Raj what it is—stealing my child. The private investigator also alleges that you were paid a certain amount of money. If this is so, then . . . I mean, to give my child to another couple, when I was there, waiting for my fortunes to change and bring him back to me. All I wanted was to give him a better life than the one I'd endured. Who better than to love my child—my child—than his own mother, whose only crime was being too poor to feed her baby?

It occurs to me now that he'll probably grow up never knowing that he had—no, has—someone who absolutely adores him. I suppose his 'parents' will keep him ignorant of who he is and never let him know that he has a real mother.

Mrs Sumitra Jones
149B Baker's Street
Sydney
Australia
31 March 2014

You may remember me. I am Raj's mother, even though I understand that he is no longer Raj. Well, I stopped communicating with you from the moment I realized that my child was stolen from me. I have come to terms with this and, as advised by my team of psychiatrist, psychologist, and therapists, I 'moved on'—I still don't know quite what that means. Nonetheless, with conscious effort, I started to live in the present moment and soon, when I thought of the past, I didn't hurt as much. In time, my husband and I were given the greatest blessing of all, as I conceived naturally and gave birth to our only child, a little girl we've named Rajkumari May Jones

Still, I was thinking the other day about my Raj as nothing can prevent a biological mother's heart from grieving. He is already twelve years old. He'll be getting his Identity Card now, I suppose. I wonder if he knows the truth. I never 'abandoned' him as the private investigator so cruelly put it years ago. I maintain that I only ever gave Raj to you on a temporary basis to be looked after until I was able to bring him back. I will not go into this. What I will ask is that as an act of humanity, if ever Raj realizes that he's adopted and one day wants to know his past, please give him my address. I'm told that his new parents are Christians and I imagine that this would be the Christian thing to do.

I know the answer to this, but let me ask it anyway—please, will you one day ensure that Raj knows that I'm his mother? I would like to meet my son in this lifetime.

Tong Chin
Ipoh
22 April 2015

Thank you so much for your recent letter. I'm delighted that you managed to read that article in the national newspapers. I admit that my wife and I were reluctant to participate in the interview because it would expose our Paul to the public. But our Paul, himself, wanted to be involved because of one of his 'brothers', the little boy in the story called Tajuddin.

It was World Autism Day on 2 April and we were invited to the celebrations at a national level at the Malaysian National Autism Society. We had sent our Paul a few days earlier to practise for the events. So, Pearly and I were early when we arrived at the centre in Petaling Jaya. What happened is so cute that I would really like to share it with you, if I may.

While we were waiting, there was a little boy popping in and out of a nearby room. We didn't want to spook him. So, we smiled and said nothing. We didn't even make eye contact. But we knew that he was observing our every move. When other children arrived at the centre, he joined them around a table, which had been set up for them with drawing paper and crayons. A teacher turned up and she introduced herself as Teacher Marliana. She told the children to start drawing images for the celebrations.

Surrounded by his friends, this little boy began to open up. We learned that his name is Tajuddin. I knew he was coming out of his shell when he came up to me and his first words were, 'MH17 crashed in Ukraine on 17 July. There were 298 passengers. They all died.' He added that he has ten friends in his class in school. He recited all their names and then told me, 'My sister bufday on 1 November 2012.'

When I smiled and asked him if he liked school, poor thing, he became all flustered.

'He is like a walking calendar,' Teacher Marliana said. 'He knows when his father started work, when he went on holiday, how long he was on holiday and when he came back.'

Tajuddin then took a pen and on a piece of paper wrote something that was mighty important to him: 'Tajuddin was chased by Ahmad on 28 September 2013.'

Oh, I recognized all these things. They were exactly the same things our Paul has been doing from as far back as we can remember. He can rattle off facts but struggles to process the information in a meaningful manner. Still, our Paul, I would hazard a guess, is a little less autistic than Tajuddin.

When our Paul walked into the centre some ten minutes into this class, I cannot tell you how proud we are of who he has become. He said his hellos to us and immediately turned his attention to helping the little ones with their tasks.

One of the girls began to cry and our Paul rushed over to comfort her. Apparently, she was being teased and bullied in school. The other students in school laughed at her when she gave the wrong answers.

Later, when I asked our Paul why he rushed to offer comfort the girl, he said, 'I feel so *kesian* for her, lah, Papa.' My heart swelled with such pride for his empathy.

Right at that moment, Tajuddin gave us an 'update' on the MH17 tragedy and told us how many people died.

Once all the children arrived, the teacher got them all into a group and we, together with the other parents who'd arrived, were given a concert of sorts. Twenty children on different parts of the autism spectrum sang for us. Several of them had, apparently, been on a recent trip overseas. They were part of a choir that sang at the Tokyo Special Music and Arts Festival. None of them seemed to suffer from stage fright. All the words were enunciated and I cannot help but say this—our Paul was pitch perfect. I got the biggest shock when, suddenly, the teacher announced that the next song was dedicated to Pearly and me. It was Sudirman's 'One Thousand Million Smiles' and, I swear, I just about wanted to cry.

The moment it was over, Tajuddin reminded us, once again, about MH17. This time, he added facts about the MH370 tragedy as well.

Everyone became sad. But this was tempered when our Paul lifted everyone spirits and rallied everyone to give us an encore performance.

I cannot emphasize that he's really a joy to us. Our world has become so much larger, better, and brighter with him in it. We do love him very, very much.

Tong Chin
Ipoh
15 August 2018

Thank you for your many letters. When our Paul attained the age of eighteen, my wife and I decided that it was time to tell him the truth. We sat him down and explained the circumstances of his birth. We were absolutely stunned when he said that he'd known for several years now. When we enquired, he said that the day we applied for his NRIC, at the Registry Department, there was a moment when I had to top up the parking metre and my wife needed to use the lavatory. In those few moments, an officer had accidentally mentioned that he was an adopted child. From then on, whenever we left him alone at home, he would rummage through the files we thought we'd kept safely under lock and key and found all the papers. He also used a website to find out his genealogy and learned about the circumstances of his birth and adoption.

He kept the matter a secret all this while, partly because he needed to process what happened to him and partly because he thought we'd be upset. Thank God we have the Church because he went to see the priest and sought his counsel.

Until now, it has been our decision that there should be no contact with his biological mother. Now, our Paul has said, himself, that he no longer wishes to meet his biological mother. Yes, he is grateful to her for giving birth to him. But his thought is this—her greatest sorrow is his greatest blessing. He would like to live his life in gratitude for all his blessings and hopes that his mother will be at peace with the decision she made a very long time ago.

Also, he's now poised to go to Manipal in India where he's secured a seat to study medicine. I cannot tell you how proud my wife and I are of him.

I have tears in my eyes as I write this. I am a simple man who lived simply with Christian values. Our Paul, our son, has given us the pleasure of bringing him up and for that, I am ever so grateful to God and to you.

From the very bottom of our hearts, thank you.

Golden Illusion

Often, social factors can underlie depression in older people, especially the loss of a spouse, social isolation, boredom and financial problems . . . Frequently, they may experience depression after other major life events, like a medical diagnosis of a heart condition or the death of a loved one . . . When socially-isolated individuals lack emotional interaction and support, they can become emotionally numb. Studies show that loneliness and social isolation are associated with higher rates of depression and death wishes.

—Professor (Adj.) Dato' Dr Andrew Mohanraj

'Salomé.'

It was barely above a whisper and useless. Salomé, her domestic helper, was never going to hear Maya. Maya couldn't hear Maya.

The mornings were the hardest.

Thank God for the remote control that Salomé had left by the bedside table. Curling her gnarly fingers around it, Maya used the forefinger of the opposite hand to press a button. She sighed deeply, relieved she'd succeeded in switching off the ceiling fan.

Oh dear God! How she hated this windowless room.

Don't complain. At least this was a whole room. Nowadays, people have no joy. So many lost everything and were living under a bridge. There had been a time when she had a whole house to call her own. A garden. And friends.

Get better and you can go home to Penang.

That's the mantra Maya recited every so often to make herself feel better.

The door opened then and Salomé, her domestic helper, entered the room. Holding a vintage mahogany serving tray in one hand, she closed the door with the other.

Something wasn't right. Her eyes were puffy and her cheeks were red. She must have been crying all night. There was a phone call from the Philippines the day before saying that the patriarch of the family, Salomé's father, had contracted pneumonia. In the blink of an eye, he was gone.

With clinical precision, Salomé put the tray down on the bedside table, bent to pick up the bedpan, and walked into the en suite bathroom.

Horror of horrors! It had to offend, that stench from the contents of the bedpan now alien to Maya because she'd lost her olfactory sensitivity after a recent course of antibiotics.

'Thank you,' Maya whispered after her, desperate for Salomé to feel her gratitude.

Maya closed her eyes, praying that she could pierce the invisible veil and travel to the astral plane.

* * *

Towards the end of the 1960s, a couple were about to board the P&O liner, *The Chusan*, in Madras, India. Eighteen-year-old Maya looked at the intricate bridal henna design on her hands. Was she doing the right thing, following this almost stranger she'd married to seek out a new life on the western coast of the Malay peninsula? With their two suitcases in either hand, Ram was ahead of Maya. About to step onto the gangway, he turned to look at her. In those gold flecks of his irises, she recognized his tenderness and knew that all would be well.

'Maya-Maya,' he called out to her.

How her elders had giggled at her husband's peculiar habit of calling everyone twice. Still, she couldn't help but blush when she reached his side and he said, 'Maya-Maya, you're too beautiful. An illusion. My dream.'

Maya needed a week to find the word to describe the single-storey house assigned to them in Hargreaves Circus on the island of Penang. In her considered opinion, it was the perfect time—one that allowed her to meditate upon it because the word had to express the serenity that came with having a stunning backdrop of a hill that she could see from the windows of her bedroom. Yet, it needed to promote the busy activity of the many birds and insects in their garden at dawn and dusk. Ram called it a swamp, but in the end, she came up with the simplest one of all: Home. And here, in 1972, she gave birth to their only child.

'What do we name her?'

'Swarnalata,' Ram replied. When Maya blinked, surprised at how certain he was, he said, 'I thought about it for a long, long time.'

'I love it.' Maya smiled bright and happy.

With 'swarna' meaning gold, Ram gave his darling baby the nickname, Goldie-Goldie. It was only a matter of time before she became GG.

Having inherited Maya's grace and Ram's love for the outdoors, the carefree child basked in her father's love. Her ferocious temper was placated whenever Ram told her one of his fanciful tales. In them, the protagonist traversed huge plains and deserts. Sometimes, he was trapped in dark and lonely caves with nothing more than a candle to light his path. Always, he struck bargains with Malayan tigers, tapirs, pygmy elephants, or the odd proboscis monkey to let him go so that he could fulfil a promise made to a little girl with golden hair to be home for her dinner.

Dinner proper with GG, however, was often fraught with tension.

'Eat, don't waste,' Maya would plead daily. 'Think of the millions in India starving,' she would add, knowing it made absolutely no dent in her child's deliberate resolve not to finish her meal. Maya was aware that when she turned her back, her husband and daughter rolled their eyes in solidarity.

Nonetheless, through the years, there were surprise parties to celebrate birthdays, holidays, ceremonies, and all events associated with joy. The happiest one, by far, was the day GG married her sweetheart from law school in Singapore. By then, Ram and Maya, having saved enough money, owned outright the only home they had ever known. Preparing for the traditional Tamil wedding, Maya had old saris draped over the branches of the full-grown angsana tree to temper the glare from the spotlight directed at the marriage dais. Cooks they hired were taught to use yoghurt as a meat tenderizer before adding the cuts of mutton and chicken to the biryani. 'You wait and see how the meat falls off the bone,' she told the head cook.

Ram leaned on his many contacts to ensure that there was a steady supply of *thani* so that his friends were suitably sloshed throughout the celebrations.

There were no celebrations four years later, though, when GG filed for a divorce. She had chanced upon her husband and his secretary trading sexual favours in his swanky office in Singapore's Central Business District.

Maya travelled to the island nation to help GG pack her things. In those thirty days together, during quiet moments when they accidentally made eye contact and their collective sadness threatened to spill over, both hurried to the kitchen to prepare something to eat or drink. By the time Maya returned to her husband's side a month later, she was an expert on the kind of boxes, glue, and bubble wrap removal companies used. And GG was well on her way to becoming one of the foremost corporate lawyers in Malaysia's capital, Kuala Lumpur.

'Maya-Maya, why have you refused so many invitations to parties?' Relaxing on their bed for the siesta, Maya turned her head, ever so slightly, away from him.

'What's the use? I'll look at all those babies and know that I'll never be a grandmother. Everyone will blame me.'

'Blame?' Ram whispered the word.

'I failed as a mother. My daughter inherited this failure.'

Unable to meet her husband's gaze, Maya did not see the bewildered look on his face.

* * *

A year later, Maya stepped out onto the veranda, expecting to see Ram. He'd gone to buy some hokkien mee because it was her lazy day when she didn't cook and allowed food from outside to be brought home. Instead, two policemen—one lanky and the other squat—stood in front of her. Officious and clinical, they seemingly focused on their shoes when they said that Ram had been hit by a taxi and died on the spot. The accident happened on the main road. The squat one handed over two packets of noodles, while the lanky one said, 'If you want to take action against the driver, here is his name and IC number.' And they left.

In the kitchen, Maya blanched the noodles in boiling water, tossed them into a ceramic bowl, and stirred in the condiments and sauce. She carried the bowl back to the veranda, sat in Ram's planter's chair and ate every morsel.

It was bad to waste food. Think of the millions starving in India.

Three months after Ram's death, when Maya arranged to prune the branches of the angsana tree, GG made a big fuss halfway because Maya was 'getting rid of Papa's tree.' Maya relented and, henceforth, the house was identified as the one with a tree that had branches growing only on one side. A month later, GG abandoned a meeting and flew back to Penang, as though she'd been summoned for a medical emergency. Instead, she spent three days rearranging a bundle of 'Crocodile' brand long-sleeved shirts, cotton undershirts, and new sarongs in Ram's almirah. Maya had made the mistake of telling her that she wanted to donate them to an orphanage. When it came time to commemorate the first anniversary of Ram's death, as though she was reciting the rosary, Maya repeated the Gayathri Mantra 108 times before she ventured to discuss the necessary arrangements with GG. Maya wanted it to be postponed by three days to a weekend so that outstation friends and relatives could attend.

'Who cares if they come or not?' GG commented in a frosty tone 'They never came when he was alive. You think they will come now? No need.' The ceremony was held on a Thursday with only Maya, GG, the priest and his little helper in attendance.

'You're so far, Mama. Who's going to look after you if anything happens?' GG asked Maya two years later.

What was this? A show of concern?

Maya couldn't believe it. Perhaps, this could be the start of a new kind of relationship between them.

'You can't expect me to leave everything and come running each time, you know.'

Then again, maybe not.

A week later, Maya opened her front door to welcome Salomé. GG had arranged for the rotund woman to stay with her, as though Maya was incapable of managing her own home. Could it be an indirect slight at how little money Maya now had, with having to organize her finances around a government-funded widow's pension? No. Instead, it was her daughter's way of showing she cared for her. At least that's what Maya told herself for her own peace of mind. Still, it was tedious to remember to say, 'Thank you,' each time Salomé completed a task to her satisfaction. That was, until the gods (for Maya was sure they alone were responsible) conspired to show her that the one whose presence she saw as an unnecessary extravagance, became a necessity for the preservation of her increasingly solitary and fragile life.

Help me!

Maya wanted to reach out her hand to Salomé's but couldn't lift it. No words came out of her mouth either. Instead, she felt her world becoming darker.

Thud!

Maya heard the shuffle of feet and saw Salomé's before everything went completely black.

When she opened her eyes, she was looking up at a fluorescent tube light.

'Mama. You're awake.'

Maya turned her head to look into GG's eyes. In her daughter's voice, she'd heard something other than the usual irritation. She couldn't decide if what she saw in her daughter's eyes was fear, desperation, or concern. It could even be love.

'How long has it been?' Maya whispered.

'Ah! You've been asleep for three days,' GG said. She then explained that when Maya had collapsed from her stroke, Salomé telephoned her at once. GG immediately arranged for an ambulance to be despatched. Mercifully, Maya responded to treatment and was now well on the road to recovery.

Upon her discharge from hospital, Maya was transferred to a new, state-of-the-art rehabilitation facility in Kuala Lumpur whereupon her every need was met. Meanwhile, it was three months before Maya understood the gravity of all the 'arrangements' that GG promised she was making for her. On a sunny morning, the ambulance dropped off Maya at GG's condominium complex.

'Mama, this is the best option,' GG said when she entered Maya's windowless room to say goodnight after the temporary night nurse left. 'And I'll be close. My condo is next door. I bought this one specially for you. Renovated it also. This room is supposed to be the best according to feng shui. Problem solved. Don't you think so?'

Maya's silence was misunderstood as acquiescence with GG's unilateral decision. 'Great!' GG said and kissed her mother on her forehead before leaving the room.

Maya tugged at the ends of the pillow case in sheer frustration until there was a small rip in one corner.

A problem solved?

She was *a problem*?

Must work harder to get better.

Must go home.

To life in Penang.

Still, Maya was powerless to stop a feeling replete with sadness and detachment from all she'd known for decades covering her being like a gossamer blanket.

* * *

Why was her astral plane never dark, dingy, cold, and miserable?

Instead, Maya always walked into a sun-drenched garden. Drawn to the small pond in the middle of the garden, she studied her reflection in the clear water. Her hair was thick, unbound, and silky, and the hands on her skin smooth. Suddenly, a mob of men in white *kurta–pyjamas* crowded around her. Each had gold flecks in his irises. 'Go back!' they said in unison. Whenever they lifted their hands, as though to hit her, she fled.

Maya rubbed the grit in the corner of her eyes before opening them.

The shrill ringing of the telephone startled her. It rang another five times before she was able to answer the call.

'Where are you, Mama? Why no answer? I thought something happened to you.'

There it was, that concern in her daughter's voice. It was that husky tone, the same one she had inherited from Ram.

'Don't forget, Mama. Today is the day for the vaccine, yes?'

Maya's eyes widened in disbelief. She'd forgotten.

'I can't come. The government only allows two passengers in the car. Salomé will follow. Okay?'

'Yes, yes,' Maya said, a little breathless, pushing her elbows into the mattress and raising her body a little.

'I have to go. My assistants are in front of me, waiting,' GG responded and Maya exhaled deeply, releasing some tension in her body. Then, she heard the words her daughter said, seemingly to someone else: 'She's such a burden. Like she's got dementia, I tell you.'

Maya held her breath. She wanted to say, 'Go away, child. I don't want to talk to you any more.' Only, GG had already ended the call.

Maya threw the phone's receiver aside. She closed her eyes.

First, a problem. Now, a burden.

How could anyone, let alone her only child, say this?

Where was the fault in her upbringing.

Oh, the pain . . .

The words reverberated in her mind: *Get better and you can go home to Penang.*

An hour later, having stood under the hot shower for what seemed like ages, her body felt supple. She secured her hair in a tight bun at the nape of her neck and lined her eyes with a charcoal face mask.

'Salomé?' Maya called out once she heard her footsteps in the hallway.

When there was no answer, she walked into the kitchen and saw that the woman was hunched over the table. When she looked up, Maya said, 'Salomé, I called the taxi. I'm going to get the vaccine. I'll wait outside, okay?'

Salomé's eyes widened. As comprehension dawned, she started to apologize, but Maya interrupted, placing a hand on her shoulder.

'It's okay. You don't need to worry. Just rest.'

'Okay, Madame,' Salomé replied, sitting down. 'Sorry.'

There was hardly anyone at the taxi stand outside the condominium complex. Maya lifted her head to the sky and felt the heat of the mid-morning sun on her face. She inhaled deeply, placed a palm on her chest, and whispered, 'Please dear God, forgive my baby. I know her. She works to hide her sorrows. This is not my daughter. My Swarnalata. And that awful thing she said was from a place of pain. Please bring her someone who will make her happy again. I want to hear her laugh. Just one more time . . .'

Suddenly, she heard a familiar voice. Softly at first, then becoming louder by the second. Maya lowered her face and opened her eyes. He was there, on the opposite side of the road. Dressed in a white kurta–pyjama, Ram's smile was as dazzling as the dancing flecks of gold in his eyes. The only thing she heard him say over and over again when he opened his arms was, 'Come home, Maya-Maya my illusion. Come home.'

Maya ran to her husband and right into the path of a speeding taxi.

Say Hello to Yama

> Every year, individuals and communities are affected by natural disasters that disrupt their economic and social development, as well as jeopardise their mental health and well-being . . . Disasters may put the victims in a state of despair and shock. This traumatic experience disrupts the normal functioning of the victims and severely impacts individuals, families and communities. Families face a loss of their identity by being placed in temporary shelters. The loss of privacy, resources and social support, and the lack of control over one's own possessions, are all associated with elevated levels of acute psychological distress. Additionally, family separation, lack of safety and loss of livelihood, also contribute towards this decompensation. Most people affected by emergencies will experience feelings of anxiety, sadness, hopelessness, fatigue, irritability or anger, as well as difficulty sleeping.
>
> —Professor (Adj.) Dato' Dr Andrew Mohanraj

Oh my! A pewter grey sky with stunning mandarin clouds criss-crossing throughout was more than the necessary drama in what promised to be the tail end of two weeks of misery.

The repeated warnings of flash floods, constant worry, and having to obey RELA officers' instructions gave way to this sight that could only be described as a painting by the Divine. It was one thing to brush my teeth at a shared sink in the relief centre. It was quite another to change underclothes knowing that nothing but a thin curtain separated me from a leering and wrinkly, albeit harmless, infirm man.

It was good to be back in the village, however geologically unsafe Kampung Sungai Tua still appeared to the authorities. Besides, I would be here for a short while, a few nights at most.

'Stay inside as much as possible,' the officers had instructed before I left the relief centre.

I needed water, though, and to collect the pouch. Yes, there was a water pump from which to fill my plastic water bottle, but the pressure was not strong enough. So, there I was, squatting behind the village mosque, holding my breath to quell the stench of rotting debris from the landslide and contemplating the path I was about to take. There was a time when I wouldn't have known the difference between *tembusu, mersawa, kapor,* and *merbau* stacked by the riverbed waiting to be transported to the lumber mills at the mouth of the river. Now, with a single glance, I knew that it was logs of *cengal* that floated downstream.

The notice from the meteorological department two weeks ago warned of possible floods. No one anticipated that it would be the worst floods that the inhabitants of Kampung Sungai Tua had ever faced. They were considered lucky because the water surge that began upstream on Gunung Induk triggered landslides that resulted in the destruction of several villages nearby.

'I am going to accept the government's offer to relocate,' said Kak Tom, my neighbour and landlady, a week after the notice arrived. Poor thing. She'd been looking for her missing child, Suriani, for a year now to no avail. I had to keep the girl's whereabouts a secret, though, in the same way I had to keep my own.

I glanced at the logs one more time, careful to avoid bringing too much attention to it lest someone was watching me. I caught a glimpse of the pouch's strap peeping out from the hollow between the logs.

It was safe.

I was safe.

I was alive.

Perhaps, to die was better.

Maybe, the day would come when I'd see H—I refused to say my husband's full name—body floating among the logs.

Because of H, we ran for our lives.

Because of H, we gave up all creature comforts to live as one of the hard-core poor.

Because of H, we'd pretended to be part of a religion we weren't born into.

This was what happened to a Convent girl who, at eighteen, abandoned higher education and fell in love with a lowlife, instead.

I looked out at the river once more. The water flowed at a sedate pace, taking with it filth collected along the way.

It was time.

I stood up, arranged the folds of my kaftan and held the Tupperware close. It still hurt down there. I wasn't ready, yet, to seek any form of treatment. Sighing and wincing in equal measure, I strode, duck-like at first, and then with increasing confidence. I was eager to eavesdrop on the *cakap-cakap* by the water pump. All the way to this gossip session, I couldn't help but lament how my once-charmed life had come to this.

***

The gunpowder grey sky was punctuated by twinkling stars the night it all began. He received a phone call from an *ah long*. The loan shark informed H that he'd splashed red paint on my father-in-law's house night before. The Chinese man also threatened grievous bodily harm if H didn't settle his debts as soon as possible.

'It's your fault,' H said.

'Why?'

'You wanted us to have that big fancy wedding. Call that Panditji fellow and all. And you couldn't get along with my mother. So, we had to live here. Pay rent and all. I am only twenty-seven, you know. Where was the money going to come from? My parents didn't give any *ang pow* for the wedding also. I borrowed, lah. Now, see what has happened.'

Ang pow? I didn't know that H had expected the gift of a ceremonial red packet full of cash from his parents. I poured the tea back and forth briskly from stainless steel jug to ceramic mug until it created the teh tarik's foamy head. I plonked the mug on the dining table. When H picked it up, he slurped the brew, unaware of my angst.

When a shiny new *parang* was left outside our front door with a note attached to it saying, 'U R Next', He insisted that, for our safety, we leave the flat under the cover of darkness. Still a new, obedient, and petrified bride of no more than six months, I obeyed H. Within seventy-two hours, we emptied our meagre savings, abandoned his Proton Saga, packed our bags (including the parang) and changed our identities—me by donning the hijab and H by growing a beard. We boarded the next available bus out of Alor Setar. We got off when it stopped outside a mosque in the middle of nowhere. We remained silent when Wahab, the *penghulu* of Kampung Sungai Tua and pseudo-Imam, assumed that it was his moral duty to offer us shelter as fellow Muslims.

'If you don't mind doing a bit of housework and helping the other villagers,' Wahab said, 'our sister, Kak Tom, has a small place next to her house. You can stay there for a while.'

As we lay on the mat spread out on the floor that first night in our new home, H turned to me and whispered, 'Just imagine. From being Harry, I'm now Hamid. And you, from Bhoomi, you're now Putri. So easy. If we stay like this, when I die, I have a chance to have seventy-two virgins in heaven.' If I could have killed him with my looks, I'd have officially been a widow that very night.

With icy blue skies for days on end, H took to kampung life like a proverbial pomfret to the river. Together with Wahab and the other kampung folk, H ventured into the jungle behind the village, taking with him the parang to hack the overgrown foliage along the way.

'There's this interesting thing up there, you know,' H shared after a week.

While I doled out his dinner of rice, kangkung sambal, and fried anchovies on to tin plates Kak Tom had lent us, H described a place the villagers had discovered six months earlier. Referred to by the rather unimaginative name of 'The Hut', it was situated on a plateau three-quarters up the hill. When I went with H a week later, I realized that it was neither a hut nor a shed. It was something in between, for the floor was nothing more than dried cow dung, as was the practice in the kampung. The walls were pieces of wood leaning against each other to form what architects called an A-frame structure. There were carvings on these walls such as names of people, row upon row of four straight lines that were struck out to mark the passing of five days each, little hearts with arrows. There was one of a boat with stick people half in, half out, and some upside down. In an urban studio, these might have been regarded as art. Here, they were more like scratchings of the desperate, especially when we learned from a forest ranger called Boon Teong that this had once been the temporary shelter for Rohingya women, waiting for middle men who promised them safe passage to their waiting menfolk in Sumatra and beyond. Instead, they were shipped off to *mamasans* in Bangkok and Kuala Lumpur who accepted these nubile maidens for work in the brothels. Once this prostitution and human trafficking ring was busted, the villagers used The Hut as a place to rest whenever they went in search of herbs and other medicinal plants in the jungle.

'I've got new work,' H whispered, one day about four months after we'd first arrived. 'Some people need to clear the jungle. They want the land to create a latex clone forest farm.'

'A what?'

'It's about rubber trees. But the trees will later be used for wood also.'

'Who told you all this?' Nothing was mentioned about this during the latest cakap-cakap either.

'Remember Boon Teong? Chinese man. He guessed that I am actually Chinese.'

'How?'

'I don't know.' He looked at the kettle with boiling water bubbling away.

'This is dangerous.'

'No lah. No need to be so frightened. He is nice, one. I want some tea. Make for me.' He picked up the parang and started to sharpen it. 'This will protect us. Don't worry. He wants to help me get extra money to pay off the ah long and go home.'

'He knows about the ah long?' I put the kettle back on the stove.

'Aiya, no need to think so much, okay? See this?' He held up the parang. 'With this, I can do anything, anytime, and anywhere. So, no need to worry.'

H raised his voice. I knew better than to speak at that moment. Instinctively, I pulled the ends of my sleeves to hide the fading bruises on my forearm. Had I the courage, I would have asked him, 'How does that parang help you?' Instead, I quietly made his teh tarik.

The day the government changed a year later, supposedly for the better, we had a marbled sky of bright blue with streaks of dull grey. The new politicians' promises were for cleaner and more transparent management of all matters under the purview of the government, both local and federal. In Kampung Sungai Tua, this called for a gathering—far more serious that the usual cakap-cakap—at the school hall.

Dispensing with preliminaries, Wahab called the meeting to order.

'There have been logging activities upstream. Do any of you know anything about this?'

I glanced at H. He looked straight ahead, unblinking. Using layman's terms, Wahab said that the forest reserve at the top of Gunung Induk had been cleared. The land, at one thousand metres above sea level, was what experts called a high hill dipterocarp forest and was deemed environmentally sensitive.

'Do you all know what's going to happen?' When no one replied, Wahab explained, 'It's like this. Put a hen and a few chicks on some grass. Pour a drum of water on them and they will run here, there, and everywhere, but the grass will absorb the water. Now, you take away the grass and make it a cement floor. Put the same hen and chicks there. Throw water and, what happens? They will be washed away, like a strong current is pulling them.'

Shoulders started to droop.

'What do you think will happen to us when there's heavy rain now? We'll be like those chickens. We will be washed away.' Pointing in the direction of the river, Wahab said, 'And, that place will become full of mud.'

No one said a word and everyone hung their heads low.

Petitions were organized and I helped by writing letters to the authorities. Well, at least to the district land officers. When the officers responded six months later by making a visit to the kampung, yet another gathering was organized in the school hall.

Once again, had I the courage, I would have narrated, in chronological order, the environmental crime playing out before my very eyes or at least from whatever H told me. You see, Boon Teong, looking to side hustle wanted investors for a plan he'd conceived. Once he found them, a company was set up. Mercifully, H had the sense to decline Boon Teong's offer to become one the directors of this company. The standout point of this meeting, however, was that, for all his talk and warnings of the environmental disaster at the doorstep of Kampung Sungai Tua, Wahab had given in to his avarice and become part of Boon Teong's new cohort. Smiling from ear to ear at the top table, Boon Teong must have been overjoyed because with Wahab, he'd acquired a race-based *bumiputra* director, thereby, allowing this new company to get preferential treatment in all government-related matters.

'Sad, lah.' He clicked his lips, satiated from the dinner of laksa I'd made using the eel H caught from the paddy fields nearby. 'If I didn't want people to know about this ah long thing, I would have become a director also. Win-win, you know.'

Why didn't H see that we would never win? The villagers would never win. Even Boon Teong wouldn't win. The company was nothing more than the instrument by which these middle men could launder their earnings off Mother Earth. Their role as district officers who acted as watchdogs would be dismantled. Mother Earth would be betrayed.

Cakap-cakap

'What happened to the latex clone forest?'

'Not enough money. New company sold the land to the operator of a durian orchard.'

'Durian? Our kind of soil, can or not?'

'Sure can. If anything happens, also, they'll say it's geology, lah. Government before, lah, or, God's work. No one will point-point finger.'

'Why, ah?'

'Wahab said because the company got director who is *krabat*. You know, lah, with royalty, everything will be okay what.'

'Ya, lah.'

'But now, ah, must help Kak Tom.'

'Why?'

'Her daughter, Suriani, missing. Dunno where she went.'

'Ya, lah. Must find her fast-fast.'

The day the trees were completely uprooted for the farm, the sky was ash grey without a single streak of silver. Soon, the kampung folk were buying gunny sacks of rice from farmers in a neighbouring village. Their previously water-logged plots of flat paddy land were now mud-logged testaments that their source of irrigation had become unsuitable for cultivating rice.

'How could this have happened?'

'Don't ask so many questions, Bhoomi.' H opened the leather pouch and counted the notes inside, then sipped from the tumbler of *tuak*, an alcoholic drink made from fermented rice.

'This is not good. The gods will be angry. Then how? Yama will come.'

'You and your Yama. You married me, okay? A Buddhist. No need to bring all these Hindu-Bindu gods. Especially the one of death,' shivering, he showed his disgust for my faith by adding, 'eeee . . .'

I looked away. Something wasn't right. I could feel it.

'Forget all this. Let's put something in there.' He pointed at my belly. Our daughter, for H was sure it would be a baby girl, would be named Meera Sarah, after our mothers. With the money he'd saved—RM4,000 at last count—H figured that it was time to think about leaving Kampung Sungai Tua. His plan was to go home, pay off the ah long, and then come back for me. Financially free, we'd return to our families, seek forgiveness, and show off our baby.

Before I could beg, 'When you go, take me with you,' H said, 'You stay here first. I clear everything.'

Although couched in terms that offered to protect me, it was the moment when I first had an inkling that there would come a time when I would need to gather my wits about me.

Cakap-cakap

'*Selamat petang.*'

'Wat chu wan?'

'Where you going?'

'Why you wanna know? You see people chop trees and take away. You say nothing. Why?'

'Don be angry, lah.'

'All wanna make big-big money. Spoil Mother Earth only.'

'Mother Earth?'

'Look around. You think that you can take so much and nothing happens?'

'Dunno.'

'You talk about chickens washing away. No chickens, lah. We are the chickens. No. Not we. Only me and others like me. We are the chickens.'

'No need to be like this, Putri.'

'Putri? Ha. Ha. Ha. I'm no princess. I'm Bhoomidevi, Mother Earth. You take what's ours, make it yours and then use it against us.'

'Huh?'

'Ya. Take out the "devi", put prince, and then become bumiputra.'

'But you also bumiputra what, Putri. You and your husband, Hamid?'

'Aiya! Useless talking to you.'

The rays of the sun shone on the spot where H said signboards should have been erected for this new durian orchard project. However, since there had been no public announcement about the actual terms of reference for Boon Teong's new company, this requirement under the local laws was dispensed with, especially since there was a need to speed up the project and a reservoir was already in place to irrigate the orchard. Reservoir was too posh a word, though, to describe what was nothing more than a gigantic hole in the ground.

'Did they at least plant vegetation to cover the exposed area? I mean, this is being built on a slope, no?'

'Where do you get all these questions from, Bhoomi?'

'Aiya, you just look at Google also, you will know what to ask.'

'No need to ask so many questions. As long as I get paid, I don't care what happens.'

True enough, no one seem genuinely bothered that the dislodged soil from the orchard and giant hole in the ground had made its way into the river. None of the kampung folk bothered that they could no longer harvest paddy, catch fresh pomfret or eel, or simply allow children the luxury of splashing in the water on a hot afternoon. Having food delivered from the town to a new mini market—another one of Boon Teong's side hustles—became the norm and, in some instances, preferable. Some, like Wahab, dabbled in the illegal trade of pangolins, his role as the guardian of moral behaviour within the village be damned.

Life bumbled along until the day I couldn't see the sky through the fat raindrops. As the twilight hour began, H rushed back from The Hut.

'I saw him, Bhoomi. I saw him.'

'Who?'

'Him.' When I stared, perplexed, H shook his hands, frustrated. 'The ah long.'

'W-h-a-?' I cleared my throat.

'Boon Teong brought him to the durian orchard. Showing off his new Hilux. This ah long fellow is his friend, lah! Die-die, I tell you.'

As I watched H gather his things into a plastic bag—one shirt, a pair of trousers, phone charger, and toiletries—it dawned on me. H was packing for one.

'What about me?'

H stood up and held my shoulders.

'I said, didn't I? I go first. Pay this ah long fellow.' He continued to pack his meagre belongings.

Suddenly, H started hitting his head with his palm. '*Alamak*! I forgot the pouch.' He began pacing. 'It's in The Hut. I go back there to get money.' One more squeeze of my shoulders and H added, 'But I will leave some money there for you. RM500. Enough for you. Very easy to find. On the shelf, near the table.'

The next thing I knew, H was gone.

I stood there, in the middle of our 100 square feet dwelling for the past five years, accepting my reality for the first time ever. I had married a useless, self-centred, good-for-nothing who didn't care an iota if I lived or died. I was on my own.

The speed of H's disappearance from my life turned out to be somewhat of a blessing, as H may not have left had I shared my news. At least that's what I'd like to think. Within twenty-four hours of H's departure, the pain in my belly was too much to bear. I screamed and Kak Tom arrived. She saw my need, took me in, and summoned the faith healer. 'Nothing can be done,' Kak Tom said and held me as I wept.

When she pulled back, though, in her eyes, I saw the words she couldn't bring herself to say: 'Poor thing. Husband supposed to look after. Husband gone. Now, baby also gone.'

The unspoken words in my eyes commiserated with her actual loss: 'Now I know what it's like to lose a child.'

The fading inky blue sky like rubbed velvet didn't help light my path up to The Hut to retrieve the money H said he'd left for me. If it had, there was a possibility I could have been forewarned. As it transpired, it was Boon Teong's left hand I saw first when I stepped into The Hut. It was without the ring finger. It seemed, H said months ago, Boon Teong had lost it at a goldsmith's. Irritated with Boon Teong's constant refusal to pay his debts, the owner had caught him off guard during one of his visits by holding him down and cutting off his finger, gold wedding band and all.

The next thing I saw was the leather pouch.

'Ah, there you are.'

I should have held my breath instead of crying out.

'There is a lot of money here. 5,000, lah. That Harry made a lot, ah?'

For a long while, I watched him. Then, I put my palm out and all but whispered, 'Yes. We saved our money.'

'What do you need so much money for?'

I didn't owe this man an explanation.

'Please, give me my money. My husband's money.'

'Your husband?' He sniggered.

I remained quiet.

'My friend saw him the other day. Said he owes him money.' Sniggering, Boon Teong added, 'My friend, ah, not so kind one, you know. And money still here, what? So, dunno if husband still alive. Maybe . . . you know . . .' Using his forefinger, he pretended to slit his throat.

I held my breath.

'Now, all alone.' Turning to fully face me, he asked, 'Do you m-i-s-s him?'

We made eye contact then. A brief encounter—one that left me uncertain if he knew my true identity, but certain of what he was implying.

I tried to grab the pouch from him.

'Ah, ah, ah,' Boon Teong deflected.

'Give me the money.'

'Oooo . . . can get angry, one.' He lifted his chin, egging me on. Clenching his jaw, I heard his breath, short and loud. I glared. Our stand-off lasted precisely twenty-two seconds, after which he stepped forward until he was no more than two feet away.

'Tell you what—here,' he said, handing the pouch to me, 'take it.'

I blinked three times.

'Take, take, take.'

He did not let go, though, when I put my hand on the pouch.

'I want something in return.'

I should have let go of the pouch then. But I needed the money. Besides, it was my money, no? My husband's money? Our money?

The pointy tip of the pouch was rough against my cheek. 'Pretty. Just like that Suriani. She was much younger, though. Bangkok mamasan said she's very popular.'

What would H have done if he knew what happened next? Then again, how would I have explained it to him? Or to anyone else for that matter? What would I have said? That I reached out for the pouch anyway? That Boon Teong then pushed me until I fell backwards on to the table? That he turned me on my stomach, yanked my kaftan and . . .

When I couldn't even say it to myself, how was anyone going to believe a word I said?

'Ah,' Boon Teong said when it was over. 'Here. Give you ang pow. RM500. I will keep the rest. Keep safe for you.' Zipping his pants, he said, 'You come back next Wednesday. I give you more money, okay?'

With each step back down the hill, I recited a mantra to the spirits watching and begged for forgiveness for defiling their space. At home, I took off my kaftan, turned the tap on, and poured icy cold water on my being. No one must know that I shivered from what I'd been forced to endure to stay alive.

A thousand curses to H. He'd taken the parang with him and I had nothing but my wits to defend myself. I heard the rumble and opened my eyes. Peeping through the gaps in wood, the sky was a canopy of velvety black. I must have dozed off. Quickly, I switched on the solar-operated emergency flashlight. Turning my back to the apology for a door hanging off its hinges, I opened the pill box and dropped the tablets into the plastic bottle of tuak. Watching the effervescence, I prayed that the RM300 I'd paid for the pills would be worth every sen. The faith healer promised that three pills were enough to knock out an elephant.

The door opened. A gust of warm night air filtered through. I looked at the three men by Boon Teong's Hilux. Three very different types. One scrawny with no bum but an enormous pot belly and the second with a smallish bum and love handles. Boon Teong, with his ill-gotten money, had eaten himself into plain fat all over.

I heard their words.

'Good-good, lah. Nice face also.'

'Yah.'

'How much? Hundred?'

'No, lah. No need so much. Fifty each enough. This orang kampung only. Give this durian also enough already.'

The bastard meant to short change me. There was only one thing to do—if he halved what was due to me, I would double what he thought was due to him. I slipped all the pills into the jug, making it three pills each for these lecherous souls. I then called out to Boon Teong. He turned, saw me holding out three tumblers, and rushed forward. In less than a minute, all three men gulped down the tuak.

They all fell down.

* * *

Cakap-cakap

'Putri. You smiling. Why ah?'

'Why? Cannot smile is it?'

'No, lah. Have you heard or not, what happened?'

'What?'

'Two Chinaman and one Malay fellow died, lah.'

'Oh.'

'Wahab found them near The Hut. But all hush-hush because the Malay fellow is related to *krabat.*'

'Oh . . . You want? Fresh durian.'

'Wah! Nice Tupperware also. Where you get from?'

'Got, lah. Somebody give.'

'Wah! Delicious. Sad, ah. Kak Tom already left. What you going to do now?'

'Dunno yet. Must think.'

Under the fading dawn sky, chequered in shades of pale yellow and powder blue, I squatted next to the logs by the river.

I pulled the pouch from its hiding place. It was all there—the old notes H had collected and the new ones I'd taken from Boon Teong and the rascals. It was enough to leave this God forsaken village and start over. I also unfolded the cut-outs of the newspapers that I'd kept from my time at the relief centre.

> Kupang: The newly elected Energy and Natural Resources Ministry's Secretary-General, Datuk Salleh Yassin, extends his condolences to the villagers who have lost loved ones surrounding Gunug Induk. The Minister also convened a task force to investigate the matter. The report states that the tragedy was a 'cascading of geological processes'. Heavy rain, landslides, debris flows, and floods have been identified as the main causes of the worst floods in Kampung Sungai Tua's history. The task force also discovered that the erosion that occurred in the secondary forest was due to the conversion of land for cultivation. Even though his administration cannot be blamed for approving the durian orchard project, which has resulted in siltation causing the river to become shallow, the Minister has communicated with his counterpart in the Health Ministry. Psychological help and counselling will be provided to all the victims of this tragedy.

Rubbish!

Counselling wasn't going to help one bit.

It was time to help myself. Putting the pouch into a plastic bag I had brought back from cakap-cakap, I stood up. Crumpling the piece of newspaper, I flung it into the river. At that very moment, a body floated past. Face down, it was bloated, caked in mud, hands akimbo, and fingers splayed. The ring finger on the right hand was missing.

'Say hello to Yama.'

The Weathermen—A Love Letter

> Due to Covid-19, we have all gone through the misery of isolation and physical-distancing, and it has had a negative impact on our mental health . . . Staying connected is, after all, the very essence of good mental health.
>
> —Professor (Adj.) Dato' Dr Andrew Mohanraj

Anjali
Kuala Lumpur
24 October 2020 (Start of Scorpio Season)

Dear Roshan,

Last night, my mother wanted to know about the progress of the revised *jadagam* report from the astrologer after we gave Panditji your wrong time of birth. To paraphrase Shakespeare, if what I told Mummy were played upon a stage now, I could condemn it as impossible fiction. It would have been criminal not to record what I said to her in my sometimes journal and share it with you. Hence, this letter. And, yes, sometimes journal, because I've struggled to keep one since university. Forget that. I promise you that this is a light-hearted read compared to the prolonged uncertainty of muddling through Covid-19 and the possibility of Emergency being declared in Malaysia.

You see, Daddy was a man of few words. However, what he did say was often so meaningful that it remained for life with those who heard him speak. Like when he referred to astrologers, numerologists, and palmists as, 'The Weathermen'.

'Those jadagam things they create,' Daddy decided, 'are as accurate as a weather report. When they say eight out of twelve "houses" are good between a couple, look at the four that aren't.' My mother grumbled at his pessimism, but I learned from this. The fact of the matter is that I couldn't care less what these reports say. I usually agree to get them done to please others and follow procedure. It's like preparing for my court cases. Any lawyer worth her salt will tell you that although the paperwork is properly done, she must always be aware of being ambushed during the proceedings. I equate those four 'houses' that won't work in any union as an ambush in court. Will a marriage work in spite of these non-matching houses? That's the question, Roshan. More importantly, will ours?

That's another thing. Why do the aunties think that a wedding is the same as a marriage? Just because we're a doctor–lawyer union doesn't mean it's necessary to have a huge wedding to please the relatives. My newly-converted Christian ones stole cash donations made during Daddy's Hindu funeral. A grand temple wedding with them in attendance will be my wedding from hell. Thank God for all the social distancing rules and restrictions on big groups.

I digress.

Panditji is probably sulking that we were careless with your time of birth. On the eve of the *atma shanti* prayers for the repose of Daddy's soul two years ago, Panditji insisted that I buy some flowers. I'd asked him to bring absolutely everything, as I had no clue where to get things like long-lasting camphor, betel leaves, turmeric paste, and pure ghee. I rushed to the only florist whose roadside stall was still open at 7.30 p.m. When I told him what the flowers were for, he practically snatched a few wilting stalks out of my hand and marched to a cooler inside the shop lot.

'Panditji, ah?' he asked when he returned and began rolling a large bunch of fresh purple and yellow daisies in old newspapers. Adding a few stalks of rosebuds to the bunch for free, he said, 'Take this. All new one.'

I smiled. All of Alor Setar was petrified of this cantankerous priest whose reputation for not tolerating mistakes preceded him.

How to push him, Roshan, for our revised jadagam report? He'll scold me.

That's why I asked Krishnan for help. He's so funny. He makes me keep it a big secret that he's a devout Catholic. He's aware that I will tease him because it's the Bible-toting ones who will swear that they don't believe in all these *jadagam-badagam* things but will also be the first to want their horoscopes read. Like your Anglican reporter friend in Pantai Hills. When we visited her newborn baby, she showed me the child's birth chart. 'For extra protection,' she said, placing it in the baby's cot next to the sealed brass tumbler of holy water from Lourdes. Putting her finger to her lips, she whispered, 'Don't tell others. I got this from Kerala yesterday.'

Speaking of God's Own Country, I'm on the verge of giving up on Krishnan's 'astrologer contact' in Kerala. After six weeks, Smokey (as I've decided to call this astrologer) is probably still roaming the countryside looking for the ideal palm leaf, smoking it so that it's smooth, sharpening his quill, and preparing the ink. Every time I ask Krishnan what's happening, his WhatsApp message is two words, 'Please wait'.

Finally, I turned to the friend whose name is listed as 'The Wizard' in my phone's contacts. A pukka Ceylonese, imagine a seventy-eight-year-old man with sparse white hair that is styled with Brylcreem gel. He wears starched cotton shirts like the civil servants of the British Raj used to. From elbow down, though, he's a 1970s hippie espousing flower power. He wears at least three bracelets on either wrist made of various beads. On the right, he has amethyst to activate his crown chakra and rose quartz to harmonize the energies in his heart chakra. On the left, there's topaz to . . . I forget for which chakra. In his house, he has converted the space where the skylight used to be into a windowless bedroom to align with the energies of *Vaastu* geomancy. That's The Wizard for you.

I gave him our details (the correct ones this time) but didn't dare tell him that this was all upside down. This jadagam thing should've been done before we met. That's the norm, no? First the report, then the parents meet, then the couple meets, then marriage. Like a proper Tamil drama.

How to tell The Wizard that we've known each other for two years already? He asked me which hospital you were working in. I told him that you've been in Mauritius for six months because of the pandemic then changed the subject.

The first astrologer The Wizard suggested was Master Yuvaraj from India. With Covid-19, Master's gone high tech. For RM250 (which I can send to him via PayPal because he's been approved by the Government of India to be able to accept international remittances), Master will present his report via Zoom, and I am allowed to ask as many questions as I like.

I opted for a local and cheaper weatherman. However, he's going to take time because I sent our details to The Wizard on a Tuesday. The astrologer can only accept WhatsApp messages on a Friday. That was yesterday. In the literary footsteps of Robinson Crusoe, I've chosen to name this one 'Friday'.

It seems that since we're in the throes of Navaratri, everyone is ultra-busy. Even readers of Western-based horoscopes are saying, 'It's Mercury retrograde until 3 November. You'll have delays in communication.'

Incidentally, I can't understand why so many people are upset about the wrong time of birth issue. Like your mum telling me to take things easy. With all my insecurities, I wonder if she's annoyed with me. The thing is, I feel for her. Poor thing. I can barely remember details about my dachshund Gulabi (closest I had to a child). Your mum has six children. Her giving me the wrong time of birth was bound to happen. If she knows the ridiculousness I've been through, she'll see that this is really nothing and very funny.

For example, there was Notchy (I don't bother remembering the names of previous suitors and I freely admit that I sometimes get them mixed up). His father was adamant that we meet only if our stars were aligned. Since we had ten 'houses' that matched, it was permissible for 'the boy' to call me. He spent a quarter of an hour describing his Amma's finger-licking *vengayam columbu*. Also, his darling niece was so clever because she could blow soapy bubbles when she was all of one. His only question was if I was willing to cook the same onion curry as his Amma.

Later in the day, he texted to inform (his word, not mine) me that we should 'take it up a notch'. I asked what this meant. He wanted me to go with him to Kluang to attend the wedding of the son of the lady who'd introduced us. That's like 250 kilometres from KL. I was expected to travel outstation with a stranger, stay overnight in a town I've never been to, and attend a wedding of someone I've never met. Would you do this, Roshan?

I responded with, 'Let me think about it.' I've learned never to reply with a firm no. Or even in the affirmative, for that matter. Always be non-committal, as whatever 'the girl' says, however intelligent or honest, will inevitably be wrong and backfire.

Next, I put on my Spidey sensors, sent out feelers, and made enquiries.

As it happens, Notchy was a little naughty.

Notchy had a twenty-year-old daughter from a previous shotgun wedding. It had been a *thali*-tying temple wedding that was never registered, thus rendering this child illegitimate. Now that he was fifty, he wanted legitimate children and his Amma was desperate for him to settle down. Notchy saw my photo and figured that I was worthy enough to be his baby-making machine. More so since two matching 'houses' were intimacy and family.

The other was Borty, some management-level person at AIG Insurance. Our charts matched in nine houses. Since

I'm in my forties, he wanted me to buy medical insurance that covered fertility issues. He was worried that our children wouldn't be perfect and expected that I must be willing to terminate an imperfect pregnancy. I am opposed to aborting a foetus for trivial reasons; if it's God's will that I care for an imperfect child then I will. That didn't go down well.

Honestly, which child is perfect? Look at my cousins. They were born supposedly perfect—the right caste, fair, intelligent, and became professionals. They made fun of me, the imperfect one, because I'm adopted and my father belongs to a different caste. The younger one was obsessed about inheriting the family house throughout the terminal stages of Aunty Shanta's battle with cancer. 'It was a matter of upholding the principle of equality among children,' my cousin said. All this talk paled into nothingness when she let her mother die lonely and made her brother—her own flesh and blood—feel that Aunty Shanta didn't love her firstborn child.

Maybe I should have had the gumption to ask Aunty Shanta for all the details about my adoption. In 1972, my parents had been so thoroughly busy cuddling their bundle of joy that they didn't care to ask for any details about the baby such as its caste, if its biological mother wanted to be in touch, etc. By the time I was old enough to comprehend the circumstances of my birth, everyone concerned, except Aunty Shanta, was dead. I never felt the need to ask her, though. Now that she's gone, I will always wonder if my time of birth is correct. Honestly, who is born right on the dot at 9.00 a.m.? That is why I always tell people that I make my own destiny.

Again, I digress.

Back to Notchy or Borty. Keep in mind that I never met them in person. Everything was via phone and text messages.

I want to confess something, Roshan.

Shy-shy but must tell.

Remember Nandaram? Well, in May last year, during one of his you-were-told-that-it-will-not-work-with-Dato-Dr-Matthew phases, he urged me to undergo a ritual. By this time, you were not simply Roshan to him, but full-on Dato Dr Matthew Roshan Shankara. He was (still is) enamoured with all your titles.

Nandaram's intention was to dig a hole on the beach in Morib and bury me up to my neck in the sand because my *mooladhara* chakra was out of whack. My unexplained weight gain, becoming irrelevant at work, and constant fear were all because I needed to ground my energies. Mercifully, he changed his mind. Instead, I took part in a sort of *atma shanti* puja to get rid of the 'old Anjali'. The new Anjali emerged from that quaint, provincial temple completely yellow for a few days because buckets of turmeric-laced water had been tipped over my head to cleanse me.

Sounds like I'm ungrateful and making fun of Nandaram. I promise you I'm not. I sincerely believed him and in him. The operative word being 'believed'—past tense. It took me this year of healing to accept that what I sought was spirituality, not religion and ritual. I resented being told what to wear for festivals at the *ashram* or the food restrictions because the Divine had seemingly chosen me for ascension to a higher spiritual plane. Most of all I hated being asked to my face, 'Are you clean?' It was to make sure that I wasn't on my period and could participate in prayers. It never occurs to a man that he wouldn't exist if his mother wasn't 'dirty'. Would he dare ask his mother, 'Are you clean?' Would you, Roshan?

I'm resigned to the fact that Nandaram will always oppose our union.

Mummy knows that my heart sings for you in ways that it's never done for any other man. Both our mothers can see how I glow from within whenever I talk about you. It is this joy that I wanted to share with Nandaram. He didn't want to know. Instead, he reinforced his disciples' notions that I was toxic in mind, mouth, and mood and a metaphorical death alone was my salvation.

At least I only had a turmeric-laced bath. I didn't have to marry a banana tree like Aishwarya Rai. This also was mild compared to a prayer many years ago at the Nageswari temple in Bangsar. Imagine me, who suffers from ophidiophobia, shaking from head to toe presenting a six-inch-tall cobra made of silver to the goddess whose name roughly translates to champion of snakes. Apparently, I had the curse of a snake in my subtle being—*naga dosham*—and that's why my sharp tongue repelled men. By making this gift to the goddess, the snake and I were free to find mates. How can I explain to people that since this invisible reptile's departure, my words are probably more cutting now?

In all this, I still don't know what that word jadagam means. I thought it meant a report that sets out the suitability of a romantic match between two suitors. Now The Wizard has used a new one—*porutham*. My feeling is that no one genuinely knows what these words mean and I'm probably the first inquisitive one to ask.

What now, Roshan? I mean, The Wizard doesn't just dabble in numerology. He's seriously into it. He even told his staff to change the spelling of her name from Tamilselvi to Thamilselvee. Maybe, it works, lah, because this girl got married. Just like that.

Anyway, The Wizard said that we must not delay. I wouldn't rely on it, though. He once told me that to achieve success (because I'm obviously a failure right now), I had to change how I spell my name. It should be Annejelly. People will call me Jelly, Roshan.

Echoing Panditji's first supposedly inaccurate report, The Wizard also pointed out the obvious when he invited me for tea—you and I are both no longer young. Nevertheless, there are chances that we'll become closer in 2021. The full moon is coming and, apparently, it's special because it's the first time this whole year that there's a full moon twice in one month.

Also, I forget, but The Wizard said that some star is supposed to be in some planet right now. Probably Shani in Rahu and Keth, as they are perpetually in my life. While sipping his piping hot teh tarik, The Wizard declared, 'The time is right.'

But right for what?

And what does 'must not delay' mean?

I was desperate to seek clarification but didn't dare.

Can you imagine what would have happened if I'd said, 'Yes, yes, we will not delay. If God wills it, Roshan and I will get married and procreate NOW!'

Naturally, my imagination ran wild. Although there's currently a whole ocean between us, you will marry me and somehow impregnate me this very night—an immaculate conception, at best. Still, Roshan, in nine months, we could have our own Christ-like child who will be highly intelligent with a lovely smile.

What are we to do when our weathermen—Panditji, Smokey, and Friday—eventually send their reports? Naturally, I expect to receive them after my birthday on 4 November because that's when Mars goes direct and communication is back to running smoothly.

What if we're not at all a match? What happens if one weatherman says we're a good match and other two say we're not? Do we choose the best of three? Do we never see each other again? Or, do we do Tamil drama style and elope? Must we sacrifice ourselves for love à la Shakespearean tragedy?

Maybe, to brighten any uncertain forecasts all round and make sure that our marriage is a resounding success, I should consider first marrying a banana tree, complete with that cobra from my subtle energies to bear witness to this sacred union. What do you think?

Muddles, cuddles, and bubbles, my darling.

All my love,
Anjali

The Incredible Tragedy of the Indian Man

> . . . In many cases, moral and religious obligations are the reasons for staying in the relationship . . . Some may worry that if they leave, their spouse will harm their children or prevent them from having access to them.
>
> —Professor (Adj.) Dato' Dr Andrew Mohanraj

'We're up here.'

The voluptuous woman raised her head. The man waved. She nodded and proceeded to walk into DrinksRUs. This was the first time she was going upstairs to the restaurant section of the local bar. It was a warm February afternoon—the lazy part of the day when the lunch crowd had gone back to work and the tea-time one was yet to arrive; the time when bored housewives of diplomats, having completed Pilates at a nearby gym, had a quick meal before rushing to pick up their children from the international school nearby. Precisely two such women sat at the table closest to the stairs. They watched as the woman walked over to the table in the balcony.

The man was fifty-seven years old but looked forty-five. Dressed in fancy Chinos and a monogrammed collared t-shirt, he glanced at his Tag Heuer, the accessory of choice when he was out to impress. The woman with large brown eyes was seven years younger and dressed in a store-bought cotton kurta and jeans. Next to the man sat a little girl with dainty features and translucent skin that stretched over pinchable five-year-old cheeks. He was Joseph Murali Danker. The girl was his daughter, Mel, whose full name was Melissa Abe Danker. The woman was Sunita Chopra, or Nita as she asked family and friends to call her.

Certainly, they were stunning: Mel, on her own, and both Joseph and Nita. The couple glowed from within in each other's company. They had been lovers ten years ago and parted with a good deal of sorrow. Neither had been able to entirely give up on the memory of the other. Even though all forms of communication broke down between them for a while, especially when Nita moved to Langkawi while he stayed in Labuan, they were bound to each other as if they were still together. The source of this bond was of little interest to Joseph. He felt it as a power to push and pull—he'd pull Nita when she was out of sight and push her away when she was in his vicinity. Nita spent the whole year of their affair being stupefied by how easily she dropped everything whenever something as mundane as his WhatsApp messages came through.

* * *

They met under curious circumstances—at a funeral of the mother of a mutual friend. At the time, Nita was still living in

Kuala Lumpur. The coffin was placed in the main hall, which was on the lowest floor of a five-storey house. Nita stayed near a group of ladies singing a set of *bhajans* for the repose of the deceased's soul. When she looked up, there he stood, the bald gorgeousness that was Joseph, staring down at her. She glared at him, daring him to come forward. He glared back and made his way down the stairs. After he'd paid his respects to the deceased, he stood in front of her and said, flippantly almost, 'Hello.' Nita was smitten.

It was Nita who made the first move. She invited him to a show and was taken by his quick reply: 'I'd be delighted.' Although pleased, she already sensed that if, in future, she showed her enthusiasm to engage with him, his responses wouldn't be as forthcoming. Putting aside such negative thoughts, in the months ahead, whenever Joseph came into town, under the pretext of attending a meeting at the head office of MalayanBank, he'd call and they'd meet for coffee, dinner, or even a game of poker. You would have seen them huddled in the corner of Alexis Café sharing a chocolate mud cake or drinking from the same glass during the intermission of a concert at the Petronas Philharmonic in Kuala Lumpur City Centre. He took her on the test drive when the bank offered him a Mercedes Benz as part of his emoluments. Thanks to Joseph, Nita became an expert at baking meringue pies because they were his favourite.

'Tuk, tuk, tuk,' he called a mortar and pestle, not knowing how to refer to them, the very first time he came for dinner to her place.

'You know,' he said, taking a bite out of the last bit of homemade pizza, 'I want to be a Freemason, lah.'

'Huh?'

'Ya. You know tha—'

'I know what Freemasons are. But why suddenly?'

'I have always wanted to join.' He swallowed half the glass of wine from a bottle he'd brought with him.

'What's stopped you?'

'Nothing . . .'

'Obviously something is bothering you about it. Spit it out, Joseph.'

He took a deep breath before saying, 'I have all these people in my family, lah. My friend, Teresa.' Putting down his glass, he said, 'Actually, she's Datin Teresa. She is not Catholic, but all Church people said her husband—I think his name is Rajan Koshy—got Datoship last year. So lucky, I tell you. Things are so much easier when you have one of those.' Shaking his head, he added, 'All these Church people won't approve.'

'Huh? What do they have to do with you making these sorts of decisions?'

'Aiya. I am Catholic.'

'So?'

'Freemasons ask us to believe in the one, true God.'

'And?'

'Catholics believe in the Holy Trinity.' He raised three fingers for emphasis.

'Dear God, you're a coward,' she wanted to say to him. Instead, Nita remained silent. She focused on swirling the burgundy-coloured liquor in her glass, eager to avoid laughing at him.

He shrugged. 'Anyway, I just wanted to share.'

'Okay.' She took his empty plate and was halfway to the sink when she had to stop upon hearing what he said next: 'You're so easy to talk to, lah, Sunita. I feel so comfortable.'

Oooo . . . comfortable. No man had ever described being in her company in such terms before. Intense, yes. Opinionated, yes. Blunt, yes. But comfortable? That was a new one. There was hope yet for a relationship with this man. Joseph snuffed it out.

* * *

With Joseph's marriage had come a new roster of joys, gossiped the insurance agent who once sold them policies, some three years after Nita stopped communicating with Joseph. According to the agent, Joseph's wife coddled him into increasing her clothing allowance from RM200 to RM1,000 per week. It didn't seem to mind Joseph, for he revelled in the planning of luxury holidays to such places as the Barrier Reef, the island of Capri, or Waitomo. He didn't actually go snorkelling, ride in a cable car, or descend into the caves lit by fireflies. He simply loved that she felt free to charge his credit card to plan these trips with her girlfriends.

'He's stupidly happy,' the agent divulged. Apparently, Joseph had taken out a RM2 million life insurance policy with his wife, Toriko Abe, as the sole beneficiary.

'So embarrassing, lah.' The agent wouldn't stop sharing, oblivious to Nita shifting in her seat to avoid any more mention of Joseph. 'I invited him to a restaurant for lunch. Actually,' he looked around the lush décor and said, 'this restaurant, lah. Same-same. But, I t-e-l-l y-o-u! He cannot even decide for himself what to eat.' Mimicking Joseph making a call, he put his pinkie to his lips and thumb to his ear and said, 'Tori-tori, what can I order, ah?' He shook his head, embarrassed by, for, and of Joseph.

Nita had but one thought—Joseph had a nickname for his wife.

'Why, ah, Indian men all so Queen-controlled when they have Chinki—in this case, Japanese—wife? They see fair skin only, they become stupid.' He paused to shovel—there was no other word for it—pasta carbonara into his mouth. Having swallowed, seemingly without chewing, he said, 'I think, ah, these men, their Ammas all don't teach them how to talk nicely to Indian girls. When they become boss also, it's like that.'

'Huh?'

'If the boss is Indian, he will *maki* the Indian girls like don't know what.'

'Hmmm . . .'

'True, I tell you. Look at my friend, ah. He's a lawyer. Got own company all.' Raising two fingers on one hand and his forefinger on the other, he added, 'Two Indian girls and one boy working for him. The girls? He will call bitch lah, *pishashi* lah, pariah lah. All bad-bad words. The boy? He's one judge's son, what. You know? Tan Sri Alagasundram? His son. My friend very nice to him.' He shook his head. 'Then, got one new Chinese girl. Tight-tight blouse, short-short skirt.' He hit his forehead with the palm of his hand. '*Habis* I tell you.' Nita scarcely took a breath before he said, 'Quieter than the *tikus* to the Chinese girl. If my friend marries her . . .' He shook his head. '*Habis*. He will give money, house, family, dog, cat, *biawak* . . . everything.'

Nita put her hand up to get the waiter's attention. She was in need of a refill for her glass of iced water.

'You look at two brothers, ah. If one got Indian wife, he won't even look at his wife when he is talking to her. She must walk behind him. The one with Chinese wife? Nose in the air all the time. Like that Joseph fellow. Walk holding hands all. All the time saying, "I love you Tori-Tori."' Shuddering, he said, 'Eeee . . . *Malu* only.'

'Okay. Okay,' Nita put her hand to stop him. She'd had enough of his tirade.

'I stop. But, I tell you, Ms Nita. Better you forget Indian man and find Chinaman.' He put his hand on his heart, 'We always, always, always nice to Indian girl.'

'Okay. Fine. Now, let's get back to my insurance. Policy okay or not?'

'Ah, okay. Okay. Back to work . . .'

* * *

Polite. Dignified. Distinguished.

None of these were words Joseph used to describe Nita's exit within the hour of knowing about Toriko's presence in his life. Angry was a good word, but Joseph didn't know why. After all, he hadn't made any sort of commitment to Nita. When he had been at home, it was the vision of Nita that floated in front of his eyes before he went to sleep. He thought of her big eyes and wide smile. He composed WhatsApp messages to Nita, sharing articles he'd published, and the people he met. He didn't want to share details of his life, which she seemed to want from him from the questions she sent in reply. With Toriko, though, it was different. It started with what he called 'office teasing'.

'I only have to look at her, lah, and I f-e-e-l things,' he'd said to a colleague.

Joseph received a letter from Nita a week after she was out of his life. A letter, mind you. Not a message sent over WhatsApp. He remembered every word of it but didn't see what prompted it and sent a series of WhatsApp messages.

'Why such bad words?'

She didn't reply.

He sent another four subsequent messages.

'Datin Teresa invited us to dinner. She says that Toriko is elegant.'

'Toriko said yes to becoming Catholic. You will stay . . . actually, what are you? Hindu isn't it?'

'Toriko is almost fifteen years younger, Sunita.'

'She is fresh.'

Blue ticks for them all.

He knew Nita had blocked his number when his, 'I hope you understand' never went through. In any event, it didn't matter any more because twenty-seven-year-old Toriko was now making googly eyes back at Joseph. He wanted the mother of his child to have a safe and healthy delivery. At forty, there were no guarantees that any child Sunita carried to term, if she could even manage that, would be born normal. And, if a prenatal scan were to show that the foetus was indeed malformed, he would never consent to an abortion, however strong the medical grounds were for such a procedure. Besides, to him, it was as plain as the crystal-clear water dispensed from the thousand-ringgit machine Toriko made Joseph gift her for their third-month anniversary that she loved him.

* * *

Within a month of Joseph's departure from her life, Nita emptied her flat, rented it out, and moved to the island of Langkawi. She accepted part-time work as a HR manager at the Sheraton. She enjoyed the fixed hours, as they gave her plenty of time to explore the many nature trails on the island. In those moments, standing in the boot-sucking mud of a mangrove, she would remember Joseph refusing to introduce her to his 'good friend, Datin Teresa' (his words) because he didn't want his privacy invaded. Foolishly, she'd assumed this meant that what they had was sacred. The one time she had texted him to ask if their relationship was going anywhere, he promised to speak to her about it in person. Only, when they did meet, he said, 'I'm overwhelmed,' pulled her into his arms and shut her up with a kiss. When she had looked into the source of her deepest love, she saw man deeply conflicted, but she knew not with what or whom. She'd resolved to love him with all her being until he couldn't help but admit that he loved her.

* * *

The women near the stairs continued to look at Joseph and Nita, albeit surreptitiously. Who wouldn't? The women gossiped and eavesdropped at the same time. Groceries threatened to fall out of the canvas bags they'd placed, in a peculiar habit of the East, on another chair. As they leaned their elbows on the table and sipped coffees that cost RM17, they were witness to a pure and endearing moment: Nita turned to the girl, smiled brightly, and pushed a lock of her curly hair behind the child's ears.

A unit of three. An unbreakable bond.

'Remember when Mama bought you the hair band. Where is it?'

'I don't know, Papa,' Mel said.

'Okay. Mama will know. You can ask her when she comes back from Tokyo.'

At this, the women near the stairs kept their cups to their lips, looked straight at each other, and swallowed. Lowering their cups to the saucers, some charm had gone out of the scene. The woman wasn't the girl's mother after all. This nuclear family wasn't perfect. A man—still married, separated, divorced, or status unknown—was here with his child. The woman who sat with them was . . . well . . . pathetic.

Had Nita looked at the women, she might have wondered what right they had to pass judgement. Then again, she might not have. She already knew that there were others among Joseph's circle of friends who thought him a beach-bum-looking man. He had beady eyes, full cheeks, and now, as a father, a beer belly. When they had first met, though, he'd been awkward in his movements, like a lanky teenager who didn't know where to place his hands at any given time. Nita hadn't changed—she was still twirling the curly ends of her hair around her forefinger, still had mocha-coloured skin, still weighed no more than fifty-eight kilogrammes.

* * *

Consider the one time Joseph surprised her. It was three o'clock in the afternoon, the hottest time of the day. He rang the doorbell an hour earlier. When she opened the door, in his hands was a Styrofoam box with mee goreng from the hawker stall. He didn't know if she'd be in and took a chance. This was no mere whim, though. He'd thought about coming to see her for months. He'd even said so, many times. And all because he had a lot to say to her. In her presence though, he said nothing.

Instead, in the single luxurious item in her flat, a round mirror six feet in diameter, their reflections portrayed their strained profiles.

'Joseph,' she whispered.

'Sunita,' he replied.

She blinked. 'Call me Nita. Everyone does.'

He shook his head. 'Sunita.'

She wanted to scream: 'Why the formality? Like a "kind regards", message.' Instead, with sweaty palms, not making eye contact, saying nothing, she wondered if she should forget this late lunch, take his hand, and guide him to her bed.

* * *

This was their first meeting since rumour of Joseph's impending separation from Toriko had filtered down the grapevine. Time apart had not dimmed the fact that it was a struggle for Joseph and Nita to take their eyes off each other. There was chemistry, for sure, but it was a longing mixed with regret. Their affair had marked them but in different ways. When alone, they'd go over the details—parts of her body he touched or words she whispered. They never remembered time or the places, though. The problem was where her love was all-consuming, he was sharing his with another.

'Why did you ask me to come here, Joseph?' Nita finally blurted out.

'Hmmm . . .' He looked at his daughter. 'Mel, why don't you go and see those fish?' Pointing to the aquarium, he added, 'Come back and tell me what fish they are. I want to speak to Sunita Aunty for a while.'

'Okay, Papa.' The child sure was obedient.

'So, what do you want?'

Nita then watched this man as he gathered his thoughts, words, and deeds about him. She wondered what he'd say. This was the kind of meditation she'd become accustomed to from her years on the island, especially when she took on a part-time job of shadowing a virologist to help him create a monograph about the resident bee population. Clad in a protective white suit and hat, she'd reach out with a gloved hand to capture a bee in a small vial for the virologist to take back to his lab. His goal was to identify early warning signs that bees in a particular hive were under stress, thereby, recovering their hives before it was too late. This was to avoid the phenomenon called colony collapse disorder. Affected bees were often infected with a virus that deformed their wings, grounding them, thereby making them subsist on liquid honey rather than the stores of honey that the bees would have amassed had they been healthy.

There wasn't a moment, when carrying out these tasks, that Nita did not think about Joseph. He hovered over her as she entered the data that the virologist had collected. He sat next to her in the *sampan* when she accompanied the virologist into the geopark. She caught herself converting a statement into a question with the word 'right' in exactly the same way that Joseph sometimes did. The more she mulled over Joseph, the more she accepted that, yes, there was a part of him that did care for her.

* * *

Consider what happened about three months after they'd met.

A pigeon laid an egg in a potted plant on her balcony. She took a photo and sent it to him.

'Look after those,' he texted back, issuing an order, almost.

In the next two months, she changed her schedule to make sure that she was only ever away from her flat for no more than an hour. She named the one she thought was the mother, Lola. The father was Compass, because the colours of the feathers on his tail made the shape of the single most identifiable symbol of Freemasonry, the square and compasses. The babies, when the eggs hatched, were named Jack and Jill. One stormy night, when Compass hadn't returned to keep Jack and Jill warm, Nita stayed up until midnight, fretting. What if Compass never returned? Where was the closest pet-food shop, still open at midnight, that would give her the food needed to nourish these birds? She pulled out all the things from her cupboard in search of an old table lamp she no longer used because the bulb emitted heat. Joseph would never forgive her if Jack and Jill didn't survive. It would be evidence of her potential failure as a mother to any children they could create together.

Nita spent her lonely hours wondering what it was like to live with Joseph. Did he reach for his phone first thing in the morning? Did he have music on while he shaved? Did he choose his clothes the night before and set them out? What was breakfast like? The most intimate thing they could do, she always imagined, was having a cup of coffee together and sharing bits of the newspapers. Meaning, he'd read the news and politics, she'd read the feature articles and letters to the editor. Then, they'd switch and drink their second cup of coffee. Quite simply, Nita, an intelligent girl who favoured the rational and orderly, could not believe that Joseph did nothing to take their relationship further. Her expectations were conventional, old fashioned in fact. So, of course she forgot how mutually exclusive this sort of intense emotional drama and a nice life were.

* * *

'So? What is it?'

'I want you to know, Sunita, that I care about you.'

'What?'

'Yes.'

'Err . . . Toriko?'

He sighed, strained, as though there was something weighing on his mind.

'Spit it out, Joseph.'

'This was the problem with you, Sunita. You are always so blunt. Want people to say things. Force them to admit feelings they are not ready for.'

Nita made to stand up.

'No! Stay. I'm sorry.' After she relaxed in her chair, he added, 'I really need you.'

'Need me?' Nita raised one eyebrow, puzzled by this confession of sorts.

'Need a friend, I mean. I have no one to talk to.'

'Oh . . . okay.'

'Well, Toriko isn't . . .' Taking a deep breath, he said, 'She didn't turn out to be . . .'

Joseph seemed to be struggling to find the right word.

Nita tilted her face and said, 'Fresh?'

He looked directly at her. 'Oh, you remember that?'

He's an obtuse ass, for God's sake. There wasn't a woman alive who would ever forget words uttered with the sole intent of hurting her.

'No. Toriko was certainly . . . err . . . fresh.' He paused. Pointing in the direction of where his child stood, he said, 'See that little girl?'

Both of them turned to look at Mel, now approaching two women seated near the staircase to say hello.

'Pretty little thing, your daughter.'

'Did you not wonder about her?'

'Huh?'

He paused, then blurted out, 'Toriko only wanted my money.'

'I could have told you that,' was what she wanted to say. She bit her lip, instead.

Once he started to speak, it came out in one glorious outpouring of emotion.

'I wish I could have seen all this before. I have been nothing but miserable since the day we got married. I hate it. But I couldn't do anything about it. Despite begging—actually begging—nothing. Toriko would say nothing. She has no empathy at all. I haven't met anyone more selfish than her. She is the stereotypical materialistic girl. There was a third person. But I think there were many third parties. I wanted children. I found out that she was taking the pill.

I had to wake up every night to make sure that she didn't take the pill. When she became pregnant, I was beyond happy. But I also wondered if this child is mine. So, I did a DNA test. Thank God Melissa is mine. But Toriko never became Catholic and she will not allow Mel to become one. Only wants the girl to follow her side. Truthfully, I don't know where Toriko is. She told me she was a PA. But, I think—this Japanese culture and all—she was actually a geisha the company brought to Labuan. She also talks about tea-houses all the time. She demanded her freedom. So, now, at night, I look after Mel while my wife goes out. With her friends, it seems. I still cannot believe that she would do this to me.'

He took a break.

'From the time we married, my life has been a joke. Outwardly, it has appeared like the ideal life. Instead, it has been untrue. A pointless marriage and colossal waste of the best years of my life. The only good thing has been Mel. But, poor thing . . .'

'What do you mean poor thing?'

'Can't you see it?'

'See what, Joseph? This is the second time you're saying it. I still don't know what you're talking about. She looks fine to me.'

He took a deep breath then said, 'She's not completely right. I didn't know it, but Toriko didn't want children. So, she was taking medicines—other than the pill—and when she became pregnant, it affected the baby. My child is not completely okay. She has excessive blood in her brain and her development will be slow. She looks okay now, but her growth will be stunted. She may never see adulthood.'

They sat in silence for a long minute.

Reaching out to take her hand, he said, 'I miss you.'

She kept her hand where it was and her mouth shut.

'I love you. You can marry anyone else, but I will always love you, Nita.'

It wasn't that this was the first time he was saying the three words she'd longed to hear him say. It wasn't, even, the sudden awareness that the women by the stairs had heard his impassioned confession. It certainly wasn't that the waiter had completely forgotten about her order of a cappuccino. It was that Joseph had called her 'Nita'.

A certain peace came over her. In that acknowledgement of his adoration for her, Nita's yearning for him evaporated. In its place was pity. He was the kind of man who'd observe others being in the 'loving care of their wives', thereby revealing his desire for one. When Nita had presented herself to him on a silver platter, pledging to be devoted to him, Joseph had done all in his power to push her away and look down on her. He'd chosen, instead, someone Nita called cosmetically correct: fair, ever-ready to fan his inflated ego, and, obvious to everyone except Joseph, was only after his considerable wealth. He'd gone down a path of becoming isolated, deceived, betrayed, and being mocked. Nonetheless, he almost got what he wanted from Nita that day: a powerful and brilliant sucking of her energies to boost his frayed emotions. The moment he had her eating out of the palm of his hands, though, he'd leave her in soul-engulfing sadness under the pretext of returning to the mother of his child. Rumours of a separation were hogwash. As a devout Catholic, he would forever be trapped in a loveless marriage to Toriko to keep up appearances before his good friends. Such was the incredible tragedy of the Indian man.

Nita pulled her hand from under Joseph's when Mel returned to stand by her side. She reached out to stroke Mel's pink cheeks and said, 'You're an absolute sweetheart, Melissa Abe Danker.'

Nita stood up, straightened her back and looked at Joseph one last time. She would love him all the years of her life, for sure. But there is love, and there is love.

It was a long time that Joseph sat in contemplation with an expression that was begging, 'Come back, my love.'

The women near the stairs paid their bill. One of them stood up and stopped to stare at the party of three. She couldn't help herself.

'How absolutely lovely,' she muttered to her friend. It wasn't often you saw three people who fit so beautifully in what could and should have been a perfect family.

Nuns and Roses

> Dialogue across religious divides plays an important role in weakening the sense of dehumanisation that often serves as the basis of extreme antagonism and violence. Discourse provides a space for people of different backgrounds to meet and exchange perspectives and understand one another, rather than relying on stereotypes and mistrust.
>
> —Professor (Adj.) Dato' Dr Andrew Mohanraj

'kɒnvənt gɜ:l'

If you've spent any time at all in a mission school for girls, you must recognize these words, know what they mean and how they are pronounced. If, however, your response to them was, 'Errr . . . Don't know', I'd worry for you. Either you have to refresh your memory (quickly!) or risk having to hear the alumni's familiar rebuke of, 'Don't bluff!' If you did recognize the words, then you're a credit to the Sisters of the Infant Jesus who once taught us Phonetics.

By the way, when spoken, 'kɒnvənt gɜ:l' translates to 'convent girl'.

That said, the memories of my lessons in Phonetics with the nuns pale in comparison to what happened one sunny day in 1980.

First, though, it's important to keep in mind that the Convent in Alor Setar wasn't a convent in the proper sense of the word, but a contraction of the official name of my alma mater: 'Sekolah Rendah dan Menengah St Nicholas Convent'. What this meant was that when Alor Setar folk asked each other, 'Your daughter go to which school?' the answer was most likely to be nothing more than, 'Convent'.

On any given school day, the one-way street outside the Convent was a chaos of vehicles from fancy cars, modest ones, motorbikes belching smoke, weather-worn trishaw riders, all jostling to drop off girls between the ages of seven and seventeen at the Convent. At 7.30 a.m. on the dot, the six-feet high gates were closed to the outside world under the pretext of order being established within the school's compound. Little ones carried their school bags in one hand and held a friend's hand in the other as they walked to class. Older ones, full of teenage angst and burdened by much heavier backpacks, walked in groups and avoided eye contact.

As I said, in June 1980, none of this was of concern to me. A far worse horror was playing out in the presence of one I doubted I could ever look at again—Sister Alphonse.

Although she was ancient by my standards, Sister Alphonse must have only been in her early forties. Less than a year ago, she'd moved into the house given to the nuns—Sisters' House. Every day, my classmates and I, a group of precocious girls, each born into religions that were far removed from Catholicism, would visit her. She would guide us to the chapel inside Sisters' House, where we'd dip our tiny fingers into a bowl of holy water, bend a knee at the altar, and make the sign of the cross. Frankly, if Sister Alphonse had asked us to dip our whole bodies into the holy water, we would have. We adored this bride of Christ. She listened intently as we shared our grievance of the day, which was invariably something seemingly monumental, like who used whose eraser without permission. On occasion, we would steal roses from our gardens and bring them to her to place at the altar for Jesus because Sister once told us that, 'When you love someone, you shower them with gifts, like roses or flowers.'

In her beige habit, Sister Alphonse was a woman whose proportions weren't quite right. Despite having a slim trunk, her limbs were stocky, like a skinny doll wearing puffed up sleeves and stuffed trousers. There was no way of knowing her hairstyle under the habit she wore. Was her hair shorn to within an inch of her scalp? Or, was she hiding a bob? What was certain was that she was Eurasian because they were the only people I had come across who had that web of broken capillaries that fanned out from a bulbous nose. She also had a good set of teeth, which was surely because the good nun had placed them under the care of the best dentist (in my opinion) in town—Mummy or, as everyone in town called her, Dr Patsy.

On that awful morning, though, I didn't want to see those huge pearly-white incisors because it meant that Sister Alphonse was repeating, yet again, those most offensive words. I looked, instead, beyond Sister's Alphonse's face and the open louvers of the windows. Even though the ceiling-to-floor doors of this classroom, used only for Catechism classes on the weekends, were open, the air was still. There was one girl standing in the middle of the vast playing field.

Poor thing. What had she done to deserve such severe punishment?

Not worn the regulation dark blue ribbon to tie her hair?

Not passed up her homework?

Spoken when she wasn't supposed to?

Maybe she needed something to drink.

She was going to faint at this rate.

'Are you listening to me, Asha?'

I nodded, turning my attention to the present moment.

Stop talking, Sister.

Just stop.

I wanted to scream, but no sound came out.

Mercifully, the bell rang. Without seeking the nun's permission, I threw my pencil and eraser in a case, grabbed my bag and stood up. My chair fell back as I mumbled, 'Thank you, Sister,' turned my back to her and escaped from this torture chamber.

'What did you learn today?' Mummy asked during our drive back home.

Wanting only to wipe out the memory of what had happened, I ignored her. It was some days before I shamefacedly admitted the real reason I refused to return to those one-to-one lessons with Sister Alphonse.

'I cannot, Mummy,' I begged.

'Spit it out, Asha. What happened?'

'She . . . she . . .'

'She what?'

I sighed. I didn't know how to say it. I mean, how could Sister Alphonse, who was the bestest of the best and the wonderfullest of the most wonderful of all the Sisters say this bad, bad word?

How could she?

Of all the people, to me.

'I was bad, Mummy.'

'Huh?'

'Yes.' Big eyes stared at Mummy, tears threatening to fall onto bigger cheeks.

'W-h-a-t h-a-p-p-e-n-e-d?'

'Sister said a bad word.'

'What bad word?'

'S-e-' I swallowed. A moment later, I blurted, 'Sex.'

My mother stared at me for a long while.

In my defence, in 1980, I was all of seven years old. I didn't know how to tell Mummy that I *did* understand that Sister Alphonse had been explaining that to know if something was male or female, I needed to know its gender or sex. It was a lesson in English grammar and nothing sinister. Still, the thought of the word alone was difficult to bear. That Sister Alphonse, a nun who had taken the vows of poverty, chastity—I repeat, chastity—and obedience was too much. It shouldn't be something she should be considering in thought, word, or deed. And here she was, saying the word. And saying it out loud. To me. My Sister Alphonse was going to be cast into a world of sin without absolution, no? Forget redemption.

It was too much, I tell you.

To everyone else, this was but a huge anticlimax. Whatever the case, I've never seen my mother laugh as long and as hard as she did that day.

After this, the time-lapse between the commissioning of such 'sins' in this home-away-from-home for eleven years and confessing to the said sins increased. In one particular case, it was twenty-five years.

Imagine.

It was a dreary day in September 1981. At about 10.25 a.m., an announcement was made over the PA system. The unfriendly voice said, 'Asha Pillay from Class 3 Green, go to Miss Sibert's office now.' Classmates who dared to, looked at me as though they were commiserating with a death row inmate about to make her final journey to the gallows.

Five minutes later, I stood before our headmistress. On Miss Sibert's table, that horrible thing called the report card was open as she scanned my academic performance for the month. I swallowed the lump in my throat, aware that I couldn't plead for mercy on account of the fact that Mummy and Miss Millicent Sibert had once been classmates in Light Street Convent, Penang.

Was it true that Miss Sibert ate naughty girls for breakfast and lunch?

Would she eat me?

No, lah.

How?

Maybe I would be caned.

But for what?

And, there was no *rotan* in sight. I hated that malleable bamboo stick that I am still convinced the school's gardener also used to kill snakes.

Something was not right.

Miss Sibert looked up, pushed her straight hair behind her ears and said, 'Asha, are you interested in learning Mandarin?'

Huh?

Interested?

Mandarin?

A question?

No scolding?

I stared at her.

Miss Sibert rotated the report card clockwise so it was the right way around for me to read. Pushing it closer, she pointed to the column marked 'Mandarin'. That month, I'd achieved a grand total of 10 marks out of 50. Previously, my average had been 45 marks.

I cannot remember my response. In fact, I wonder if I said anything at all.

It was several decades before I confessed my sin.

'Miss Sibert,' the thirty-year-old me said during a visit to her house in Penang, 'I didn't dare tell you then that the girl who used to sit next to me wasn't there. She was sick and didn't come to school that day. So, I had no one to copy from.'

The seventy-something-year-old Miss Sibert looked at me with a benign smile and said, 'Yes, I knew what you girls were doing all along. I just wanted to see what you would say.'

Mortified, I closed my eyes.

All this time . . .

And she had known what we had been up to.

Every time I reflected on these stories, my long-held belief that these women, though cloistered and unmarried, were not dumb, stupid, or out of touch with reality was reinforced. Streetwise, knowledgeable, and quite business savvy, they were strict with us but also incredibly kind. And, they were very open-minded.

I mean, during a lesson on religions of the world, Sister Alphonse had asked us to share a story about a spiritual being from our own faiths. I chose to tell my friends and the nun about the deathless saint, Kriya Babaji. Born as Nagaraj in 203AD in a village in South India, he was kidnapped when he was five years old by a slave trader. Once his owners set him free, he joined a group of *sanysins* and, at the age of eleven, found Siddha Boganathar in Katirgama, Ceylon. When his training under this man was complete, he sought initiation from into the ancient art of Kriya Kundalini Pranayama from none other than the *rishi* called Agastya. Once his training was over and he had earned the right to be initiated, Nagaraj acquired a new name—Kriya Babaji.

'They still live here, Sister Alphonse.'

'What do you mean?'

'Aji once told me that Agastya lives in Gunung Jerai.'

'Aji? That's your—'

'My grandmother. Sometimes, he gets a visitor, Kriya Babaji.' I said this with the kind of conviction that booked no opposition. 'And I am telling you, Sister, one day, I will meet Kriya Babaji. I promise you, I will meet him.'

Sister Alphonse looked at me. The devout Catholic didn't make an attempt to dismiss a little girl's fervent hope or laugh at her desire. In fact, she recognized a yearning so great to come into communion with an elusive higher power that no logic, ritual, or stricture would allow this child to deviate from her belief. She did the only thing that came naturally to her—she put her hand on my shoulder, looked deeply into my eyes, and said, 'And so you will.'

Of all our activities involving Sister Alphonse, though, the highlight had to be the celebration for the Convent's Golden Jubilee in 1984. As the chairperson of the organizing committee, she also oversaw the production of *The Sound of Music* at the Dato Syed Omar stadium in town. Although the entire school was involved in this, I recall that members of the larger Catholic community in Alor Setar also gave of themselves to help make this a joyous occasion. For a few days in August 1984, members of the Kedah Royal Family and the public watched as we morphed into tiny, Malaysian Maria von Trapps. Singing our little hearts out, we serenaded everyone about the 'hills being alive', momentarily forgetting that Alor Setar was surrounded by utterly flat paddy land.

In spite of these happy memories, many at the school bore witness to a brutal reality taking shape during the 1980s. For one, the large cross hanging above the office building was pulled down by authorities for fear that the very sight of it might influence students to embrace Catholicism. New school badges were engraved with a forgettable motto in Malay to replace the one that Convent Girls the world over knew (and still know)—*Simple in Virtue. Steadfast in Duty.* And, when Sister Alphonse died on 20 June 1989, Mummy wrote to me in boarding school to tell me that only five sister nuns were allowed to attend a mass said for her at St Michael's Church in town. The authorities had decreed that Malay girls, some of whom were now prominent politicians in their own right and members of royal families, were no longer allowed to enter a non-Muslim place of worship. They had developed and were promulgating the phobia among 'their own kind' that their sensitivities would be affected if they stepped into a Church.

Quite simply, the spirit of the Sisters of the Infant Jesus who served at our school was systematically whittled away until one day, fighting back tears, one of the nuns said, 'We have to go. Our mission here is over.'

By the mid-1990s, the nuns left the home they'd known for more than fifty years. The first thing the authorities did was raze to the ground Sisters' House. Gradually, all the buildings in the school were also destroyed. In time, the site of what had once been the premier girls' school in Alor Setar became a nondescript supermarket.

In spite of all the brouhaha—funny, sad, and malicious—no truer is a statement than this verse from the Holy Bible: 'And now these three remain: faith, hope, and love. But the greatest of these is love.' I speak for the majority of former kɒnvənt gɜːls in Alor Setar when I say that we carry in our hearts an immense gratitude and love for these Catholic women who made it their mission unto God to shape the women we have become. I pray that the intangible values they inculcated in us will live on in future generations.

Reference List

'Federal Court also Orders NRD to Remove 'bin Abdullah' from Birth Certificate', *The Star*, February 14, 2020, https://www.thestar.com.my/news/nation/2020/02/14/federal-court-also-orders-nrd-to-remove-bin-abdullah-from-birth-certificate (accessed November 2023).

'Matters Of The Mind (Datuk Dr Andrew Mohanraj)', *The Star*, n.d., https://www.thestar.com.my/lifestyle/viewpoints/matters-of-the-mind?bycat=643_1634091356 (accessed January 2024).

Chung, C., 'You're Obsessed and Compulsive . . .', *The Star*, January 22, 2018, https://www.thestar.com.my/news/nation/2018/01/22/youre-obsessed-and-compulsive-people-with-ocd-cant-help-but-have-unwanted-and-disturbing-thoughts-i (accessed November 2023).

Karim, K N., 'Federal Court Rules Unilateral Conversion of M. Indira Ghandi's Children to Islam Null and Void', *New Straits Times*, January 29, 2018, https://www.nst.com.my/news/crime-courts/2018/01/329867/federal-court-rules-unilateral-conversion-m-indira-ghandis-children (accessed November 2023).

Menon, S., 'Be Strict to Combat Bullying Culture, Say Experts', *The Star*, January 14, 2022, https://www.thestar.com.my/news/nation/2022/01/14/be-strict-to-combat-bullying-culture-say-experts (accessed November 2023).

Mohanraj, A., 'The Pain of Grief', *Dr. Andrew Mohanraj – Mainstreaming Mental Health*, August 12, 2015, https://andrewmohanraj.com/2015/08/12/the-pain-of-grief/ (accessed November 2023).

Mohanraj, A., '8 Behaviour Patterns that Children Ape from their Parents', *The Star*, May 4, 2018, https://www.thestar.com.my/lifestyle/family/2018/05/04/children-ape-their-parents (accessed November 2023).

Mohanraj, A., 'Finding Ways to Adjust to Uncertain Times', *The Star*, August 2, 2021, https://www.thestar.com.my/lifestyle/health/2021/08/02/finding-ways-to-adjust-to-uncertain-times (accessed November 2023).

Mohanraj, A., 'I Am Addicted to Substances for a Reason', *The Star*, February 8, 2022, https://www.thestar.com.my/lifestyle/health/matters-of-the-mind/2022/02/08/i-am-addicted-to-substances-for-a-reason (accessed November 2023).

Mohanraj, A., 'Turning to Spirituality to Lessen Mental Health Problems', *The Star*, May 3, 2022, https://www.thestar.com.my/lifestyle/health/2022/05/03/turning-to-spirituality-to-lessen-mental-health-problems (accessed November 2023).

Mohanraj, A., 'People with Autism Need More Support at Community and Societal Levels', *The Star*, August 9, 2022, https://www.thestar.com.my/lifestyle/health/matters-of-the-mind/2022/08/09/taking-community-and-societal-action-on-autism (accessed November 2023).

Mohanraj, A., 'Depression May Present Differently in Older Adults', *The Star*, September 6, 2022, https://www.thestar.com.my/lifestyle/health/2022/09/06/depression-may-present-differently-in-older-adults (accessed November 2023).

Mohanraj, A., 'Thinking about Dying Can Spur You to Live a Better Life', *The Star*, October 4, 2022, https://www.thestar.com.my/lifestyle/health/matters-of-the-mind/2022/10/04/thinking-about-dying-can-spur-you-to-live-a-better-life (accessed November 2023).

Mohanraj, A., 'Power Can Be Addictive for Politicians', *The Star*, November 13, 2022, https://www.thestar.com.my/news/focus/2022/11/13/power-can-be-addictive-for-politicians (accessed November 2023).

Mohanraj, A., 'Dealing with the Psychological Trauma of Disasters', *The Star*, January 3, 2023, https://www.thestar.com.my/lifestyle/health/matters-of-the-mind/2022/01/03/dealing-with-the-psychological-trauma-of-disasters (accessed November 2023).

Mohanraj, A., 'Mental State of the Nation and Malaysians', *The Star*, January 2, 2023, https://www.thestar.com.my/lifestyle/viewpoints/matters-of-the-mind?bycat=643_1634091356 (accessed November 2023).

Mohanraj, A., 'Feeling Stressed Out? Practise Self-Care and Have Support for Stressful Times', *The Star*, February 7, 2023, https://www.thestar.com.my/lifestyle/health/matters-of-the-mind/2023/02/07/practise-self-care-and-have-support-for-stressful-times (accessed November 2023).

Mohanraj, A., 'Elderly Women Targeted for Financial Security', *The Star*, February 15, 2023, https://www.thestar.com.my/news/nation/2023/02/15/elderly-women-targeted-for-financial-security (accessed November 2023).

Mohanraj, A., 'Discourse and Contestation of Ideas to Address Islamophobia', *Dr. Andrew Mohanraj: Mainstreaming Mental Health*, March 10, 2023, https://andrewmohanraj.com/2023/03/10/discourse-and-contestation-of-ideas-to-address-islamophobia/ (accessed November 2023).

Mohanraj, A., 'When a Man Is Abused by His Wife', *The Star*, October 2, 2023, https://www.thestar.com.my/lifestyle/health/matters-of-the-mind/2023/10/02/when-a-man-is-abused-by-his-wife (accessed November 2023).

Nazlina, M., 'The Grounds of Judgment in the Indira Gandhi Ruling', *The Star*, November 29, 2019, https://www.thestar.com.my/news/nation/2018/02/09/the-grounds-of-judgment-in-the-indira-gandhi-ruling (accessed November 2023).

Nijar, G. S., 'Review of the Indira Gandhi Decision', *The Sun Daily*, February 12, 2018, http://www.thesundaily.my/news/2018/02/12/review-indira-gandhi-decision (accessed November 2023).

'A Malaysia for All', *New Straits Times*, November 19, 2021, https://www.nst.com.my/opinion/leaders/2021/11/746600/nst-leader-malaysia-all (accessed November 2023).

Parvan, L., 'Malaysia: Animal Assisted Therapy Stands Up for Physical and Emotional Support of Patients', *Bodyreviewers.com*, August 17, 2017, https://www.bodyreviewers.com/malaysia-animal-assisted-therapy-stands-physical-emotional-support-patients/ (accessed November 2023).

Solhi, F., 'Keep Pressure Mounting on De-Criminalising Suicide Attempts', *New Straits Times*, October 8, 2021, https://www.nst.com.my/news/nation/2021/10/734818/keep-pressure-mounting-decriminalising-suicide-attempts (accessed November 2023).

Sundararaj, A., 'In the Shade of a Mango Tree - Interview with Dato' Dr. Andrew Mohanraj (15 January 2019)', *How to Tell a Great Story*, January 13, 2019, https://howtotellagreatstory.com/blow-your-own-trumpet/in-the-shade-of-a-mango-tree-interview-with-dato-dr-andrew-mohanraj-15-january-2019 (accessed January 2024).

Acknowledgements

I remain deeply grateful to the many editors who have read my work and deemed it fit for publication. It's a humbling experience to know that my words have had an effect on others. Therefore, if you'll allow me, I would like to take this opportunity to acknowledge them here. Different versions of the stories listed below won competitions or were longlisted, shortlisted, and/or published in various e-zines, magazines, journals, and/or websites.

'Tapestry of the Mind' was published in *Livina Press*, Issue 7 (2024) and LitSphere (2024).

'Visitation Rights' was published in *Livina Press* (Issue 1), *Erato Magazine* (July 2022), and *The Elpis Letters* (June 2023), and also by Michelle Francik. It was also longlisted in Strands International Flash Fiction Competition 15 and shortlisted in Glittery Literary.

'Metopia' was shortlisted for the Write Time Anthology (2022) and published in the *Indian Periodical* (2022).

'kumbavishaygam' was longlisted for the 2023 Yeovil Literary Prize and published in Akéwì Magazine (2024).

'The Interlude' was published in *Story Nook* (2022), was listed as honourable mention for the Strands International Flash Fiction Competition 17 and was a winning story in FemmeFluenza 3 by WriteFluence.

'Lolita' was published in *The Minison Project* (2022) and included in the anthology *Crimson* by WriteFluenza (2023)

'Exchange Marriage' was a winning story in *It Was A Queer, Sultry Summer*, a resultant publication of the winning stories of our Sentence Expansion Extravaganza contest (September 2023)

'My Final Tapasya' was longlisted for the 2022 Yeovil Short Story Prize, the Strands International Flash Fiction Competition 14, listed as honourable mention in Strands International Flash Fiction Competition 16, shortlisted in WriteWords 22 by The Phare, selected for Secret Attic Challenge (2022), and included in Moss Puppy Magazine (2022).

'Unchartered Waters' was longlisted for the Bristol Short Story 2023 award, published in Issue 2 (October 2023) of *The Hoogly Review*, which nominated it for the Pushcart Prize 2024 – Fiction and PorchLit (January 2024).

'Golden Illusion' won the first prize in the H E Bates Short Story competition (2022) and was the Winning Story in FemmeFluenza 2.0 by WriteFluence.com. It was also published in *Karma Comes Before* (2023).

'Say Hello to Yama' was published in Issue 4, Spring Issue (2023) of *Livina Press*, *Usawa Literary Review*, Issue 9 (June 2023), *The Afterpast Review* (June 2023) and shortlisted for Aesthetica's International Creative Writing Award 2024 (December 2023).

'The Weathermen—A Love Letter' won the Trisha Ashley Award in 2022. It was also published in *Livina Press* (2022), *The Paper Crow* (2022), and the *Elpis Letters* (2023).

'The Incredible Tragedy of the Indian Man' was published in Issue 5, Summer Issue (2023) of *Livina Press.*

'Nuns and Roses' was included in *Asian Extracts* (2021) and *Spare Parts Lit* (2022).

While the words are mine, I would like to also thank those who have made this collection a reality, in particular, Kuah Sze Mei, Dr Sharon Zink of Jericho Writers, Nora Nazerene Abu Bakar, Thatchaa, Divya, Sneha, and the team at Penguin Random House SEA. Most of all, I'm grateful to my mother for insisting that I 'must write and publish these stories anyway'.

If you're contemplating suicide, are concerned about your mental health or quite simply feel the need to talk to someone, please do not hesitate to reach out to:

Mental Health Psychosocial Support Service: +60329359935 / +60143223392

Talian Kasih: 15999 / +60192615999 on WhatsApp

Jakim's family, social and community care centre: +601119598214 on WhatsApp

Befrienders, Kuala Lumpur: +60376272929 / email sam@befreinders.org.my

AWAM: +60378774221 / +60162884221 or awam.org.my

WAO: +60379575636 / 0636 or wao.org.my